Outside Child

A novel of murder and New Orleans

BY

A L I C E   W I L S O N - F R I E D

KOMENAR
publishing

Cover design by KOMENAR Publishing

Interior design by BookMatters

OUTSIDE CHILD. Copyright © 2007 by Alice Wilson-Fried.

For information, address KOMENAR Publishing, 1756 Lacassie Avenue, Suite 202, Walnut Creek, California 94596-7002.

Library of Congress Cataloging-in-Publication Data available

ISBN 978-0-9772081-2-8 (Hardcover)
ISBN 978-0-9772081-3-5 (Trade Paperback)

First Edition

10 9 8 7 6 5 4 3 2 1

Printed in the United States of America

For my grandchildren, Russel and Marie; Troy Jr. and the twins Alex and Jada; Alyssa and Emma, and Francie. And to my greatniece, Destini, the real HeartTrouble's only grandchild.

Never forget, kids, that love and respect are colorless, but to receive it, you must give it. Also, dare to dream, kids, and work hard to make sure your dreams come true. Remember: You are the only person who can determine what you can and cannot do.

ACKNOWLEDGEMENTS

My sincere thanks to my husband, Frank, who is always there with love, encouragement and support; to Charlotte Cook and the entire dedicated, hardworking KOMENAR Publishing crew (Jasmine Nakagawa, Alan Morris, Julia Tanner, and Clarissa Louie). Your focus and determination to qualitatively publish new voices is not only commendable in this highly competitive field, but is humbling. I am honored to be your third title. Also, thanks to my brother, Yasin Muhaimin, for always remembering our stories, for orally keeping our history alive, for reminding me of the rich legacy our ancestors left behind.

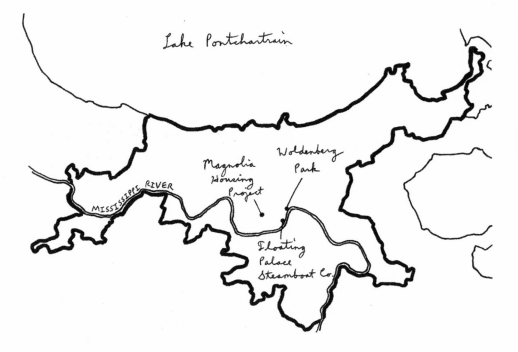

New Orleans, Louisiana

Outside Child

In New Orleans a child born from a relationship between a married man and an unmarried woman is called an "outside child." An outside child is excluded from a place of any standing in the father's family, his world, and most importantly his sphere of influence.

1

Brotherly Love

Ladonis Washington heard the front door chimes the second she stepped out of the shower. Jack? Had he changed his mind and come back to her? She stood there frozen in the moment, naked except for chill bumps. She could still see him standing in her bedroom doorway looking as if he couldn't decide whether to jump her bones or beat the crap out of her.

Why couldn't Jack understand? She'd invested a lot of hard work and sacrifice, not to mention aggravation, in her job. Why would she want to move to California? Why would she want to leave New Orleans? How many black women from the Magnolia Housing Project earned an MBA and made it in the New Orleans business world? She'd cultivated relationships. Taken every opportunity to position herself for success. And he wanted her to quit?

"I've got my foot in the door," she'd told Jack. "You know how hard it is to move up."

If she relocated with Jack to California, she'd have to start over. Really start over, and without her contacts, without her friends, without Tim.

"Ladonis," he'd said. "Get real. You're someone's assistant. The likelihood of your getting beyond that in this town is slim."

The put-down was painful in and of itself. And the hurt she felt from Jack's lack of compassion lingered. How could he say something like that to someone he was supposed to love? A loud knock on the door brought her attention back to her shivering, wet body.

"Hold on," she said, more frustration animating her words than she felt.

She toweled off, wondering if she'd done the right thing. What if she ended up without a man for the rest of her life? Would a career be enough?

"Open up, it's me," a male voice said.

Shit. She recognized the nasal tone. Her brother, HeartTrouble. Mama must've told him about the bookshelves.

She grabbed the sweats lying on a folding chair and pulled them on, then headed for the door, glancing around at the unpacked boxes. She'd been in her new condo only one day and one night. Smells of paint, sawdust and plastic still filled the air.

"I may not have a man," she declared, "but I sure as hell have a nice place to be lonely in."

HeartTrouble knocked again. She looked around for her sneakers, slipped them on and opened the door. HeartTrouble swung his lanky frame around to face her. Purple lips and pug nose, his cocoa complexion just a shade darker than hers.

"You don't have to knock the damn door down," she said.

She hated that they looked so much alike. People she didn't care to know always knew who she was. She was HeartTrouble's older sister. Lord help her.

"What kept you?" HeartTrouble said, standing in her doorway in a loud orange print shirt and brown rayon/polyester slacks.

Ladonis frowned. No time to get into an argument with her no-account, con-artist sibling. She had a broken heart to nurse. Besides, if he knew why she was dragging, he would make her feel as though she'd let the last black man on earth get away. And all because she wanted a successful career in what he and many male Caucasian executives considered white-man territory.

"What are you doing up so early?" Ladonis said to her brother. "I thought street hustlers kept vampire hours."

"What ails you, woman?" HeartTrouble said. "First you tell Mama you want to see me. Then you go lookin' for me in the Magnolia like you the fuckin' police or somebody. Now you act like I'm dog shit on your shoe."

"I gather you talked to Tiny Man," she said.

"Um-um," HeartTrouble mumbled.

She'd run into Tiny Man sitting atop a newspaper dispenser at the 7-Eleven on South Claiborne Avenue just outside the Magnolia where they'd all grown up. Her brother and his dope-head friends still hung out there. Especially Tiny Man. Some said the little man's growth was stunted because of a bout of polio. Her bet was on a lifetime diet of hard drugs.

"He told me my proper-talkin' sister was askin' about me," HeartTrouble said.

Ladonis' lips curled, her eyes rolled. Anybody who knew when to use "is" and "are" was labeled "proper-talkin'" or "white" in the Magnolia. She couldn't say which pissed her off or made her feel more like an outsider—black-folk paranoia or white-folk superiority. Everyday she had to deal with one or both. Made her life's struggles that much more complicated.

"And Mama said something about you needin' bookshelves built?"

"I do," Ladonis said. "I want to build shelves all around my living room walls. But, you know, it's honest work." She couldn't resist making the dig.

"Fine with me," HeartTrouble said. "Long as you don't think it's volunteer work. I ain't gonna do it for nothin'."

Ladonis opened her mouth to speak. The phone rang. Good. Things tended to get involved when they exchanged insults. And all she wanted from him were those damn bookshelves built. She picked up the receiver.

"Collins' office. Now," her boss, Lamar Kasdan's voice squawked through the earpiece. "We have a situation."

A situation? Shit. It had to be about her. What in the world had possessed her to go over Kasdan's head and ask Tim to present her centennial celebration idea to the CEO? She was going to lose the best job she'd ever had.

She glared at HeartTrouble like it was his fault. Then she clicked on the television. She worked in Public Relations under Kasdan, the Vice President in charge of the entire PR department. Whenever something went down, PR employees were the first called in. She prayed for some news about an incident, a "situation" as Kasdan called it, involving the Floating Palace Steamboat Company. A picture of one the Floating Palace's two paddle wheelers, the *Bayou Queen*, flashed across the screen. Her heart raced. But it was only a commercial, one she'd written, in fact. She sighed and recited the text along with the announcer:

"Steamboatin'—the serenity and adventure of life on American rivers, is kept alive by the Floating Palace Steamboat Company, owners and operators of the only two paddle wheelers that travel through America's heartland . . ."

Well, no situation there. She probably was about to get canned. She turned the television off in time to see HeartTrouble toss a gym sock atop a stack of dirty laundry.

"Girl, you messier than that junk man, Fred Sanford on that TV show," he said. "Better not let Mama see this place."

"Yeah, well, I'm not Mama," Ladonis mumbled. "To me, house-proud means owning it, not cleaning it."

HeartTrouble gave her the shame-on-you glare, her talking about Mama like that. But what was on her mind was more pressing. Could she talk Kasdan out of firing her? If she didn't, she'd have to do what she'd told Jack she didn't want to do. Start over.

"Look," she said to her brother, "I need you to build the shelves, but not today. I've got somewhere to be right now."

"Who said I'm gonna do it?" HeartTrouble's expression was a smirk somewhere between no way and maybe.

"What else have you got to do?" she said.

HeartTrouble's response was that Magnolia-style taunting, tooth-less grin. Ladonis felt a shiver. Thanks to the First and Claiborne Avenue dentist willing to provide dental care—extractions and gold teeth only—to uninsured and/or unemployed project folks at least HeartTrouble's smile wasn't unique. And by the grace of God, Ladonis had never needed dental care of that kind.

"Thanks for coming by." Ladonis picked up her purse and car keys from the kitchen counter. "I'll get in touch with you later about the bookshelves."

"Girl," he said. "You're a head case. You know that?"

Silence. Would it shut him up or egg him on? She couldn't let him sucker her into one of their usual I've-got-to-have-the-last-word fights.

"Can't a big shot like you," he added, "pay some licensed carpenter to build your fancy bookshelves?"

HeartTrouble was provoked, and he'd put her on the defensive. He'd gotten to her. What was it with the men in her life? First, her dad gone. Then her first love, Calvin. Now Jack. HeartTrouble was still around, but always putting her down for wanting to get ahead.

It was all she could do, not to blast him. Instead she opened the door for him to leave.

HeartTrouble walked out to the carport. Ladonis locked the wrought-iron screen door behind her, sticking to her decision to offer nothing but a mute response. She hurried to her Chevy Geo and backed out watching her gold-jewel laden, Super Fly throwback brother stare after her. She'd deal with him and the bookshelves later. Right now she had a problem at work. Either she was going to be fired or something big was going down at the Floating Palace.

2

Deliverer

Where was Kasdan? Ladonis made her way into the executive suite of the Floating Palace Steamboat Company. Cigarette smoke hugged the pale white walls and the floor-to-ceiling windows overlooking the Mississippi River. Dying white carnations collapsed in the crystal vase on the credenza. A stale-water odor filled the room. What a morning. Her boyfriend, her brother and now her boss. How much bad air could a person take before 9 A.M.? If only she could open a window.

She turned, afraid to leave, afraid to stay. The screech of rubber soles on the tiled hallway floor caught her attention. Lamar Kasdan walked in. A strapping man with a military erect posture. The muscles in his face were drawn so tight under his whiter-than-usual skin, his veins looked as if they were about to burst.

"You're here," Kasdan said, frowning, his eyes poring over her tattered sweat suit and bandana-clad, uncombed hair.

What did he expect? It was Saturday and he'd ordered her to come in pronto. Did he think she could go into a telephone booth, spin around and walk out in a three-piece suit and a freshly permed hairdo?

Bret Collins dashed in shortly afterwards pushing up his shirt-sleeves. His body got her usual quick, don't-catch-me-watching perusal. She'd been attracted to the CEO's rugged good looks since the day they'd met. Nothing to do about it though. She knew the rules of the game. Anyway, where was Tim?

"Something terrible has happened," Bret blurted out. "Tim fell overboard, off the *Magnolia Belle*." His voice cracked. "He's dead."

"Sweet Jesus." Ladonis' hand flew to her open mouth. "Tim? Dead?"

Her knees slacked. Her body swayed backward. She grabbed hold of a leather high-back chair. Shock, sadness, feelings so overwhelming, tumbled through her mind and body like a rockslide. Then relief. God help her, she hadn't lost her job.

"How?" she whispered, gripping the chair. "What happened?"

Tim had been her friend. Her mentor in a hundred-year-old company with no blacks working in administration. She'd been a "first," and he had welcomed her, worked with her, advised her.

"We're not sure," Bret said, walking toward the wet bar. "The captain said a deckhand saw Tim standing alone on the deck above the paddle wheel swearing and drinking minutes before . . ."

"He fell?" The words stuck in her throat. Tears welled up.

"Yes." Bret's voice quivered.

She couldn't cry. Bret wasn't crying, and he and Tim were best friends. Remember: The board room is like a baseball field, no place for tears. Tim had said that.

"Of course he fell," Kasdan said. He tore off the plastic wrapper of his Marlboro cigarettes. "Tim knew the problems if the paddle wheel caught a snag or something. You think he jumped into the paddle wheel? Cause that kind of damage?" He searched his pockets and pulled out his gold lighter. "Tim would never deliberately risk that."

"Jesus," Ladonis whispered, reacting as much to Kasdan's cold, condescending tone as to hearing Tim was dead.

Kasdan didn't like Bret or Tim. How many times had she heard him complain about the pair and their superior Yankee attitudes? Ladonis had long stopped thinking Kasdan was from up north too. Maybe no local accent, but he sounded and acted like a southerner, closed mind and all.

Bret held his hand out to Kasdan for a smoke. He put the cigarette in his mouth, lit up and closed his eyes. Kasdan stared at his boss with a look Ladonis had seen so often she'd named it "old-man blues." The aging vice president had missed his chance to run the show when young Bret had been appointed CEO right out of grad school. And whenever Kasdan was around the guy, that look of anger and disappointment tainted his face.

Ladonis glanced at Bret. His eyes were sad, yet melancholy didn't overshadow his bad-boy aura, that MTV raunchiness that popular religious conservatives likened to evil. That look had a naughty, sensual effect on her. But not today. Today was about Tim.

"We've got to control the press on this one," Bret said to her. He took a long drag on the cigarette. "A lot is riding on it."

"Control the press?" she asked. He couldn't be thinking straight. "How?" she said, waving away his cigarette smoke.

"What you're asking," Kasdan said. "Favors like that are hard to come by."

Mr. PR, as Kasdan described himself, should know. If he was the southern gentleman she thought he was, he'd know that unless they had something to deal with, all was lost. Kasdan walked over and smashed his cigarette into the crystal ashtray on Bret's desk. Ladonis saw the clench of Bret's jaw.

"Yes, I know," Bret said. "And we both know how far you'll go to come by favors like that. Do you want Velcroy and, say, the FBI to know as well?"

"That only happened once," Kasdan said. "I had no choice. You know as well as I do that . . ."

Kasdan glanced around, spotted Ladonis and shut up. She wasn't sure what favors Bret was talking about, but she knew that was how things were done. How else could a handful of white families control the purse strings of an entire city, no matter what race the electorate? Kasdan's taut features and droopy eyes were dead on for a man ticked off.

"Once is enough," Bret muttered, acknowledging with a quick glance that he'd also realized that Ladonis was there. He picked up a whiskey bottle, uncapped the top, tipped the bottle for a drink, then put the bottle down without taking a sip. He walked to his desk and stood beside Kasdan.

"I don't want the press," Bret's tone softened, "or anyone digging into Tim's life."

Smart move for Bret to try to sway Kasdan to his side. The seasoned VP had a knack for finding and exposing skeletons. And, direct order or not, when he felt threatened or put upon, he would not play by the rules.

"We have to make sure the press doesn't get hold of this for awhile," Bret said. He plopped down in the black leather chair behind his desk. "Too much at stake."

What was that all about? Her friend, P.J., the mayor's niece as well as his assistant, had mentioned that the Floating Palace Steamboat Company was involved in lobbying to reinstate gambling. Could Tim's death impact that? Or did it mean that Bret was somehow personally vulnerable?

"What our young leader is saying," Kasdan said turning to her, "is that we've got to make sure this story is handled without drawing attention to the company."

"Why?" Ladonis asked. Had the company crossed some ethical line? Corporations were getting caught over that line more and more these days. Though there was no ethical line in New Orleans business or politics to cross. Just do what had to be done. "I mean, do we have something to hide?"

"Not exactly." Bret helped himself to another cigarette from Kasdan's pack.

Another cigarette? Did he have a death wish? She didn't. She fanned away the smoke filling the air.

"But I can't get into that," Bret said. "It has to do with Velcroy."

Ladonis had caught glimpses of the Floating Palace's owner, Edward H. Velcroy, a Fortune 500 businessman out of New York. He stalked the halls bumming cigarettes during his infrequent visits. To her he was a freeloading slob with enough money and power to play Corporate God from afar.

"Why is that?" Ladonis asked.

She didn't expect Bret to tell her the company secret. Why would he? She was just a token. A local black and an employee who had a relationship with the city's black elected officials. Black officials who outnumbered and, for the most part, out-ranked the whites in City Hall. Nonetheless, if he had the audacity to suggest that she could turn stone to bread, she should have the good sense to ask him why.

Bret shook out another cigarette still inhaling on the one in his mouth. He had the jittery look of a power broker about to get caught. Or one of HeartTrouble's dope-head buddies getting into a police car. Like the shady characters she'd seen a thousand times in the movies.

"You can't explain why it's important to keep an employee's death a secret?" She spoke slow and low to sound Wall-Street aggressive and not ghetto overbearing. Her grandmother, Lucille, used to say,

"It's not what you say, but how you say it." If ever there was a time to remember that, this was it.

"This is not a good idea," Kasdan whispered. He sat on the edge of Bret's desk and leaned close to him. "She's a secretary, for God's sake."

Ladonis wanted to scream that she had a master's degree. In business. Kasdan didn't. But that didn't seem to matter.

"Ladonis," Bret said, glaring at Kasdan. "No one knows what happened out there. But you grew up here. You know how things operate and who's in charge. I need you to speak with your police friends and your contact at that TV station where you used to work. Get them to hold off publicizing this. Keep this off the news until—"

"Look." She wanted to sit, but her hands wouldn't let go of the chair. Her legs wouldn't move. "Asking for publicity is one thing. It's not feasible to ask to suppress information."

Who did he think she was? Just because she'd made a few phone calls that held off the city's bureaucratic leeches a couple of times didn't mean she could part water. Knowing the system had nothing to do with controlling it. To do that she had to have access to the old, white-money power structure.

"Don't get me wrong," Bret said. "We don't want the story suppressed. We just don't want the hoopla to go on and on. Until a body is found. Or a suicide note. Or something."

Suicide note? She shuddered. It was an accident. Wasn't it? Her hands gripped the chair harder. Jesus, Tim.

"All we're asking is that they hold up on it," Bret said. "To keep the public and media speculation out of this until we find out exactly what happened."

The lines around his watery eyes bunched up. He looked older and sad. Was that distress or manipulation she heard in his voice? She couldn't tell. She'd never seen that look before.

"I don't want the company," Bret said, "and Tim's death to boost media ratings any longer than it takes to memorialize him."

"Listen," she said. She'd almost called him Bret, even though she'd never addressed him that way before. "My reporter friends monitor the police radio for story leads. Suppose they tune in to Coast Guard calls as well?"

Bret's eyelids jumped. He hadn't thought of that, huh? Must be the cigarette smoke clogging his brain. Kasdan paced behind Bret sitting at his desk. Ladonis recognized the old-guy's condescending glare and knew what he wanted to say, what she'd heard him grumble many times before, "Boy, get your head out your butt."

"Two hours and no press," Kasdan said. "They'd be here waiting for the *Belle* to dock if they'd picked up on a Coast Guard signal. Evidently, you and the New Orleans cops are of like minds on this one—keep the press out of it for as long as possible."

"Makes sense." Bret sighed. "The cops tend to be cautious with news reporters on high-profile matters." He looked at his watch and turned to Ladonis. "The *Belle* is still sitting in the river a few miles away from Houmas House. Three, maybe four hours away. I'm sure the Harbor Police know that."

"Yes," Ladonis said. "And the NOPD will be here any minute now to find out all they can about Tim and . . . and whatever else they can learn before the boat gets here. I guarantee the press won't be far behind."

She saw Bret flinch when she said "whatever." What secret did Tim have that was so terrible? Or was it Bret's own secret he feared getting exposed?

"True," Bret said. "But by the time they pull something together to hit the airwaves, you can have the lid on."

Was he nuts? The reporters at WWL were CNN anchor wannabes and had hounds planted everywhere to sniff out a story lead. Especially her old classmate, Monique, who was already miffed at her for waking her up to cry on her shoulder about Jack. Suppose Monique was on the alert and she was already sniffing around? If she were still working at WWL and the riverfront was her beat, that was what she'd do.

"I'll tell you what," Bret said. "This story is yours. You'll be the company's spokesperson. You prepare our statement. All publicity must come through you."

Ladonis bristled. Kasdan let out a moan. As quickly as she had imagined the door of opportunity opening, she understood just how unrealistic Bret's request was. Sure, her friends would grant her a favor or two to put her in her employer's good graces. Particularly the city councilman who'd taught her high-school math, and especially if it took a stab at the good-ole-boy network. But the people she knew would never overstep their limits. Her influence went only as far as the we-take-care-of-our-own mentality would allow.

"If you can manage a publicity shutdown for a day, two at the most," Bret said, "I guarantee you won't be sorry."

What did he think Tim had done? What had he done? Whatever Bret was hiding had to be bad.

"Tim mentioned you have a centennial celebration plan," Bret said. "Correct?"

Her eyes flashed on Kasdan. He didn't say a word, but his eyebrows formed a grizzled line. Was he shocked at that idea? Or was he pondering his next move to put her in her place?

"Well, don't you?" Bret raised his voice.

"Yes, I do," Ladonis said.

Heat shot through her leaving her skin warm and moist. Adrenaline pumped up her ego. She couldn't help thinking about what would happen if she actually could pull off her hundredth-anniversary production idea. A new job title? A raise? Maybe a post on Presidents Row, that string of window offices overlooking the Mississippi River. Everything she wanted.

But what if she failed? Would corporate Louisiana add her to its list of blacks who couldn't make the grade? She feared this outcome the most. Her critical challenge to her climb up the corporate ladder. That, despite her preparation and hard work, success and failure were judged in terms of her blackness.

And what about Tim? His life? His death? Her brain filled with the question "why." Why did he have to die? And why wasn't that Bret's primary concern? Or was it? Suppose Tim had jumped, and she did what Bret wanted? Maybe she'd be the first to find out why he did it. That way, if it were bad for Tim and thereby the company, she could. . . Could what? Hide it from the world?

She glanced at Kasdan. He leaned against the credenza near the door staring at the pencil he twirled through his fingers. He looked up. His eyes swept over her. She sensed his displeasure. Not just with her dingy wardrobe. His disrespect was instinctive and as much for her being a woman as for her being black. If this blew up in her face, she'd have to wait for that old coot to die before she got another chance to prove what she could do.

She'd learned in college and on the job, specifically from Tim, that, to move up the corporate ladder, a climber needed support in upper administration. Tim was gone. If she played her cards right, perhaps Bret would be her deliverer. But could she be his? HeartTrouble had told her once that she had a way of making everybody and everything revolve around her. Was she making Tim's death all about her? What would Tim think?

3

What's in a Name?

Argus Travers stepped from his Crown Vic and slammed the door. The humidity smacked the New Orleans homicide detective across the face. Reality hit him too, in the gut, every time he came to work. His dad, God rest his soul, had been right. The Civil Rights Bill had changed not only the leadership at NOPD, but how things were done.

"Damn," he grumbled.

If only that dispatcher had known why the captain had sent for him. He hated walking into the unknown. Especially since that new black mayor had promised to clean up the corrupt force. How many of his fellow white officers had quit or had been discharged? Too many. But why was he fretting? He'd probably been called to handle another drug-related, turf-war murder. Civil Rights or not, blacks around here still feared white cops. The kind of fear that solved cases, one way or another.

Travers had parked in the McDonald's parking lot on the corner of Tulane and Broad. He walked past a row of bail bond storefront offices towards the Broad Street Overpass, under which was the police parking lot. He told everyone the short walk a few times a day was good exercise. The truth was it gave him time to gear up for the changes he had to face inside headquarters.

He crossed Broad at Dupre Street. Police headquarters was one side of the intersection and the city jail, a three-story gray stone building, was the other. He made his way up the steps to the glass-door entrance of the police department, listening for sounds from the jail. Usually he could hear the inmates calling out through the tiny barred windows to pedestrians, but today he heard nothing.

"Hello, Laundry," a brown co-worker said, walking up to Travers. "I thought you were off this weekend."

Travers faked a smile. It ticked him off that the black guys called him "Laundry" or "Laundry Man." That they felt comfortable enough to joke about his clothes. The fabric of his wool-blend jacket shone from wear. His no-wrinkle Docker slacks wrinkled like linen and his thread-bare white shirt was the same shade of dingy as the dirty beige walls of the building. The black guys teased that his outfit looked as if it belonged in the to-do laundry pile instead of on his tall, two-hundred and fifty pound, beer-belly body.

"I was," Travers said. "Until I was paged. You know how it is."

"Yeah," the detective said, coursing past Travers. "It sucks."

Travers headed for the coffee station, a card table set up under a window that looked out at the parish prison. He poured himself a Styrofoam cup of lukewarm coffee. Chicory coffee, New Orleans-style. Thank goodness some things never changed.

He started the trek across the room to the captain's office, acknowledging every greeting he received with a nod and a closed-mouth smile designed to show that he was police-tough, all business. The bare walls, rows of packed boxes and floors covered with drop cloths indicated a physical change in the old parish precinct house. Nothing to remind him of the times he'd spent in here as a child visiting his dad, or as an eager cadet recruit, or a young officer trying to reassure his father that policing rather than lawyering was his calling. The truth was the Cajun was as uncomfortable as a grain of salt in a pepper shaker.

He looked for his new partner, LeBron Wellsburg, a "brotha" transferred from Algiers, the town just across the Mississippi River Bridge. Wellsburg. How did an uppity Pontchartrain Park brat get a name like Wellsburg? One guess.

His own family's name had been changed twice. First when President Roosevelt's battle cry "one nation, one language" thundered across the country. In their hometown, that meant Cajuns, French-speaking Louisiana natives living along the bayous. Descendants of French Arcadia immigrants mixed with every other European bloodline. The French language was discouraged. Considered a sign of illiteracy. Forced Travers' French granddaddy, married to Mary Argus, a Dane, to change his name from Travers to Argus to fit in. And to get work.

But, before the old Frenchman had died, he had begged his son, the detective's dad, to change it back. Travers' dad did just that and named his first born Argus Travers. He said that gesture was to remind Travers and his brother how their granddaddy had survived the French fallout in this country with his dignity intact.

Travers sipped his chicory. Where was Wellsburg? Surely he'd been commanded to come in too. Travers wished he hadn't. He liked policing the old way, the by-any-means-necessary technique he'd employed with his old partner, Gary Bootfel. But Gary had gotten caught on tape extorting cash from Vietnamese merchants on Canal Street. He had had to either quit or be charged. Gary had quit. And Travers had gotten saddled with LeBron Wellsburg, a college graduate who was into that understanding, compassionate cop malarkey.

Travers spotted Detective Wellsburg strutting into the captain's office. Who could miss that pressed-to-perfection suit on that gym-sculpted dark-brown body of his? But Travers was the veteran detective. He knew he belonged in cop land. Everybody knew. But was he welcome? Was he one of them? Did he want to be? He fretted over the answers every day. Him, a white guy. A Cajun. His father was a past captain of detectives. Who belonged in New Orleans—in this precinct—more than this Cajun? Now, he, Travers, was being treated like he was some outside child born with the right genes, but without the pedigree.

Twyla Toussaint rolled in after Wellsburg. Even though it was Saturday, and she was officially off duty, NOPD's first female homicide detective wore her navy police uniform, the skirt version, and her curly brown hair in her trademark French twist.

"Captain Toussaint," Travers greeted her, noting the address she insisted upon. He acknowledged his partner, Detective Wellsburg, with a nod.

Captain Toussaint made her way to her chair. Wellsburg found a seat facing her. Travers lingered at the door. Here he was, in the captain's office, his dad's old office, watching a not-so-good-looking Creole woman walk behind his dad's desk.

"Tim Ganen," she said, sitting in his dad's seat. "A corporate VP at that Floating Palace Steamboat Company went through a paddle wheel into the Mississippi this morning."

"Fucking executives," Travers said. "Probably got caught ripping the company off."

"Is that cop intuition?" Wellsburg asked.

"I call it like I see it." Travers glanced over at his partner, his grin slow and menacing. "I know these guys. My brother . . ." Travers felt heat on his face. "They steal and then apologize. They cheat and working stiffs bleed. Blood for green. That's how they jerk off."

Why did he have to bring his younger brother into this? No wonder everyone thought he hated his big shot, younger sibling who ran a big insurance outfit in Dallas. What he hated was that his brother never even called unless he had some bonus to report. Like the time he bragged about his $200,000 freebie the same day his company announced that 220 workers had to lose their jobs.

"Seems to me your attitude—" Wellsburg began.

"Okay, that's enough," Twyla Toussaint interrupted Wellsburg. "I want the two of you to get over to the Floating Palace Steamboat Company and find out as much as you can about this Tim Ganen. The Coast Guard just released the boat, and it's on its way upriver." She checked her watch. "I want a handle on this guy's life and his . . . his motivation before it gets here."

Motivation? Anybody with half a cop's brain knew his motivation. Travers gulped down more chicory.

"So far," the captain said. "We've got the drop on the press. Let's keep it that way."

"Big deal, huh, Captain Toussaint?" Travers said. "Or should I say high profile?"

He hated the hoops they had to jump through when some mucky-muck got into trouble. Meant that somebody with money and influence had to have a hand in the investigation.

"I'll say," the captain replied. "The Coast Guard woke me up. Then the chief and the DA called. I suspect the Mayor will be next."

Her testiness bemused Detective Travers. He'd long thought women didn't have the balls to be NOPD. And that all the new sissy rules of conduct were implemented to accommodate them. But could the lady captain be a cop with the old-school mentality?

"By the book, gentlemen," Captain Toussaint ordered. "I have a feeling about this one."

"Who's in charge over there?" Wellsburg asked.

"The CEO's name is Bret Collins," Captain Toussaint said. "Looks like he and the dead guy go way back."

The lady captain looked away. What was she thinking? She checked her notepad.

"And a Lamar Kasdan," she said, "heads the PR department. An Ohio transplant, I believe, considering how long he's been with the company. The dead man and the CEO came here from New York, Chicago, I don't remember which." She lowered her voice. "But I hear we have a home girl, Ladonis Washington, working in PR alongside this Kasdan fellow."

Travers tuned in to the animosity he heard in her voice. Looked up and saw her pick up a pencil and tap it nervously on the desk. Her jaw muscles clinched.

"According to the Mayor," the captain said, "she can act as a go-between. He said it's always good to have someone in the thick of things who understands our ways when 'foreigners' are involved in situations like this."

"Does the mayor know this Washington woman?" Travers asked.

"I'm sure," the captain said. "She grew up in the Magnolia Project. Graduated at the head of her class at LSU. Got some press. A real go-getter, I understand. And as connected as a sister can be around here."

More connected than the captain? The daughter of a professor who grew up in that well-to-do, black-folk Ponchartrain Park suburb? Travers couldn't hold back a grin. He knew what it meant to be Creole in New Orleans. French mixed with African. He knew that when the Creoles started marrying whites and Native Americans, the mixture created a caste system among blacks based on skin tone, dialect and family history. Ladonis Washington evidently didn't have the light-skinned Creole pedigree like the captain. But she sure as hell had something going for her.

"Friend of yours, Captain Toussaint?" Travers asked.

"No, not really," the captain said, hanging her head. "We went to the same high school is all. I believe she finished a couple of years after I did."

Travers smiled. A them-against-them-feud. Would it hamper the investigation and prove once and for all that he should have been head detective like his dad? Or just fuel the fire of discontent burning inside of him? He'd better watch his step.

"I take it," Wellsburg said, "the Coast Guard is calling Ganen's plunge murder?"

"Not necessarily," Travers said. "They always call on us when someone ends it in the river."

"That's not all," Captain Toussaint said. "I expect a lot of heat from our noble elected officials because of the gaming lobby. So get to the bottom of this quickly and quietly. If it becomes national news and fodder for late night commentary, we're all screwed. It is an election year, you know."

The captain, skin as white as his, didn't have an exquisite face, making a fallacy of the myth about the beauty of mix-breed blacks. But had her expression been the least bit agreeable, she might've appeared less unattractive. Less black.

"That goddamn CEO had something to hide and I'm gonna find out what," Travers said, an assurance that struck something in the captain. What was that look she gave him? Aggravated? Accusing? What?

"Wellsburg," she said. "You're the primary. And you . . ."

She stared Travers square into his shocked blue eyes. He held back a chuckle. What do you call putting a home boy in charge?

Funny as that was to Travers, the wrongness of it was more over-whelming.

"Keep your cool," she continued. "Don't go mouthing off about thieving CEO's and get the press all worked up. I don't want the media second guessing us on this. Before I deal with them, I want to know this guy and what happened. Any speculation or—or how they say?—rush to judgment on our part, could backfire."

"Cap, I mean Captain Toussaint." Travers' tone was not respect-ful. "I think—"

"I'm the thinker here, Detective Travers."

Captain Toussaint stonewalled him with a stare so glaring, his Klan wizard father would've shut up. She was from the old school all right.

4

Pure Evil

Ladonis pulled up in front of 20BB Industry Street. Tall grass and weeds surrounded Monique's house, making it look out of place amongst the one-story bungalow style homes with their manicured St. Augustine-grass lawns and blooming flower beds. Before the sixties, practically no dark-skinned families lived in the homes built and inhabited by the black French carpenters and bricklayers, craftsmen just white enough to get the jobs that paid enough to construct these modest dwellings. Ladonis lingered inside her car, staring forward. Why was she here? Was a false sense of purpose corrupting her integrity the way Monique's unkempt yard undermined the character of the seventh-ward neighborhood?

She stumbled onto her old friend's front porch and rang the bell. She and Monique had been challenging each other for recognition since grade school. To have to ask her nemesis for help was like blasphemy. Her eyes peeled on the caramel-colored woman watching her from the yard next door. The old lady's eyes were so green, they shone like traffic lights and bore into Ladonis like kryptonite. Could the old lady see the fight going on inside her head? But what choice did she have? Her task had been spelled out to her, along with all the possible consequences if she failed.

"Miss Laura," Monique said, when she opened the door and

saw how hard Ladonis stared at her neighbor. "Pure evil, that one. Voodoo, they say."

Monique turned and walked back into her house, Ladonis in tow. The Daisy Duke short-shorts Monique wore did little to hide the big brown liver splashes on her thick, shapely vanilla thighs. And the girl hadn't changed a thing about the house since her mom had died last year. Hadn't gotten rid of any of the stuff she'd complained about. The scratched French furniture, the worn-out Oriental rugs, the ancient starched-stiff crochet table scarves.

"Evil, huh?" Ladonis said. "The revered voodoo priestess, Marie Leveau, was Catholic. Sin and evil sure do get convoluted around here."

Ladonis sighed. Would judgments like this ever cease? Hers as well as Monique's? Why couldn't one's spiritual beliefs or non-beliefs be placed under a gag order to be discussed only between the believer and the believee?

"There you go," Monique said. "Spouting off. Just because you don't believe."

"Believe what?" Ladonis said. "You've got to admit that it's a strange kinship between God and sin in this town. Think about Mardi Gras? Where else does a wild, decadent, month-long party prerequisite a sacrificial religious season like Lent?"

As the words bounced from her lips, Ladonis wondered why she'd allowed herself to initiate a religious debate with a when-it-suits-me devout Catholic. She had her own dogma to contend with. If God helped those who helped themselves, like her Grandma Lucille said, then she'd just helped Bret set her up to fail.

"Whatever, Donnie," Monique sighed.

Stubbornness added to Monique's personal drama. A stubbornness Ladonis thought clouded her friend's rationale. Made reasoning with her a pain in the ass.

"Well, Donnie." Monique plopped down on a worn Louis XIV chair. A cocksure expression flashed on her face. "One guess why you're here."

Monique knew about Tim. Ladonis should have known. Her phone call to cancel their walk, then the call to say she was stopping by must have tipped Monique off.

"How did you find out?" Ladonis asked.

"My uncle faxed me from the boat," Monique said.

"Your uncle?" Ladonis asked.

"Yeah, you know my uncle," Monique said. "You helped him get the job on board. The assistant purser, remember?"

"Oh, that uncle," Ladonis said.

She had forgotten about him, the college dropout who'd moved to Washington State and passed for white until he had a nervous breakdown and then come back to his roots. How could she have forgotten that uncle, especially since his job gave him access to a fax machine?

Whatever else Ladonis thought of Monique, she could count on her going after what she wanted. And when it came to a story that could steer her toward Atlanta, CNN and all those professional black newscasters, Monique had the sensitivity of a hound dog.

Ladonis had been involved in the New Orleans communication machine long enough to know that information, like everything else, was transported through an unseen but definite aristocracy. WWL, the city's leading news station and a CBS affiliate, was to that machine what signal carriers were to telecommunications. The pitfall to that knowledge, however, was that Monique was her only contact in that milieu, her only shot at stopping a media deluge. How desperate was that?

On one hand, Ladonis hoped that the news about Tim's death would break. On the other she wanted to be the genius behind the game plan that kept the media from overwhelming the Floating Palace. So, now, she wasn't going to back away from the I'm-a-step-ahead-of-you-glint glaring in Monique's eyes.

"When?"

"When will it hit the air?" Monique finished Ladonis' inquiry.

Ladonis nodded.

"Not until that boat gets in," Monique said. "I can't get a helicopter out there without signaling other news stations."

Ladonis exhaled, thanking God the story hadn't gone out on CB radio. Still, Monique had her on a string. Ladonis had to be patient and find out how much time, if any, she had to alert Bret and prepare a statement. Without Monique's cooperation, she didn't stand a chance in hell to orchestrate the words and images the world should see and hear about Tim and the Floating Palace.

"I want to take this one national," Monique said.

Ladonis felt her heart sink. What had she been thinking? Keeping Tim's death off the airways was impossible for a colored girl from the Magnolia. Especially when a pretty passé blanc—what New Orleans blacks called Creole—had her heart set on doing just the opposite.

"Besides," Monique said. "I want to make sure that not one single detail gets swept under a rug."

Monique was looking for bad guys. Preferably white evildoers. Sometimes Monique's determination to show the world that there were bad white people put added pressure on Ladonis. Made her self-conscious about the thin line she straddled between her black and white worlds. Was this Creole princess more proud to be black than she was?

Monique had carried the I'm-black-and-proud chip on her shoulders ever since the two of them worked on a book-report about Martin Luther King, Jr. and Rosa Parks. Turned out a lot of young Creoles adopted that attitude after Civil Rights, when black became beautiful. To the chagrin of their elders, who loved the privilege and social standing of their light-colored skin. But why did Monique have to prove her blackness by dumping on her whiteness? And why did her news reporting always have to come down to that?

"I have a proposition to make," Ladonis said. "One that will give you first crack at breaking this story as well as give me some time."

"Time to do what?" Monique said, repositioning herself on the chair.

"Tim Ganen," Ladonis said, taking the you-get-on-my-last-nerve tone out of her voice. "The man, who lost his life, was one of the company's top VPs. My boss wants the opportunity to conduct an in-house investigation to find out what happened and why, so that the facts relayed publicly are not sensationalized to the point where it promotes bias toward the company."

"That's it?" Monique's eyes squinted.

Ladonis shrugged.

"Ah, come on, Donnie," Monique said. "You cannot bullshit a bullshitter. What's really going on here?"

"Cool the drama, Nikka." The agitated tone she wanted to avoid came gushing out. "All I'm asking . . ."

"What you're asking," Monique said, "is a crock."

One, two, three. Ladonis tried to calm herself. Think before she spoke.

"I know it's hush, hush," Monique said. "But do you think I don't know that your company is up to its favor-for-pay ass in the gaming lobby? Considering how many rich conservatives pay that exorbitant price for a nostalgic ride up and down the rivers on a two-mile-an-hour paddle wheeler, I'm sure that cutie-pie boss of yours does not want to draw attention to that."

"If you ask me," Ladonis said, "it's more about you and your anchor aspirations that you'd sell your own mama out to get."

So much for thinking before speaking. And what about Ladonis' motives? Didn't she plan to use Tim's death to open a career door? How selfish was that? Especially since Tim had listened to her, advised her, encouraged her. To top it off, he'd told Bret about her steamboatin' centennial celebration idea. Just thinking about that gave her goose bumps.

"Take the low road," Monique said. "See if I care. This is big. No way am I going to take a pass."

"Who said anything about taking a pass?" Ladonis said. "I'm offering you an exclusive."

"Far as I can tell." Monique stood up, circled the room. "I have an exclusive."

"Yeah, but I knew the guy," Ladonis said. "I know people who knew him." Her voice intonation went up. "I can make sure that you get first-hand details on the personal stuff. You know, like what was his childhood like. Who was his first fuck. The kind of 411 you reporters call news." She threw up her hands. "You can milk headlines that will impress CNN for months with that kind of information." She stopped to breathe. "Either that or I can call a press conference and open this up to every reporter in the world."

"Tell me something, Donnie," Monique said. "Why is this so important to you? What are you holding back?"

"Holding back?" Ladonis got to her feet.

"Don't do that, Donnie. Don't put on that dumb-blond act of yours. I hate it when you do that. Tell me what's involved here. Sex? Embezzling? Drugs? What?"

"Dumb?" Was this insult-Ladonis day? "What's dumb? Using discretion? There's nothing dumb about being discreet. There's nothing dumb about dying with dignity." She straightened up. "Besides, you're the one who swore that you wouldn't be another . . . how did you put it? Another media gasbag feeding into America's voyeur fixation."

Ladonis kneaded her hands. What was more important? Winning this argument or finding a way to get through to her old friend? Then it occurred to her.

The city's aristocracy with the slightest connection to the Floating Palace could be impacted by this so-called situation. Outside forces could very well neutralize the city's what-happens-in-our-house-stays-here philosophy. God forbid the New Orleans way of doing things should be exposed to a national audience. If she could keep that from happening, no telling how far up she could go.

"Can you please just not publicize this until I give you the go ahead?" Ladonis said.

"There you go," Monique said. "Giving me orders."

"No, I'm not," Ladonis said with a little less malice. "All I'm asking is for some time, a day, that's all. Twenty-four hours to make sure that the right story gets out there before you start spinning facts around."

New Orleans operated and communicated on its own terms. Despite having visitors from all over the globe and a high crime rate, the Big Easy continued to conceal its likeness to a poverty-stricken, poorly-educated third-world country. Yet Ladonis had dared to wish for the two days Bret requested. But keeping the media from a story like this for an hour was next to impossible even in New Orleans. Tough odds for an ambitious project girl. For any girl.

"Spinning facts around?" Monique said.

"Well . . ." Ladonis threw up her hands. "Whatever it is you call what you media actors do."

"Give me one good reason why I should do what you want?" Monique asked. "Why shouldn't I be the one to expose the bastards for the crooks they are?"

"Because my job depends on it," Ladonis said.

That was way more than she wanted to admit to. Though it hadn't escaped her that between the time it took the city's aristocrats to clarify their position and the time it took Monique to guarantee herself first crack at the copyright, it could very well save her career. Especially with an assurance from Monique that she'd follow her lead. An empowering thought. Though not as empowering as the task was daunting.

"Please, Nikka," Ladonis said. "Don't screw this up for me. Help me keep this close for one day. You'll get your exclusive. I promise."

"Sorry, Donnie," Monique said. "But I can't make any promises."

Ladonis' spirit sunk. Life could be a bitch. So could Monique.

"Remember when we were kids," Ladonis said, "what your mama told us that time she overheard us arguing about whatever it was we were arguing about?"

An unfamiliar emotion covered Monique's face. Monique had had a hard time getting over her mother's death. A hard time dealing with having spent much of her adult life at odds with the woman. Ladonis hoped that her rash appeal to Monique's sense of loss would turn out to be a smart move.

"She told us," Ladonis said. "That loyalty builds friendship And that friendship is the foundation of a good, happy life. Remember that?"

Monique looked away, her silence as telling as a death-bed confession. She walked to the entrance hall, opened the door, and stood there like an English guard. Ladonis' brow contracted. Her eyes grew wide. She had overstepped the boundaries of their relationship. She wanted to kick herself.

"I guess you don't," Ladonis said as she stepped outside the door.

She clutched her keys so tight, the skin on her hand broke. Not only had she exposed her desperation and vulnerability, she'd antagonized the reporter from hell. And, Lord help her, Ladonis had put her onto the scent of a Watergate. What would that do to her chance of getting an office on Presidents Row?

5

Impact

A horn honked. Ladonis sped up. She didn't see the pothole until the last minute. The water-filled dips and cracks on Bayou St. John Street were invisible. She pressed down on the brakes. Her car skidded, swerved inches from an electricity pole.

"Jesus," she muttered.

The pre-dawn rain had ebbed into a dark cloud, leaving the street slick and gray, the way her meeting with Monique had left her spirits. She thought about hiring someone to break the heifer's knees. No, she had to sidetrack Monique. Conduct an in-house investigation and get the jump on the police. Lord, Lord. How was she supposed to handle the police?

A hundredweight of butterflies, wings flapping, invaded her inners. What had she gotten herself into? Tim had plunged to his death into the Mississippi River, and she felt compelled to find out why. These were the cold, hard facts, and they were as foreboding as a category five hurricane warning.

She gasped, rolled down the car's windows. The air was thick with moisture. Both the sun and the rain were stuck in the clouds, unable to break through. She glanced at the impatiens-lined median across from City Park.

"P.J." she yelled.

The sound of her own voice gave her a jolt. Since they had been freshmen in college, P.J. had played tennis on the same court in City Park every Saturday morning. Only a storm with pouring rain stopped her.

Ladonis swung around into the park's Esplanade Street entrance as if a power had seized her. Why hadn't she thought of P.J. before? Even in Louisiana with its Catholic parishes as opposed to a county form of local government, the mayor had the power to command the police. And P.J.'s uncle was the sitting mayor.

She parked and walked past the New Orleans Museum of Art, a white neoclassical building near the green-clay tennis courts a couple of blocks away off the City Park Avenue side of the 1,500-acre park. She spotted P.J. right away, her little red pleated skirt, matching visor and jewels. That girl would accessorize her bedclothes if she could.

P.J. and three other women weren't hitting balls, but yakking and laughing. P.J. was big on tennis etiquette and had told her more than once that it was considered rude to interrupt a tennis match. The perfect time to interrupt a tennis match.

"P.J.," Ladonis called out, walking onto the court. "I need your help."

"What are you doing here?" P.J. said. "I thought you had to go to work?"

P.J.'s lips curled down from a smile. Her expression showed that she wasn't pleased by the interruption. P.J.'s tennis buddies weren't welcoming either. They headed back onto the court without so much as a good morning, beckoning to P.J. not to hold them up.

Ladonis stopped, took a step back. She hadn't expected such a glare of annoyance from P.J. She hadn't expected to become friends with the half-white, zirconium-and-gold wearing prima donna when they had first met either. But, after four years of sitting beside her in classes at LSU, she'd learned to respect P.J., even to mimic her social savvy.

"Okay," P.J. said. "Who died?"

"A friend," Ladonis mumbled, choked by a burst of sadness. "And we worked together."

Her heartbeat raced. Without any of the shenanigans, Tim was dead. No more. P.J. stepped closer to Ladonis, put a hand on her arm.

"I need a favor," Ladonis said.

"Ladonis, we agreed, remember?" P.J. said, again sounding less than a sympathetic friend.

"I know," Ladonis said. "But this is a matter of life and death."

The mayor's niece and Ladonis had made a pact at graduation. Had sworn never to exploit each other's positions no matter where they ended up working. Unlike every other successful New Orleanean Ladonis knew. Especially politicians.

"Life and death?" P.J. said, waving her racket. "Girl, please. That's what you said when you woke me up before daybreak after you let that fine ass Jack get away."

Ladonis frowned. Whatever had made her think two Creole debutantes would understand what making her own success meant to her? Everything they did was to catch a man.

"Okay," P.J. said. "Make your point."

Ladonis ran down the details she knew about Tim's death. She emphasized how important it was for the CEO to get to the facts before the media started speculating.

"Before this thing is broadcast all over the world," she said. "We've got to make sure that the Floating Palace and the city's name are not dragged through media mud."

"Ladonis, you know as well as I do that the mayor does not have a controlling influence on the day-to-day work of the police or the district attorney."

Who was she kidding? What went on in City Hall was pure soap opera. Would put life on television soaps to shame.

"Please, P.J.," Ladonis said. "This is important."

"Important to whom?" P.J. asked.

Ladonis sucked in a gulp of damp air. How could she answer that? Her conscience was still grappling with the answer.

"I don't know about this, Ladonis," P.J. said. "I don't think my uncle should get involved."

"The mayor shouldn't get involved in protecting the city's assets?" Ladonis said. "Visitors are this city's lifeline, aren't they?"

A stretch, but it might work. P.J. had a real passion for her city. For her uncle's mayoral legacy. That was why she hadn't accepted that big Starbucks corporate job in Seattle after graduation.

"Have you forgotten," Ladonis said, "that the Floating Palace relocated its successful business here to a graveyard port? And, I might add, not only brought in new jobs, but enhanced tourism worldwide." She almost choked. "Your uncle should be eager to audit the press on this, for the city. A city that banks on tourist dollars. A city that gets enough bad press as it is."

P.J. sighed. A look of surrender made its way to her eyes. Ladonis' body slumped with relief.

"This is a city emergency," Ladonis said, wavering between pride and shame at how well she'd manipulated the city's position to accommodate the Floating Palace Steamboat Company. "Couldn't you broker a meeting for sometime this morning?"

"No, I cannot," P.J. answered. "My uncle is in Washington."

"D.C.?" Ladonis asked. Deflated energy softened her tone. What else could she do? Who else could help her?

"Relax," P.J. told her. "He's expected back late tonight. But I'll get to talk to him at my grandmother's house before then." P.J.'s high-society grandmother was her mom's and the mayor's mother.

"Would you explain this situation to him then?" Ladonis asked.

P.J. waved to the three women summoning her from the other side of the tennis court. Ladonis exhaled loudly. This had to work.

"Okay, Ladonis," P.J. said. "I'll tell the mayor what you said and ask him to suggest to the police and district attorney to hold off making public statements until after he speaks with you guys."

"Thanks," Ladonis said.

"I'm not promising you he'll do it," P.J. said. "Either way, I'm sure he'll be in touch."

"Fine," Ladonis said. She wanted to get the monkey off her back. "Have him call Bret Collins."

"Ladonis," P.J. said. "Don't make this a habit."

P.J. turned to walk away. Ladonis had told P.J. the same thing last year when P.J. had asked Ladonis for a favor. Could Ladonis get the Floating Palace to donate six weeklong cruises to her grand-mother's book club? And Ladonis had, saying pretty much the same thing. But without the edge she had just heard in P.J.'s voice.

"Oh, another thing," P.J. said, turning back. "The mayor will have to know from the police how the investigation is going before he does anything."

The tone of P.J.'s voice changed from protective to authoritative when she switched from "my uncle" to "the mayor." How did P.J. do that? Remain loyal and loving to her uncle and a responsible employee at the same time?

"I know that," Ladonis said.

"Well, if the police tell him that the investigation has turned up evidence indicating foul play," P.J. warned in that protective tone, "the mayor will probably encourage the police to go public or face cover-up allegations. Which, by the way, is not an option. With all the gaming stuff going on, that kind of focus on a city already under federal scrutiny—well, that's no good for anybody."

Foul play? How could two four-letter words have the impact of a hurricane?

6

Deserted

Travers stood next to Detective Wellsburg on the steps outside police headquarters. Travers, at least twenty pounds larger and a foot taller than his partner, looked swollen beside Wellsburg. And the scowl on his face did not hide his smoldering anger any more than his wet armpits hid the eighty-degree August heat. He was the senior officer. He should be the primary. How would it look? Him following Wellsburg's lead?

"My car," Travers said, pointing, "is parked down the street at McDonald's."

He hurried down the steps. He'd do the driving for this team. He would not allow anyone—the crime-scene lab guys or any other cops—see him exit from the passenger side with Wellsburg behind the wheel. There was something commanding about driving up to an investigation.

"You know," Wellsburg said, walking toward the Crown Vic, "you could wash this thing every now and then."

"Haven't you heard?" Travers said, rubbing his day old beard. "I'm allergic to soap and water."

"So it seems," Wellsburg said, staring at Travers.

Travers glanced away. Wellsburg's blended stare of scorn and mockery was like looking in the mirror. Wellsburg slid into the passenger seat. He fastened himself in, leaned his head back and folded his arms across his chest. Travers got in beside him and slammed the door.

"I bet them fucking riverboat CEOs gonna try to hide something," Travers said.

"This insight of yours," Wellsburg said, "wouldn't have anything to do with the fact that your brother graduated from Harvard and you flunked out of Delgado Junior College, would it?"

That goddamn precinct grapevine. Travers turned the key. The engine revved. How dare this guy? What made him think he could comment on his personal life? Travers had to put Wellsburg in his place. Set some boundaries. He did not want this Algiers transplant to get the impression he wanted to get familiar.

He put the car in reverse and turned around to see where he was headed. He hit the brakes. The abrupt stop jerked Wellsburg forward.

"Just because we have to work together," Travers said, "does not give you license to get into my personal business."

"Listen, Man," Wellsburg said. "Before you get all worked up, you hear about your buddy Vince yet?"

"What do you know about me and Vince?" Travers said.

He wheeled the car from Tulane Avenue and drove toward the river down Canal Street. Not the same since Maison Blanche and Krauss department stores had gone under. The Crown Vic sank into a pothole. Wellsburg was thrust back.

"I know that he and your partner, Gary, got brought up on charges," Wellsburg said. "Gary bailed. Needed his pension, I guess. But Vince decided to fight."

"Yeah, so what?" Travers said.

"The jury found him guilty last night," Wellsburg said. "The best narcotic detective on the force and he's being sent up for drug trafficking."

Whoa. Vince was on his way to prison? Cops in this town hardly ever got convicted. Hell, he'd tried to convince Gary to go to trial. Thought he'd get a better deal. The car dipped into the next lane.

"Oops," Travers said. "There goes that low-water table again."

"I know the city's below sea level," Wellsburg said, re-situating his body in the passenger seat.

A yellow light flicked to red. Travers floored the brakes. He peeked over at Wellsburg. Wellsburg stretched his arms out to the dashboard, pushed his body back into the seat. What would it take to send him through the windshield? The light turned green. Travers pushed down on the accelerator. Wellsburg leaned forward, then back.

"What do Vince's troubles have to do with the case?" Travers said. "Or us working together?"

"The Feds, that's what," Wellsburg told him. "They're all in police shit nowadays. Ever since the hotshot new mayor promised to clean up the force. Especially the narcotics division."

He hated Admin as much as any red-blooded cop, but could not allow himself to trust this guy. No way he wanted to share anything with him. Not even a common dislike for brass. Everything hostile, malcontented, disgruntled knotted up inside him so tight he could hardly breathe.

"The way I hear it," Wellsburg said. "The Feds planted an under-cover suit close to the city's numero uno pusher who just happened to be Vince's connection."

He knew all about Vince's operations. He, Vince and Gary went way back. He'd even participated in a couple of Vince's extortion scams before Vince started drug dealing.

"Get to the punch line, will you?" Travers said.

"Vince was with this guy the night he went down," Wellsburg said. "Seems this drug lord called Vince and told him to meet him outside Commander's Palace at midnight. The undercover guy tailed Vince. He saw Vince park and wait, then stop a car. You know, with the police light."

Travers felt a rush of heat over his body. His fingers slipped on the steering wheel. He'd warned his buddies things could go bad.

"He wrote the guy a ticket," Wellsburg said. "Then walked up to a black Mercedes parked behind him. According to the undercover suit, Vince tapped the Mercedes window, got in his car and drove off. The Mercedes pulled up next to the other car, fired two shots and another dealer bites the dust."

"And you know all of this, how?" Travers asked, gripping the steering wheel to keep his hands from trembling.

"It all came up at Vince's trial," Wellsburg said.

The trial. Travers knew he should've gone to the trial. Vince had asked him to be there. Travers made an illegal U-turn.

"I hear it went down just like a *Perry Mason* rerun," Wellsburg said. "There was even a surprise girlfriend eyewitness to prove that Vince and the drug lord were cohorts. Vince was forced to confess. He had to tell all about his drug dealings. I hear he had to give up the shooter in the Mercedes or be charged with first-degree murder."

"Man, you'd think the Feds would go easy on the guy," Travers said, feeling let down. "At least he got another lowlife off the streets."

"Go easy?" Wellsburg got excited. "What the fuck you talking about? You don't spend twenty years putting scumbags away for selling that shit and then turn around and spend twenty in the slammer for doing it yourself."

"It's tough," Travers said. "Trying to dispense law and order when there's so much drug money floating around."

"That's dumb, man," Wellsburg said. "Dumber and more dumb."

"Don't you ever get tired of seeing dope peddlers piss away good, spendable cash?" Travers asked.

Travers knew it was wrong, defecting to the other side in the so-called war on drugs. But if Mr. Do-The-Right-Thing was married to a disowned Maynard steel heiress and had a kid who needed braces and private school tuition, he wouldn't think that what Vince and Gary did was so bad. Why should the bad guys make the money to live well and cops get citations to frame for their walls?

"Look," Wellsburg said. "All I'm saying is that cops are going to jail more and more. Good cops as well as bad cops. They're going down for shit nobody used to think twice about."

The car screeched around another corner. Travers wanted to shut out the sound of Wellsburg's voice. To extract him from Gary's seat beside him.

"And you," Wellsburg said, "already have priors with Internal Affairs for a bad attitude and vigilante policing."

He couldn't believe how much this college-educated jerk knew about his life. How little he knew about Wellsburg. He didn't like feeling so vulnerable.

"Don't do anything stupid, man," Wellsburg said. "We might be partners, but I'm the primary on this one, and I'm not getting brought up on any kind of charges because you're itching to bring a CEO down."

"You know what, man," Travers said. "I was just thinking how good it is to have a partner who thinks so highly of me."

"Fuck you, Travers," Wellsburg said. "Just remember what I said.

I will not have your back if your hot-headedness interferes with this investigation."

Travers gritted his teeth. Why had Gary and Vince deserted him? Left him alone to fend for his livelihood in a familiar yet different workplace?

7

Sniff and Snuff

Ladonis had learned to use landmarks to help her find her way. So today, when she glanced over and saw the archway that led onto Armstrong Park, she slowed the car. The park, known to native black New Orleanians as the old Congo Square, was where slaves had been allowed to enjoy music and dance from their African cultures on Sunday afternoons, where some say jazz had begun, and where teenaged Ladonis had read true romance magazines. She turned off St. Ann onto Rampart Street in front of the park's entrance.

Just below the shabby, pink shotgun double on the right corner, she pulled her Chevy Geo up the circular brick drive in front of the Dixieland, the Floating Palace's own luxury French Quarter hotel. Avery, a giant, red-headed, freckled-faced bellman, rushed around to hold her car door open.

"What's up?" Avery said. "Family or business?"

"Business with family," Ladonis said, handing him her car keys.

Her cousin, Big Dee, was the hotel's dispatch supervisor. The woman had organized and now ran a successful underground network of bellmen, doormen, housemen and room attendants in hotels throughout the city. For a price, they warded off jealous wives, husbands and lovers, the media, paparazzi, even the police. Ladonis' plan was to have Big Dee cut Monique off from anyone and everyone on that boat who had information about Tim's death, including Monique's faxing uncle.

Avery smiled. Rumor linked him and Big Dee romantically. Ladonis knew for a fact that he was her cousin's best friend. Her Grandma Lucille had told her that if a good friend stood with you, you could survive without family. It meant a lot to Ladonis that Big Dee had Avery to depend on.

"Where is she?" Ladonis asked.

"Her office," Avery told her.

"Anyone in there with her?"

"Not that I know of," Avery said, slipping behind the wheel of her car.

"I'll just pop in then," Ladonis said. "I won't be long. Okay?"

She didn't want Avery to park her car in the Dungeon, the hotel's underground parking area. When she finished talking with Big Dee, she had to rush to the Pelican Street Wharf. To be there when the boat docked. Her plan was to look around Tim's room and talk to her friends on board before the cops arrived. Otherwise, her efforts to "control the press" could sink deep into the river of failure.

Ladonis found her daddy's sister's firstborn, Delois Washington, at her desk working with time cards. Big Dee had the face of a child, the physical presence of a female gladiator, and the business savvy of a Louisiana politician. Perfect qualifications for running her underground operation in a city some said was the most corrupt in the world.

Big Dee brushed back her braided extensions and looked up when Ladonis entered her space. An expectant look on her face. Avery had warned her. That was the nature of the operation. Required nothing more than peon grapevine communication.

The doorman sniffed out the culprits—an enraged wife, jealous husband, or , in this case, a reporter. Warnings of the person's hotel whereabouts spread like wild grass to bellmen, housemen, even telephone operators. Then anything could happen. A room might get switched or a guest sneaked from one hotel to another. Back-alley taxi and limo service arranged. Televisions blacked out. Telephone calls intercepted.

According to Big Dee, she'd done what government had failed to do. She'd carved out a piece of the New Orleans American pie for its little people. In the city's most lucrative market—depraved behavior.

"Problem?" Big Dee said, her tone direct, without inflection.

"A whopper," Ladonis told her, plopping down on the rundown love seat across from her cousin's desk.

"Aunt Leslie Pearl?" Big Dee said, her brown eyes wide with alarm.

"No," Ladonis said. "Mama is fine. It's work related."

"Underground work?" Big Dee said.

"It is," Ladonis said.

Ladonis had learned from HeartTrouble that, to be successful in Sin City, one had to have underground connections as well as friends in high places. HeartTrouble, an underground kind of guy, had a criminal file so thick, it filled three file-cabinet drawers in the Criminal Courts records room. Yet, because Grandma Lucille cleaned house for a couple of judges and a city councilwoman, he'd served little to no time in the Orleans Parish jail on Tulane and Broad streets. And no time at all in Angola. But HeartTrouble was small-time.

Big Dee's body straightened. She unlocked her desk and pulled out her little black journal. She'd organized her band of sin protectors after she unwittingly destroyed a priest's life. She told Ladonis that a tabloid reporter paid her fifty dollars to snitch on a hotel customer's liaisons with call girls. The customer turned out to be a priest devoted to the city's poor. After the holy man's community fallout, Big Dee decided that if fifty dollars could ruin a man, she could make a fortune protecting reputations.

"Who, what, when and where?" Big Dee said, her voice growing stronger.

"You remember my classmate, Monique LaFaye?" Ladonis said. "The reporter?"

"I saw that Negro wannabe sniffing around here a couple of days ago." She rose from her chair, walked to the small refrigerator and took out a Coke. She held the can out in offering to Ladonis. Ladonis shook her head no.

"Whose life is she screwing with now?" Big Dee asked, uncapping the soda.

"Mine," Ladonis said.

"Ain't you too black to be on her hit list?" Big Dee gulped down a couple of swallows of the drink.

"Yeah, but I'm in the line of fire," Ladonis said. "Tim . . . you know Tim don't you? Tim Ganen? The finance guy?"

"Your friend," Big Dee said. "I see the two of you 'round here, talkin' all the time."

"Well, he died in a paddle wheel this morning."

The words came out easy enough. But the reality was still as shocking and painful as the first time she'd heard them. How long before that ache went away?

"That explains why the boat so late," Big Dee said. "I'd better get the staff prepared. The passengers will be all wound up and needy as hell."

Big Dee reached to pick up the phone, then hesitated. She leaned back in her seat and looked squarely at her cousin.

"But that's not why you here," she said, her tone softer.

"No, it's not," Ladonis said. "I need your help."

"To do what?" Big Dee asked.

"I need you to make sure that nothing about what happened to Tim on that boat leaves this hotel," Ladonis said. "Bret Collins asked me to keep things quiet for a while. Give him time to find out what happened so that we can be in control of what gets printed and viewed on television about all of this."

Ladonis' words sounded logical and trivial at the same time. Made her feel stupid as well as important. Did she believe what she was saying?

"The only problem," Ladonis said, "is that Monique's uncle faxed her from the boat. She knows about Tim."

Big Dee's operation only recently included the Floating Palace's two boats. If the boat's crew worked nearly as diligently as the hotel personnel and was half as dedicated, Monique was in for a professional hard time.

"She hasn't wired the story in yet," Ladonis said. "She wants this scoop to jumpstart her national newscast career and is savoring the first interviews for herself. Because once the news gets out, the big names will be all over it and their bylines will obliterate hers."

"She won't talk to anyone who gets off that boat," Big Dee said. "Not even her uncle. I'll see to him personally."

Confidence was her cousin's most admirable attribute. Even when her ex, a fireman, had beaten her that one time, she had been confident enough to leave him.

"Good," Ladonis said. If Monique's uncle wasn't the problem, he would've faxed Big Dee about Tim. Not Monique. "I suspect

Monique will be here any minute now, ready to pounce on the passengers as soon as they set foot in the lobby. So keep an eye out."

"I'll put Avery on it," Big Dee said. "He'll alert the staff. Including the receptionist and the bartender. We'll know every move she makes the minute she gets here. And," she added. "Her uncle won't be sending any more faxes."

Ladonis and Big Dee had been inseparable as children. As adults, Ladonis and her cousin were about as different as night and day. Ladonis, all permed, tapered, manicured and educated, liked the spotlight. Big Dee hadn't graduated high school, never applied make-up, owned at least a hundred gray and navy of the same sweat suits, preferred to work behind the scenes.

"We'll start monitoring all the calls that come through the switchboard," Big Dee said. "Turn off the power to all the computer lines. Hijack computer batteries. Everybody gonna have a hard time gettin' the word out for two, maybe three hours."

Two hours wasn't two days, but it was something. Ladonis rose to leave. Depending on what she learned onboard, she could arrange a press conference and submit a press release by the six o'clock news. That was the best she could do. Hell, that was the best anyone could do with a hot story like this.

"Got to tell you though, Donnie," Big Dee said. "We ain't found no way of stoppin' people from usin' those damn cell phones except to 'misplace' them for a spell. And a lot of guests carry them nowadays so they don't have to pay these high-ass hotel phone charges."

"I know," Ladonis said. "I thought about that. Good thing they're out of range on the boats, and the signals are bad on the dock too, or . . ."

"The lobby would already be full of reporters," Big Dee said.

"Yes, it would." Ladonis exhaled loudly.

"And you better hope none of the passengers on the boat have one of them satellite phones either," Big Dee said. "Avery always readin' up on that stuff. He told me that those satellite phones can pick up signals from anywhere."

"I'm banking on the fact," Ladonis said, "that since our passengers are older and willing to spend a fortune for a trip back in time, they're not too keen on modern technology. All I need is a couple more hours. Let's hope that what you do will give me that."

"Let's hope," Big Dee said. "I liked Mr. Tim. He was cool." She tossed her empty Coke can in the trash. "Donnie."

"What?"

"You know somethin' really bad must be behind all this," she said. "Them askin' you to keep everythin' off the news and all. Your friend coulda been pushed off that boat."

"Foul play," Ladonis whispered.

Big Dee nodded.

Ladonis hadn't considered the criminal realities those words conjured up when Bret had asked her to help him with Tim's death. She'd hoped that Tim's probable misdeeds were more like misappropriation or misrepresentation. Worthy of reprimand. Perhaps even loss of his job. Like what had happened to the Enron thieves. But to get killed? That added a new dynamic to her quest. And a new fear.

She felt as though she was on a cliff. If she made one wrong move, she might fall off. She could hear her grandmother's voice in her head saying, "Watch your step, girlie. You about to step in a pile of shit."

8

Bitch

Ladonis walked out onto the dock headed for the *Magnolia Belle* now being tied to the wharf's embankment. She had to get to the bottom of whatever it was Bret wanted to hide before anyone else. Particularly since the word *scapegoat* came to mind. She wasn't going to bear the blame of other's actions just because she was there. She needed to do her own digging and get the upper hand to avoid being blindsided by what she hadn't been told.

The closer she got to the Mississippi River, the lower and thicker the clouds hung, darkening her view like shades being pulled down on a window. Thank goodness Kasdan's car was missing from the parking lot, and he wasn't there to look over her shoulders. The old man had had no qualms about taking credit for her simple company newsletter proposal. She didn't want him to take ownership of the first thing she'd been asked to do by an official higher up than he was. Then again, maybe she did.

When she arrived, Mr. Taylor, the bony, blue-black, white-haired daytime security guard met her at the entrance with a memo from Bret announcing Tim's death. It read:

All employees are expected to cooperate with the police, but keep rumor and innuendo about Mr. Ganen out of the investigation. Integrity is a virtue to be applauded, and this company rewards integrity.

What "rumor and innuendo" about Tim had Bret so spooked? And why had Bret insisted on her involvement? Kasdan was supposed to be one of the best spin doctors in the business. Was it her so-called clout at City Hall? There had to be more to it.

Ladonis saw the *Belle* with its red and white welded-steel hull and superstructure and felt protected and afraid. The same way she felt when she entered the red bricks of the Magnolia Housing Project. And the sight of the four-story paddle wheeler sitting still and isolated on the river reminded her of something Grandma Lucille used to say—"Livin' here in this beautiful city, in this here project, black folk still shut out, even if they is livin' dead smack in the middle of town." Could the *Belle* shut out Tim's secrets? Would the *Belle* let her in to find out what they were?

Ladonis watched the debarking passengers load their belongings into waiting taxis and buses. An extended stay in the Crescent City at the Dixieland until cleared to leave by the NOPD was procedure after mishaps on board. She stepped onto the red carpeted gangway of the boat's bow. Fried bacon, toasted breads, and coffee scented the air. Eating was still a priority.

"Hey, Ladonis," a male voice called out to her. "What's up?"

Bill Greenville lunged up the gangway. Ladonis gave the bouncy, balding blond man a smile. He was a Cincinnati native who worked as a galley steward on the boats every other semester to take a break from school and to find himself. At least that was what he'd told Ladonis. She'd learned that many of the boat's white personnel had similar objectives. But, to the blacks, these service jobs were as natural as rain and just as necessary.

"Is it true?" Bill whispered, leaning in toward her. "Did Tim kill himself because the Floating Palace is going public and he didn't want to get caught embezzling?"

Embezzling? She'd learned growing up in the Magnolia not to dismiss messages from a rumor mill. Gossip in the projects was like baseball, as natural to the social environment as apple pie is to American culture. And the grapevine between the office and the traveling boats could put the Internet to shame. Was that the rumor Bret didn't want to get out?

"Ah . . . ah . . . we haven't made a public statement yet," Ladonis said. How would it look to Bill or anyone if she, the PR person in charge, wasn't privy to such information? "I can't comment or discuss that until we do."

If what Bill said was true, it would explain a lot. A senior employee killing himself could prove problematic to the Floating Palace going public. There was the search for stockholders to consider. The Securities Exchange Commission evaluation, which included checking the accuracy of registration statements. If the SEC discovered that Tim had his hand in the till, they could put a hold on the public offering pending an investigation to protect investors. That could certainly screw things up. Especially a gambling deal.

She didn't want to give Bill time to figure out that she was in above her head. That would minimize her credibility as an executive. An image she'd worked hard to establish.

"Have you seen Captain Girardeau?" Ladonis asked.

"Try the pilothouse," Bill said. "He works on his logs around this time. He acts like he's making notations directly into the history books."

Ladonis headed for the pilothouse and ran into Captain Girardeau rounding the corner. Portraits of past captains on the boats and in the office portrayed men remiss in the looks department. Except this guy. He could have been a centerfold with his bulging muscles, full head of dark hair, and smooth olive skin.

"May I speak to you a moment?" Ladonis asked.

"I'm on my way to the Purser's Office," the captain said. "I just got word the police are headed onboard."

"I'll come with you," Ladonis said. "That way we can talk."

She'd hoped to know more before the police showed up. To find out Tim's secret. How could she stay a step ahead now that they were already here?

She turned, and the captain followed her down the spiral fire escape stairwell to the third deck. The Texas Deck. The third deck on all steamboats had been named for Texas when it was admitted to the Union in 1845.

"Captain, did Bret tell you that I'd be—"

"Yes," Captain Girardeau said, interrupting her. "He told me that you would be around."

Either she'd heard someone say or she'd read someplace that the captain of a boat was like the mayor of a city. Judging from the captain's flat tone and the look on his face, Captain Girardeau felt that a command from administration was an assault on his sovereign right to run his own ship.

"I have to prepare a statement for the press about what happened," she said. "Can you fill me in?"

"I've already talked to Kasdan," the captain said. "Ask him."

She felt the chill coming from his ice-blue eyes. She'd always been wary of these river types. They tended to be nostalgic for vintage southern ideals and attitudes. And working with the top guys, like Kasdan.

"I was instructed by the president of this company to ask you," she said.

The captain wasn't impressed with her show of authority. His glower made that clear. However, he'd respond like the company man he was. Ladonis knew that.

"A couple of deckhands say they saw Tim board in Natchez," the captain said. "But no one's seen him since. Except Mr. Turkson."

"Mr. Turkson?" Ladonis asked.

"Yeah," Captain Girardeau said. "The passenger who said he saw Tim fall overboard."

"A passenger saw him fall?" Ladonis said.

"And a deckhand," the captain said. "Well, the deckhand didn't see him fall exactly, but he did see him drunk hanging over the paddle wheel."

So it was an accident. Tim hadn't killed himself. He'd gotten drunk and fallen.

"Did Tim usually drink a lot when he came on board?" Ladonis asked.

"Who knows?" the captain said. "Most times when he was on board, he stayed in his cabin."

"Which cabin was that?" Ladonis said.

"Two one nine," the captain responded.

"Two one nine?" Ladonis said. "I thought the numbers went up to two one eight."

Captain Girardeau frowned. The lines across his high, straight forehead merged, painting an annoyed expression on his face.

"Before this boat was remodeled in '89," he said. "Two nineteen was part of the boiler room."

"The boiler room?" Ladonis said. Was he pulling her leg?

"That's right," the captain told her. "The boiler room."

"Well, how did it become 219?" She could be ornery too.

"It was just wasted space left off the remodel plan," he said. "By the time anybody noticed it, the remodel was almost done. The Coast Guard wouldn't approve refitting the space alone, and it would've cost too much and taken too much time to redo the plans. So they just closed it off."

"Okay," she said. "How did Tim make it into a cabin?"

"He was in the Boathouse Library one day. Saw the plans. Next thing I know, Velcroy had approved his bootleg fix-up."

"How did he do that?" she asked.

"He built a couple of walls. Put in a bed, a computer hook-up. Just like that . . ." He snapped his fingers. "Cabin 219."

Ladonis followed the captain into the lobby, stepping onto the classic thick Axminster carpet. Whenever she came into this area, her thoughts drifted back to the south's nineteenth century. She could see herself descending the grand staircase wearing fine clothes and jewelry, carrying a lace-trimmed parasol. She would be every bit as elegant and willful as that great belle, Scarlett O'Hara, on her way to trifle with the affections of some handsome, wealthy suitor. Even if that heroine was white.

"Hello, child," a familiar male voice said, bringing her back to the present painful mess.

Mr. Cairo, the chief purser, peeked through the brass wicket-covered casement that resembled an old-fashioned bank teller's window. The gentle old man had given Ladonis the same warm greeting since the first time they had met.

"Mr. Cairo, hi," Ladonis said.

Mr. Cairo stepped from behind the counter, his wiry gray hair tousled. His spectacles perched on his nose. He wore a red bow tie affixed to a white shirt. According to passenger surveys that she reviewed regularly for promotion ideas, his riverboat tales were as important to steamboatin' as steam power was to the paddle wheel. He kept the history buffs coming back year after year.

"Sad thing about Tim," Mr. Cairo said. "Isn't it?"

Ladonis nodded.

"Going to the galley," he said. "Need nourishment. I eat aplenty when I'm sad."

Ladonis waved goodbye to him. She turned her attention back to the captain. She still had questions.

"Captain," she said. "What time did Tim generally come up for air when he was onboard?"

"In the evenings, mostly," the captain said. "After the last dinner seating."

"Did he have dinner in the main dining hall that night?" Ladonis asked.

"I don't know if he did or not," the captain said, giving her the eye.

Did she sound like a third-rate private detective? Better that than a laughingstock. It was important that she come across as smart and professional to find out what she needed to know. Luckily her voice sounded more assured than she felt.

"But," Captain Girardeau said, "I do know that Tim was a creature of habit. As a rule, he took his meals in his cabin or down below in the employee mess hall."

The captain strode over to a tall gray file cabinet. He peered up at the postings on a bulletin board. Ladonis tried to see what he was reading, but his body blocked her view.

"Tim would go to the Propulsion Lounge," the captain said, still reading what was on the wall. "Just before Shirley and Joe's last ragtime set. He'd have a drink or two at the bar, and kid around with the attendant. When I'd make my late-night rounds, I'd find him and the Red Hot Mama clowning on the dance floor while Joe played the banjo."

Ladonis tried to imagine Tim dancing. They'd spent a lot of time together. But she still had so much to learn about him. Or from him. Now she never would.

"This always happened," Captain Girardeau said. "Long after the bar had closed at 2 A.M. I would watch them belt out a coupla bars of 'Dixie' and 'Old Man River,' do a coupla dips and twirls. Then I'd send them off to bed."

Captain Girardeau stepped inside an area the size of a closet. He made a phone call. Ladonis could hear but could not make out his mumble.

"Did Tim come aboard often?" she asked when he returned.

"Fairly often." Girardeau looked sideways at her. "He told me he got more work done on board. No phones or staff meetings to deal with."

Girardeau led the way back through the purser's counter, through the lobby, out onto the boat's stern. She followed close behind and bumped into him when he stopped to observe his crew perform their chores. She'd wanted to ask what he knew about the going-public rumor and how it could've impacted Tim or his death. But Tim had said never to confront a potential problem without the facts. Particularly in a hostile environment. Was the Floating Palace a hostile environment? The captain sure was. She needed a better understanding of the going-public process in relation to the company before asking more.

"Did anyone accompany Tim on these little trips?" she asked.

"No," Captain Girardeau said.

Since the words *foul play* had come up, Ladonis had wondered if maybe Tim had problems in his love life. But she couldn't recall ever seeing or hearing anything about Tim and his personal relationships. Not like his best bud, Bret. Rumors that Bret was a hot, bona fide love-'em and leave-'em kinda guy spread like wild fire.

"But, you know," Captain Girardeau said, "the crew sometimes teased Tim about that because he spent a lot of time cooped up in his cabin. The guys said he sneaked in his piece and kept her stashed in the boiler room to keep her hot and ready."

His piece? Ladonis flushed. Sounded like a sexist remark Heart-Trouble and his ignorant thug friends would make. She knew how she'd respond to them. But how should she respond to the amusement that flickered in the captain's eyes? He certainly didn't appear sorry that his raunchy humor embarrassed her.

She averted her gaze and recognized Bunnie Sinclair walking toward them. Bunnie was a little woman but a big pain in the ass. Ms. Sinclair lived to upset any woman's plans to succeed past her at the Floating Palace. Ladonis had better get her answers quick. Bunnie Sinclair was sure to crowd up the path and complicate her mission.

"Captain," Ladonis said. "Which deckhand saw Tim board the boat in Natchez?"

"That would be Nate Blenner," Captain Girardeau said. "He's the one who talked to the Coast Guard investigator. You best ask him what he saw."

The captain looked past Ladonis onto the dock. Was he beckoning to Bunnie? Ladonis could feel Miss Steamboatin' getting closer, sucking up the air around her.

"By the way," the captain said. "Somebody saw Tim talking to a tug pilot. I don't recall who at the moment. Guess you got to find that out, too."

"Is this man, this tug pilot, someone Tim had talked to before?" Ladonis asked. "A friend, perhaps?"

"I can't say," Captain Girardeau said. "Personally, I avoid tug-boat pilots. They're not real river men."

"You know, a Fred Way type," Bunnie interjected.

Captain Girardeau acknowledged Bunnie's arrival with a smile. Ladonis bit her lip, annoyed by the condescending tone in Bunnie's voice and the captain's gesture of approval. As if Ladonis couldn't know about Fred Way, the patriarch of the Mississippi Valley's rivers.

"Captain," Bunnie asked. "Was the tug you mentioned called the *Jackstaff*?"

"You'll have to check that out with Burl Decatur," the captain said. "Or, better still, with the deckhands. They'll know. They can tell you the name and operator of every tug that pushes barges on these rivers and to which ports."

If there was one thing about Bunnie Sinclair that drove Ladonis mad it was the fact that Bunnie knew the ins and outs of steam-boatin' better than anyone. She'd been hired two years out of high school after she had wandered into Cincinnati following some guy. Bunnie had been around longer than anyone who worked there, including Kasdan. So who better to ask about river barges and activity on the river?

"What's the *Jackstaff*?" Ladonis asked Bunnie. She felt like she'd cut herself with a knife.

"You're the hot-shot MBA Nancy Drew here, aren't you?" Bunnie said, sporting that pompous prep-school look of hers. "You tell me."

Bunnie had the advantage. Her toothy grin made Ladonis feel like *My Fair Lady's* Liza Doolittle in need of Henry Higgins to teach her to speak. Something tingled in her chest. A body-warning signal? Her grandmother had put great stock in the body's ability to forecast doom. She gritted her teeth to the rhythm of the gold-plated, solid-brass pipes of the calliope serenading the debarking passengers.

Bitch.

9

Praise the Lord

Ladonis strode off the *Magnolia Belle* with Bunnie Sinclair on her tail. Her mood alternated between practical and emotional. Between reality and a dream. Rising and setting like the rotating tropical sun through dark-then-light-gray clouds. She looked around for the cops. How could she manipulate the press if the police found out what had happened to Tim before she did?

Bret Collins flanked by one white man and one black man, approached from the terminal/office building. Ladonis' heartbeat sped up. As badly as she wanted Bret's mandate to be a career opportunity, she couldn't shake the feeling that he needed someone to take the heat when the truth came out. Someone to take the fall if the truth hurt.

Damn. If her thoughts stayed in this dark place, no one—Bret, Kasdan, or that pain-in-the-ass Bunnie Sinclair—would need to undermine her efforts to move up. Paranoia would. She hated to admit that her brother, HeartTrouble, could be right about anything philosophical. But, like he often said, paranoia is just as much a part of a black person's legacy in America as slavery. Even more so in multi-colored New Orleans.

"Where's Kasdan?" Bret asked Ladonis.

"He's not with you?" she said. Who was she? Kasdan's keeper?

She looked past her hunky boss and saw Kasdan. He strutted toward them. His stride swift, his eyes focused ahead.

"He's on his way," she said.

"Mr. Kasdan and Miss Washington here work in Public Relations," Bret said to the detectives. "They are our company's spokespersons."

The black detective, Detective Wellsburg, nodded. Ladonis stood near his white partner, Detective Travers, a middle-aged man about average height with a scowl drawn to perfection on his face. She shook his sand-paper hand, his grip so firm her knuckles crunched. Something she felt—but couldn't see—in his blue eyes, unnerved her.

Kasdan advanced, hands outstretched. His drooping cheeks and his eyes, sunk deep into their sockets, mirrored disapproval. He'd worn that same expression when he'd slammed out of Bret's office muttering, "You're a fool to hand a company crisis over to the hired help." He had been talking about her. That displeasure still showed on his face. Had aged him even more.

"Hello," Bunnie said, extending her hand across Ladonis. "I'm Bunnie Sinclair, the office manager. How can I help?"

"Ms. Sinclair," Detective Wellsburg said.

Bunnie strained her neck to look up at the detective. Not even her spiked heels raised her high enough to look into Wellsburg's dark eyes. Ladonis wished a strong wind would come and blow the petite Ms. Sinclair away.

Bret, acting as guide, led the way onboard. Ladonis hung back. For the time being, observing was more important than being in the thick of things. And the road leading to her success was getting crowded. Bret, Kasdan and now Bunnie. Way too many white folks with personal agendas that could knock her off the road.

Bret pointed out the spot on the Dixie Deck where Tim had

allegedly fallen. Where Mr. Turkson, the eyewitness, had watched. Ladonis trembled. What had Tim felt? Her mind and body froze in that thought.

~

When Ladonis reached the Propulsion Lounge on the Texas Deck, the detectives were talking to a deckhand. She recognized the deckhand right away. Nate Blenner. The crew called him Preacher Man. He was born again and fancied himself some kind of spiritualist who had direct contact with Jesus. The crew treated him like a comedian.

Preacher Man looked out of place standing by a table in the plush bar that overlooked the giant red paddle wheel. His soiled bright-orange coveralls and muddy work boots clashed with the fire-red cushions of the chairs. Dirt smudged his tanned white skin. His stringy, dirty-brown hair hung limp under his black and gold New Orleans Saints cap.

"Mr. Tim got on board," Preacher Man said, "whiles we was in Natchez unloadin' shrimp offa the barge *Jackstaff*. I seen him come up the gangway, drop his grips, and walk over to talk to that tug pilot. Praise the Lord."

"You know the tug pilot's name?" Detective Travers asked.

"Can't say's I do. Praise the Lord," Preacher Man said. "He the one who chews tobaccy, though. Teeth browner that sh—" He stopped himself. "Always spittin'. Praise the Lord."

"Do you know what they talked about?" Detective Wellsburg asked.

"Wasn't listenin'," Preacher Man said. "Couldn't hear nothin' even if I was of a mind to. Too much goin' on. Peoples gittin' on and off the boat. Peoples yellin' back and forth. The black guys sin-gin' and jivin' whiles they s'posed to be workin'. Only thing I seen was them talkin', then shakin' hands. Praise the Lord."

Ladonis took in every word. Noticed every nuance. Did the detective already suspect Tim of something? Did he know about the rumor? That Tim was an embezzler?

"Did you ever see Mr. Ganen talk to this guy before?" Detective Wellsburg asked.

"Can't recall if I did," Preacher Man said. The deckhand took off his hat and twirled it by its rim. "Like I said, I saw Mr. Tim walk over to where we was stackin' shrimp sacks, look around some, shake the man's hand, then pick up his grips and go in the lobby. That's all I seen. Praise the Lord."

"How many, um . . ." Wellsburg referred to his notes. ". . . grips did Mr. Ganen carry?"

"Two, same as always," Preacher Man said. "His briefcase and his clothes bag."

Ladonis had seen Tim with that raggedy Pierre Cardin luggage many times. Teased him about carrying his reports and clothes around like a toddler does a favorite blanket.

"You sound pretty sure about that," Detective Travers said.

"Mr. Tim come on board all the time," Preacher Man said. "Sometimes I tote them grips down for him myself. Same two grips. Praise the Lord."

Ladonis looked at Bret. Saw his hurry-up-and-get-this-over-with expression. She watched Kasdan too. He stood off to the side, looking at them with an eagle eye. She glanced over at Bunnie, but she was inconsequential. The big boys, Kasdan and Bret, were the players to watch on this stage.

"Okay, Nate," Detective Wellsburg said. "We'll meet you in fifteen at the place where you saw Ganen and the tug operator. Okay?"

Preacher Man shook his head and rushed off. Detective Travers got in Bret's face. Bret responded to whatever he said with a frown. His cheeks turned beet red. Ladonis inched closer. Kasdan took the opportunity to corner Detective Wellsburg.

"Exactly what are you going to say to the press about this?" Kasdan said.

Ladonis stood at attention. A potential lotto winner waiting to hear that last number called out.

"Well," Detective Wellsburg said. "We haven't found the body, or any part of it. And we don't have any idea what happened."

Any part of it? His body? She felt sick to her stomach. How could he speak of Tim as if he were a missing document?

"That makes it pretty difficult to make a statement, don't you think?" Detective Travers said.

Ladonis flinched. There was something about the way Travers said *don't you think?* What did he know about Tim's death? About Tim? Had P.J. spoken to her uncle yet?

"No statements," Detective Wellsburg said, "Not until we have some idea about what happened out there. Whether this guy jumped or if it was an accident. We're keeping the lid on until we have something concrete."

Praise the Lord. Ladonis closed her eyes. She inhaled and exhaled her relief.

"But you have an eyewitness," Bunnie said, walking up to Detective Wellsburg. "Someone who saw the whole thing. Isn't that concrete?"

"Well, yes," Wellsburg said. "We do have a witness. A passenger."

Ladonis wanted to tell Bunnie to bug off. But would that give the detectives the heads up on how she felt about the she-devil? She'd read enough whodunit novels to know that a policeman could take an attitude like that and develop a federal case out of it.

"Yeah," Detective Travers said. "But according to the Coast Guard's report, the witness was legally drunk. That complicates things. Right, partner?"

"And from what I've seen," Detective Wellsburg said. "The witness was pretty far away to get a clear look even if he was sober. Particularly in the dark."

What was with these two? One sounded like he was mad with the world. And the other was mad at him.

"We got a call this morning from a WWL reporter," Detective Travers said. "She wanted to know what we knew about an incident on the river."

Monique. Ladonis stepped aside to let a worker pushing a hand truck pass by. Detective Travers moved too, into a patch of not-so-bright sunlight. Ladonis could see clearly his disheveled clothes and his unshaven face.

"What did you tell her?" Ladonis asked.

"I told her that the NOPD wasn't working on any such case," Detective Travers said. "At the time we weren't. The Coast Guard hadn't turned it over. But I'm sure she's got somebody on the boat feeding her info. And, when that happens, confirmed or not, the story gets out."

"Too bad the press doesn't operate like we do," Detective Wellsburg said. "We're inclined to hold off talking about this sort of thing until we have the facts."

With the police's unwitting help and Big Dee's operatives on the job, she just might break this story on her terms. Provided the cops knew less than she did at this point. Ladonis' soft sigh went unnoticed.

"This gives us a chance," Detective Wellsburg said. "To touch base with friends and family and to establish a relationship. And to question witnesses before the media spotlight affects their memories. But the press, now that's a different story."

Media spotlight. Monique wanted it. Bret didn't. Though spotlight wasn't the way she'd describe her desire to succeed, Ladonis wanted her chance to shine. Why did what Monique and Bret want have to impact what she wanted? Life could be so unfair.

Bret led the group off the plank walkway, his steps slow and unsure. To the elevator. Was he stalling? Then why take the elevator and not the stairs?

"I understand," Detective Travers said to Bret. "You and Tim were college roommates."

"That's right," Bret said.

A sign on the elevator said it could hold ten people. Bret, Kasdan, the two detectives, Bunnie and Ladonis made six. The tension, however added the weight of at least that many more. Ladonis crammed in to the far right, across from Bret. Every time he so much as twitched, she made note. She was determined to learn what had him wound up tight enough to explode.

"Have you gotten in touch with Tim's family?" Detective Wellsburg asked Bret, squirming in his snug spot.

"No, I haven't," Bret said. "I thought I'd wait . . . to make sure, you know. Tim and his father weren't on speaking terms. I see no reason to tell him anything until we are absolutely sure about what happened."

"What else do you know about his family?" Wellsburg asked.

"I know that they're from the Midwest," Bret said. "His mother died a year and a half ago. His father hasn't spoken to him since he left home to go to college instead of hanging around to work on their farm."

"The disappointed parent," Travers said. "I'd like the father's name and telephone number."

Procedure, Ladonis mouthed in response to the questioning look on Bret's face. Did the business genius not read anything except the *Wall-Street Journal*? She was pleased with her mystery-novel knowledge of police behavior.

"Who knows?" Travers said. "Your friend might have written his father, telephoned him, said something to him that could shed some light on this matter. Perhaps clear it up."

Bret shrugged. He instructed Bunnie to get the information from Tim's personnel file. To pass it on to the detective. A single wrinkle line formed over Bunnie's eyebrows. Ladonis smiled. A menial task for a menial person.

⌒

Ladonis tagged along behind Bret, Kasdan and the detectives. Tim's cabin was a few doors down. If only she could have gotten inside Tim's room before the police had arrived. If only she had some idea what they might find. Especially if it could be incriminating.

Bret, Kasdan and the detectives entered the room. The space was so tiny Ladonis decided to stand outside the door within hearing and seeing distance. But just standing on the outside looking in gave her the creeps. What had he done in there?

Or was it the metaphysical notions her Grandma Lucille said their ancestors called *raising the dead*? Could Tim be watching them? Maybe it was all the mysteries she'd read. Or maybe her Grandma Lucille was right about communing with dead people. Either way, there was something telling in that room. As Grandma Lucille would say, Ladonis felt it in her bones.

The detectives moved around as if they'd been there before and knew all the hiding places. Then she noticed Bret. The way his body swayed unsteadily when Detective Travers examined Tim's desk and dresser drawers. She thought he'd pass out when Travers opened the medicine cabinet. And, when Detective Wellsburg started fooling around with Tim's computer, sweat beads rose on Bret's upper lip like oil on water.

What the hell was he afraid they'd find? Whatever it was, they didn't find it. At least Ladonis didn't think so until she saw Kasdan turn dusting-powder white when Detective Travers bagged Tim's computer discs.

10

Gangsta Look

Ladonis doubled back to the port side of the vessel. She wanted to talk to the two deckhands she'd spotted earlier working on the gangway. After that little run in with Bunnie, she had to find out about the *Jackstaff* on her own.

Deckhands were like flies on walls. They kept to themselves. But, at any given time of the day or night, two or three could be found in every nook and cranny of the boat. And there the two were. Unfortunately Bret and Kasdan stood within earshot distance to where the men were working. And she didn't want them to hear her asking the two men what they knew about that tugboat.

Did she dare to intrude on Bret and Kasdan's little chit-chat? Should she tell Bret about the rumor about Tim embezzling? Ask Bret if it was true the company was going public? Or would that tip her hand? Also, had the company put its stock on the market? No, she'd check it out in *Barron's* before speaking with Bret. That was what Tim would do if he were in her shoes.

Then Bret and Kasdan went inside the terminal. Ladonis rushed over to the two workers. The two men tugged at the ropes that hoisted up the gangway—the stage, as Mark Twain had called the carpeted steel planks back when they were wooden and when slave crews put on shows there for the townspeople. Black grease spots and God knows what else stained the two men's orange coveralls. That oblivious look of a work-induced bliss covered their faces.

"Whew, that smell," Ladonis said, sniffing the air.

"Shrimp," one of the men said. "We unloaded it off the *Jackstaff* on Friday. Been wipin' down the deck ever since."

"Whew." Ladonis fanned her nose.

She'd better hurry up and get this over with or she'd be sick for sure. The mere mention of shrimp made her tummy roll.

"I thought seafood deliveries were made dockside?" she said. "In New Orleans."

"They is," one of the deckhands said. "Except when they run out or go bad. Then we get 'em anyway we can. Most times a tug bring 'em in."

Had Tim made a point of getting onboard because of that shrimp delivery? Preacher Man had insinuated that he had. That was what had her stumped. Tim was strictly a numbers person. The closest he ever got to a vendor was through a figure on a spreadsheet. The only words that he'd used when speaking about creditors were *paid* or *balance due*. The Tim Ganen she knew would never give hands-on attention to a routine delivery.

"Did Tim Ganen usually come on board to check emergency deliveries?" she asked, placing her hand on her queasy stomach.

"What?" one of the men said.

"Did Tim Ganen verify that tug-boat delivery?" She moved away from the odor.

"What's going on here, Ladonis?" a male voice said. "Did Bret send you?"

"As a matter of fact, he did," Ladonis said.

She turned and faced Burl Decatur, the purchasing director. A huge man. Tall and round with a grainy complexion, pores so large and plentiful, they bearded his lower face. He wore a yellow leisure shirt with fat black stripes down the front. What HeartTrouble called the white-boy gangsta look.

"I'm gathering—"

"I heard," Decatur said.

Word around the office was that Decatur was as mean as they came. Ladonis avoided dealing with him directly. Worked with Pam, his friendly Cajun assistant instead.

Decatur moved towards the deckhands. The two workers shared a strained, telling look. Decatur was not their favorite person. The deckhands walked away without giving Ladonis a second glance.

"What's PR's interest in tugboats?" Decatur asked.

"PR," she said, "is interested in everything that has to do with these boats."

Ladonis fought to hold on to her official tone. Maybe Decatur would back off at the authority she forced into her words. He didn't.

"Listen, girl," Decatur said. "I don't care who's interested. But, if anybody got questions about purchasing, they'd better ask me."

Girl? She was inclined to remind him of her name. But a little voice in her head said, "Consider the source."

"I'll keep that in mind," she said, looking him straight in the eye.

Grandma Lucille had told her once to always look mean folks in the eyes when they were aiming to intimidate you. "If they look away," she'd said, "they're nothin' but talk. But if they stare back, they hateful enough to kill." Decatur held her gaze.

"You do that," he said and stalked off.

Ladonis walked over to the boat's bow to the area the deckhands had fixed up to resemble a porch. She sat on the swing bench they used for river-view water breaks. Decatur's killer-look was etched onto her brain. A warm, humid breeze harsh enough to startle swept over her. She trembled. Took in and let out a big gulp of muggy, river air. She'd read someplace about a parallel between weather and violence. Particularly in the southern climates. Hurricanes and thunderstorms were common regional, deadly, violent weather patterns. And Decatur was a New Orleans-grown bad guy. He had to be guilty of more than a gangsta look.

Ladonis moved the swing back and forth with her hips. What was Decatur's business with the *Jackstaff*? And how would the fearsome purchasing director play into her plan to find out? But her most burning question was what was Tim guilty of. And, not just what Decatur knew, what did Bret know?

"God, Tim." Ladonis sighed. "What's going on?"

HeartTrouble had this warped street code of ethics. To get them before they get you. Should she apply her brother's philosophy to her predicament? Though lamentable, she had a feeling that was exactly what she ought to do. But how could she get somebody with a killer instinct like Decatur? The prospect went way beyond the corporate shenanigans she was willing to instigate. What would HeartTrouble do?

11

Scumbag Connection

"Damn," Travers said, exiting the air-conditioned police station on South White and Broad streets. "Cloudy or not, it's hotter than hell out here." He wiped at the sweat on his brow. "Hurry up, will you?" he said to Wellsburg who was headed back into the building.

"Don't rush me," Wellsburg said. "I've got to take a piss. I'll meet you on the corner."

"It's not me," Travers said. "I don't give a rat's ass how long it takes you. But Dugar said to hightail it on over there or be in contempt."

Travers didn't like it when judges and lawyers couldn't get their acts together and fought their battles on his time. He felt that, once he'd given a case to the DA, he was done. This was the second disclosure-of-evidence hearing in two weeks on his and Wellsburg's first collar together. Another media-friendly case involving a heroin pusher who sold to a junior district attorney who died from an overdose.

Travers moseyed down to the corner, Tulane at Broad, and waited in front of the criminal courts building. The clouds hung so low, the words *Administration of Justice is the Foundation of Liberty* across the stone building were barely readable. He pulled a piece of paper from the inside pocket of his jacket.

"Section C," he read. "Honey Man."

Travers stuffed the paper back into his pocket. But thoughts of the perp, Honey Man, remained on his mind.

He spotted Wellsburg making his way past the prison onto where he stood at the foot of the court house steps. Police headquarters, parish prison, the criminal courts building and the DA's office. The city's entire criminal justice system, all there like his Trump-minded brother had once described the hub of financial buildings on Wall Street.

"Every other day," Travers said to Wellsburg, "there's something going on with this case."

"It's a TV case," Wellsburg said, stopping in front of him. "What do you expect?"

"Yeah," Travers said. "And we've got to waste time whenever a lawyer wants to get his face on the news."

Wellsburg ascended the stairway, two steps at a time. Travers eyed the twenty-four white speckled steps. He had to spend more time in the gym. He took a couple of deep breaths before scrambling up.

"Somehow," Travers said to Wellsburg when he caught up to him. "It just doesn't seem right for us to get threatened with losing our badges just because the DA is under pressure."

"Public outcry," Wellsburg said, eyeing a tall, slender woman with a briefcase making her way up the steps. "Remember this is not about some strung-out nigger street pusher. It's about a young, white law-school graduate who died."

Travers knew that if he addressed his partner's sentiment, the discussion would get out of hand. It never failed. Put a black and white in the same space and race was bound to come up. No matter how friendly or hostile the conversation. The department's race-sensitivity shrink said that was probably because race was both personal and universal at the same time. Whatever the hell that meant.

"I was wondering," Travers said, wanting to get something more pressing off his chest. "About Honey Man."

"Wondering what?" Wellsburg asked. "That his lawyers can't get his damn trial past all the evidence hearings?"

"That too. But I've got this hunch."

The muscles in Wellsburg's face flexed. Travers didn't want to tell him. Didn't want to be chastised for working on a hunch. But he had to. Wellsburg was the primary.

"I've got this feeling about the corporate dead guy and that shrimp delivery," Travers said, making the point as much to himself as to his partner. "Him talking to that tug operator."

The sound of Travers' cowboy boot heels accompanied by a squeaky, brushing tone from Wellsburg's rubber-soled loafers created a marching melody on the marble floor. The rhythm of footsteps echoed throughout the long, quiet hall.

"Yeah," Wellsburg said. "So what?"

"So," Travers said. "The tugboat guy the deckhand told us about sounds like he could be that Popeye character Honey Man described."

"Coincidence," Wellsburg said, his confidence dwarfed by a crack in his voice and his long face.

"I'm not so sure," Travers said. "We should question Honey Man again."

"Why?" Wellsburg said. "Honey Man has nothing to do with the river case. Besides we've got a possible VIP murder to deal with."

"Sometimes," Travers said, his tone insightful. "In order to solve a high-profile case, you have to first find the scumbag connection."

"Look," Wellsburg said. "You said yourself that Honey Man is just a runner. What makes you think his running dope has anything to do with what happened on that boat?"

"I've got a hunch is all," Travers said. "Haven't you ever had a hunch? A gut feeling about something?"

"A hunch, my ass," Wellsburg said. "You want that CEO. And, if you can't get him for killing his friend, drug smuggling will do. Right?"

Travers stopped. Stood at a huge double oak door and stared up at the gold letter "C" that identified the courtroom.

"We're here," Travers said. He turned to face his partner. "What was it Jack Nicholson told Tom Cruise in that movie? You can't handle the truth, can you, my man?"

Wellsburg said nothing. The door to Section C opened. A tall African-American man stepped into the corridor. He wore a black sheriff's uniform with gold trim.

"Can you?" Travers said. A teasing half-grin crossed his lips. "Can you handle the truth? I heard Honey Man mention something about meeting some guy at a fish restaurant on the bayou. And you were in the room when he said it."

"You Travers, ain't you?" the sheriff called out.

Wellsburg clenched his jaws. Adjusted his tie. But said nothing.

"That's me," Travers said, frowning.

He really didn't want to sit through motion this and motion that. All that lawyer crap. He wanted to get to the jail and talk to Honey Man. He was onto something, and he knew it.

"The DA say get your butt inside," the sheriff said. He pointed at Wellsburg. "You, too."

Wellsburg strolled through the massive oak double door. Travers brushed past the sheriff. His trademark half-grin flashing. Primary on the case or not, he was going to interrogate Honey Man again. He was going to find out all he could about the man the jailed addict called Popeye.

12

Wrongdoing

The platform road between the office and the boat was packed with people rushing about. Ladonis spotted Decatur getting into his black GMC Jimmy parked beside the gazebo on the river side of the dock. She tracked his four-wheel drive to the parking lot. Then she made her way through hand trucks and forklifts hauling everything from food to toilet paper. Business as usual. Didn't anyone care that a man had died?

She watched Decatur exit Pelican Street wharf and drive out onto Tchopitulas Street. She hurried back to the terminal and entered through the side door. Purchasing was a two-person office on the ground level. Pam was alone. The perfect time to pump her for information about the *Jackstaff.*

"Let's give them something to talk about . . ." Pam sang off-key.

Pam walked out of her boss' office singing with the radio. She was dressed in blue jeans and a tank top that hugged her implants and exposed her pierced belly button. She stepped into her outer-office space where Ladonis waited.

"How about love . . ." Pam let out a loud breath. "You scared me, ché."

"Sorry about that," Ladonis said.

Apparently Tim's death hadn't impacted this workforce the way it had her. But Ladonis needed Pam on her side. Not upset and ticked off. Rushing in and demanding sympathy and answers, grief or not, was not the way to go.

"What can I do for you, ché?" Pam said.

Ladonis' Cajun classmates had said that *ché* was to Cajuns what *sistah* and *brotha* were to blacks. Terms of endearment. Of acceptance. At least for the moment.

"Maybe you can help me," Ladonis said. "My cousin is getting married, and she wants to serve oysters and shrimp at the reception."

Her stomach turned. The stinky smell of shrimp like the bad odor of wrongdoing filled her nostrils. Only she couldn't figure who was doing wrong. Bret and Tim. Tim and Decatur. Or Tim, Bret and Decatur. But what about the sting she was playing on Pam? How wrong was that?

"I was wondering," she said, "if you can tell me where the Floating Palace gets seafood these days. Gerald, the galley chef, told me that he got an order in the other day towed in by the *Jackstaff*. But he couldn't remember the name of the vendor."

The incense that burned on Pam's desk had a strong peach aroma. Ladonis sneezed. Pam handed her a tissue.

"Thanks," Ladonis said.

"Too bad about Tim, huh?" Pam said.

Ladonis looked down, a little too sad to share her emotion.

"I know he was your friend," Pam said. "He was always talkin' about you and how smart you are and all."

Ladonis had no idea Tim had spoken of her to others that way. He'd stopped telling her how bright he thought she was. Probably because she'd told him she didn't like being looked upon as some sort of enigma because she was female, black and smart. Put way too much of other people's expectations on her. She had enough stress dealing with her own ambition.

"Gerald told me this place sells oysters, too," Ladonis said.

She had to change the subject. The power of emotion had seized her. And this was not the time to be weepy. A man was dead, and she had to find out why.

"Gerald told me," Ladonis said. "That the oysters were processed with the new Ameripure technology. And that the shrimp are the biggest and best he's seen in a long while."

There was no shortage of seafood in New Orleans. Yet seafood restaurant owners and connoisseurs were always on the look out for that bigger, cheaper shrimp. Working in purchasing, Pam had to relate to that.

"I don't know about that, how you say, Ameripure stuff, ché," Pam said.

Neither did Ladonis. She'd read about the process of purifying oysters in last Sunday's newspaper. Thought it might give her play more credibility if she used the term.

"Gerald is probably talking about Mayflower's," Pam said, turning down the sound on the radio. "It's the only vendor I know that uses the *Jackstaff*." She pulled the chair out from her desk and sat down. "And it's the only place Decatur's been buying shrimp from these days."

"Really?" Ladonis said. "Do you have a number and a contact person at Mayflower's? I'd like to see if I can get a deal for my cousin's wedding."

"Here." Pam flipped through her Rolodex and plucked out a card. "This is the number, and . . ." She looked up at Ladonis. "The second number is Mr. Tombigbee's private line. He's the sales rep, I believe."

Ladonis didn't miss the hesitation in Pam's voice, as if she'd said something wrong or wondered if she were doing the right thing. She needed to take the pressure off the nice Cajun woman.

"I don't know how to thank you, Pam," Ladonis said in a light voice. "I'll show you pictures after the wedding."

She started to walk away, thought better of it, and turned back around.

"Ah, Pam," she said. "I don't know Decatur that well. But, if he's anything like my boss, Mr. Kasdan, he won't like my horning in on a company resource for my own private use. Especially if he didn't say it was all right. Will he?"

"No offense, Ladonis," Pam said. "But Decatur can't stand you. I mean not just you, but . . ."

"I understand, Pam," Ladonis said, choking back her emotion, pretending that her apprehension had not switched to anger. She didn't like Decatur's cracker ass either. And she didn't like it that she felt that way. That her attitude linked with his on the shackles of prejudice. "I guess the best thing to do is not to tell him. Right?"

"I won't say a word," Pam said, smiling up at her. "But I can't speak for them at Mayflower's. That Mr. Tombigbee for sure. I get the impression he and Decatur are buddies."

"I see."

Somehow Tim was connected to Tombigbee and the *Jackstaff.* She had to get the goods on Mayflower's, but without speaking to this Tombigbee guy. But finding out how could be more dangerous than she suspected. Especially if Tombigbee and Decatur were as close as Pam suggested.

Decatur was a scary dude. And, if he found out that she was snooping around in his affairs, with or without Bret's blessing, there was no telling what he'd do. She had to continue to wing this mission under the radar. Because just as frightening as what Decatur could do, was the thought of what he might have already done.

13

Freaked Out

Mayflower's was in a little area called Manchac, just past Laplace, about forty-five minutes west of the city. Ladonis figured that if she took the new ramp off the Pontchartrain Expressway, it would put her on the I-10 in no time and she could be back long before the office closed. If Bret or Kasdan questioned her whereabouts, she'd explain that she was out in the trenches working to make sure the press kept out of their business.

She drove across the Manchac Swamp, a shallow bayou between Lake Pontchartrain and Lake Maurepas, listening to the oldie but goodie station hoping that the music would take away the images she had of Tim's body being masticated in a paddle wheel. Hoping to stop the suspicious thoughts she had about Bret, about why he was so afraid of the press.

She wasn't convinced Bret had been on the up and up when he'd asked her to deal with Tim's death. Now finding out what was behind his request was even more important than accomplishing the task. She refused to be duped because she wasn't paying attention.

By the time she drove up and parked at the strip mall where Mayflower's was located, she had belted out "What's Going On" with Marvin Gaye, "My Girl" with the Temptations and "Ben" with Michael Jackson. She and Aretha had just hit the last chord of "Respect" when she saw Decatur's Jimmy in her rear-view mirror driving onto the lot. She clicked off the radio and crouched down in the seat, praying he wouldn't recognize her Chevy Geo.

She heard his car door slam. Her body twitched when he clicked on his security system and the doors locked. Footsteps, brisk and heavy, then silence. Had he recognized her car? She leaned up a tad and saw him through the side mirror. He stood a hair away from her door on the driver's side. She almost pissed in her pants.

She ducked back down. His feet thumped on the ground as his heavy frame moved alongside her car. She ducked further down. Her leg cramped. She put her hand over her mouth to keep from crying out in agony. The sound of footsteps faded. Ladonis sat up, stretched her leg to massage her achy thigh, and scoped out the area.

Mayflower's was at the end of the mall surrounded by glossy, dark-green Escallonia leaves acting as a background for rose colored, tubular flowers, protected from the sun and rain by a loud blue awning. Only two other cars were parked in the lot. A rusty old Ford pickup and a gray four-door Nova. No way she wouldn't be noticed if she went inside. But she had to find out what Decatur was up to. To see what, if anything, it had to do with Tim. Maybe his death.

She crept toward Mayflower's like she thought a cop would, sneaking up on a perp. She peeped inside the storefront window, her view obstructed by hanging ivy and a blue checkered swag. No one. White linen and one magnolia bloom centerpiece covered empty tables. A restaurant? She'd pictured a smelly refrigerated warehouse with a bunch of beer-bellied men sitting around gutting fish.

She eased around to the right of the building to another set of windows. A different angle, hopefully a better look. It was. Decatur walked further into the dining area. He went behind the bar in the far corner, got two beers, snapped the tops and sat at a table near the kitchen. She could see his mouth moving but couldn't hear through the glass. She went around back. There had to be another entrance.

At first she thought someone was practicing on a drum, the sound she heard like a brush hitting a timpani. The noise got louder as she rounded the corner to the back of the restaurant. Then she saw a yellow-brown dog closing in on her. She let out a muffled shriek, pressed her back up against the wall, closed her eyes and waited to be devoured. Nothing happened. Ladonis pried her eyes open and found the dog rummaging through the garbage tins just beyond where she stood. The air reeked of dead water creatures. And she could smell catfish frying. The smart thing for her to do was leave, but she'd dumped smart for I've-got-to-know.

The dog was preoccupied, and the seafood fumes churned in her stomach. She eased over to the opened back door and peered inside through a torn screen. She didn't see anyone. So she slipped her hand inside a hole in the screen and let herself in. She re-latched the hook lock. Habit. She'd gotten spanked too many times as a child for leaving screen doors unlocked to forget now.

"Decatur, what the fuck you doin' here, Man? You're supposed to be on the job."

"Shut up, Tombigbee," Decatur said. "Somethin's come up."

Ladonis followed the sound of Decatur's voice to the door near where he sat. She heard footsteps and retreated into a tiny space between two refrigerators.

"Yeah, like what?" Tombigbee said. "That other shit you into? When you gonna realize the good thing we got goin', Man?" Tombigbee's feet slid around the restaurant. "You in charge of the credit card. We can be in business forever if you don't get too careless."

"We've got trouble, I'm tellin' you," Decatur said. "Ganen went and got himself chewed up in a paddle wheel."

"What?" Tombigbee said. "I been watchin' the tube all mornin'. I ain't heard nothin' about it."

"It's been hushed up."

"What about the arrangement?" Tombigbee asked.

"Nobody knows," Decatur said. "Not yet, anyway."

What arrangement? What trouble? The more Ladonis heard, the more questions she had. The more tense she became. And the more tense she became, the more her stomach reacted to the smells from the garbage tins. To the fish-greasy odor in the air.

"You got the other stuff?" Tombigbee asked.

"No," Decatur said. "Ganen got hold of it. Left word that if I wanted it, I had to meet him—"

Something crashed to the floor. Ladonis shrieked. She had to get out.

"Who the hell are you?" A white woman held a pot like a weapon aimed at Ladonis. "What you doin' in here?"

"Shit," Ladonis said, wiggling from her hiding spot. She dashed for the latched screen door. Pushed through so hard, she yanked the latch from the door frame. Outside, she stopped, her insides bubbling. She couldn't go any further, couldn't stop her upset stomach from relieving itself. She puked.

"What's goin' on?" Ladonis heard Decatur ask the woman.

"Who you hollerin' at, Agnes?" Tombigbee said.

"Some colored gal was nosin' around in here," Agnes said. "Least I think she was colored. Can't tell no more with all them Mexicans you have traipsin' in and out of here. She scared me, that's all."

"What was she doin'?" Tombigbee asked. "Stealin'?"

"How the hell do I know?" Agnes said. "It happened too fast."

Outside, the trees and pavement spun around in Ladonis' head like a merry-go-round. She had to get away, but her legs could hardly hold her up. She lost her balance, but caught her fall with her hands, scraping them on the concrete. She crawled out of sight under Decatur's Jimmy just ahead. She glanced back. Decatur barreled through the door and stepped in her vomit. A split second more and she and Decatur would've locked eyes.

"Motherfuck," he bellowed.

He walked over to a patch of grass and wiped the soles of his shoes. Then he walked over to the Ford truck and looked inside, next the Nova. He moved toward her Geo.

"Shit," Ladonis said. "I'm dead."

Her day planner was on the front seat, and she couldn't be sure she had the wherewithal to lock the car door before she'd jammed the keys in her pants pocket. Two more steps and—

"Decatur," Tombigbee called. "Over here."

"You got her?" Decatur headed back toward the restaurant.

"Agnes say she's probably a kid from the school up the road." Tombigbee's feet appeared, moving toward Decatur. "She said every now and then one or two of them leave the school grounds to do a little exploring."

Ladonis saw four feet walking toward Mayflower's. Decatur followed by Tombigbee. They were moving away from her and her car.

"She must've smelled the catfish," Tombigbee said. The screen door squealed. "Damn it to hell. The bitch broke the latch."

Ladonis scooted her body from under Decatur's Jimmy, ducked down and sneaked back to her vehicle hiding alongside Decatur's car and the Nova. She examined her hands. Blood. She wanted to scream. This was the kind of shit she went to college and moved out of the neighborhood to avoid. And HeartTrouble razzed her all the time about her abnormal reaction to blood. HeartTrouble. Good thing her brother didn't know about the mess she'd gotten herself into.

"Thank God they hurt worse than they look," she said to appease herself.

She hung her head over the steering wheel and begged her aging Geo to start without its usual dillydallying. No such luck. The Geo choked and growled loud enough to wake the dead.

She glanced up. Tombigbee blasted out of the restaurant. He spat. The engine turned and sputtered. She kept her head low so that he couldn't see her face and drove off as well as her trembling knees and bloody hands would allow.

14

Throwed Off

Ladonis scuttled into Kasdan's vacated office, closed the door, slumped down into his chair and stared out the river-view window. The lazy sun had stalled over the Mississippi River Bridge, casting an orange shadow over the still muddy waters. Everything slowed. Only her thoughts ran rapid.

Was Tim a crook? Was Bret? What was Tim's business with the *Jackstaff*? And how did that god-awful Decatur fit into it all? Questions. Suspicions. But no answers.

It was time to get the word out. But what was she going to say? Any number of things could've happened to Tim on that boat. All bad from the little she knew, for Tim and the company. Of one thing she felt certain, danger lurked. If she kept on this mission, there was no telling where she could end up. She had to figure out her next move.

The door flew open. Ladonis sprang up, positive that Kasdan had returned. Bunnie sashayed in wearing a Madeira Mexican skirt, the flare swinging in step with her lively strides.

"Velcroy will be in town tomorrow," Bunnie announced, "and he wants to see you in his office at 9 A.M. sharp."

"Jesus H. Christ, girl," Ladonis said, "what is your problem?"

"And don't be late," Bunnie said, glaring at her.

"You are throwed off," Ladonis said. "You know that?"

The thumping in Ladonis' heart gave her chest pain. She had had enough of Bunnie's superior attitude. And it was time to let Bunnie know it.

"Forgive me for not responding to that remark," Bunnie said. "I don't have my urban-bush translator handy."

Ladonis wanted to kick herself for forgetting where she was. There was no way Kasdan—or Bret, for that matter—would credit her with being bilingual if they'd heard her other dialect. Equal opportunity or not, she'd be relegated to hauling coffee and filing. But it was Bunnie who had confronted her. Tact didn't count with her.

"I take that back," Ladonis said, unable to contain her defensive offense. "You are not confused. You're stuck on stupid. Can you translate that?"

"Not so stupid as to kiss up to the boss," Bunnie told her.

"You know what?" Ladonis said. "Word is you've got the hots for pretty-boy-blue-eyes. I bet you're just jealous because he's paying me some attention."

Ladonis reared back in the chair, squinted her eyes, her chin in the air. Bunnie leaned forward on the desk, her body anchored with her hands.

"You know what?" Bunnie said, looking straight into Ladonis' eyes. "You're exactly what I thought, a common trollop."

"Honey Child," Ladonis said, leaning forward into Bunnie's face. "You ought to know. Every time a man comes near you, your mouth hangs open like a dog in heat."

"That's disgusting," Bunnie said, rolling her eyes over Ladonis' body. "You're disgusting."

"I'm disgusting? Everybody knows you're the executive slut."

"And everybody knows you're a fool."

Ladonis pounded the desk. How could she succumb to her own temper like that? Nothing exposed vulnerability and self-doubt like fits of anger.

The phone rang. Ladonis yanked the receiver from its cradle. Bunnie passed her a taunting I-had-the-last-word grin and stalked off.

"What?" Ladonis yelled into the earpiece. "Oh, Twyla, I mean Captain Toussaint, hello."

She sank down into the chair to listen to what she knew was going to be bad news. By the time she hung up, she'd gone from being mad as hell to sad as could be. She rushed down the hall to Bret's office and found the young executive pacing the floor, nursing a glass of whiskey.

"They've found Tim's body," she said. "At least enough of it to know that it's him."

She felt something shake inside. There was no longer any doubt. Tim wasn't coming back. The silence was so loud, she couldn't hear herself breathing.

"I'm sorry." She sighed. "We can't keep this quiet any longer."

Hearing the words made her feel as though she'd been released from a locked room. Maybe now she could shake the feeling that the world was about to cave in.

"No," Bret said. His eyes expressed sadness as well as desperation. "I need more time to . . ."

"To do what?"

She ignored the little voice inside coaxing her to ask him if the rumor about Tim being a thief was true. If he was in on it. If that's what he needed time to cover up.

"Until we're absolutely certain about what happened," Bret said,

"I don't want Tim's death to put this company in the middle of a media circus."

"Neither do I," Ladonis said, her tone practically scolding. "But it's official. He's dead. And he died in a paddle wheel. There's nothing left to do except get our statement out. Try to gain control over what is said."

Especially if he was a thief. She swallowed the thought and looked at Bret. She expected a response that didn't come.

"It's just a matter of time," she said, "before the news hits the airwaves and papers. It will be better for the company if we break the story."

"And say what?" Bret said. "That Tim fell overboard in a drunken stupor?"

"Who knows?" Ladonis said. "That just might be enough information to keep the news hounds from going on a feeding frenzy."

"Or send them on one," Bret said.

And what will they find? Ladonis' stomach fluttered. That was the problem.

"That can't happen," Bret said. "You keep this from the media like we discussed, or you're fired."

15

Three Faces of Ma

Bret had apologized for threatening her job, but Ladonis still reeled from the feeling of failure she had experienced when she'd heard the words *you're fired*. She arrived at her mother's without having made a statement to the press and without having been approached by any reporter to make one. Yet, she was wound up tight enough to snap. Did she expect her mother to know what she should do about the situation she'd gotten herself into?

Ladonis came up the walkway of her mother's two-bedroom bungalow on Paris Avenue, in an old Gentilly neighborhood. The television blasted a greeting. She didn't bother to knock or ring the bell. Her mother had a hearing problem and, in all likelihood, would not have heard her, especially with her good ear tuned into her favorite soap.

Ladonis could smell vanilla, sugar and margarine before she opened the door to her mother's modestly furnished living/dining area, the furniture covered with plastic. She walked into the kitchen, the center of her mother's home. The large yellow room was three times the size of the kitchenette she'd endured for twenty years in the Magnolia Housing Project.

"Hi, Ma," Ladonis said. "Baking, huh?"

Mrs. Washington grunted and mumbled something Ladonis

couldn't make out. The senior Mrs. Washington leaned her tall, hefty frame against the counter, a big crock bowl hugged under her breasts by one arm. Was she ignoring Ladonis? With all she'd been through today, Ladonis wasn't surprised. She could still hear Bret's ultimatum. Hear his rambling on about the stress he was under. Did he think she was on a joy ride?

She looked over at her mother stirring the batter, the way the sagging flesh of her arm flapped with each vigorous stroke, the way her lips curled up into a pout. Bret had no idea what it was to deal with stress. Stress was the shit her mama dished out.

"Ma," Ladonis said.

"Ma, what? Can't you see I'm busy?"

"Don't be so grumpy, Ma," Ladonis said. "What're you baking?"

"I'm baking Kemp a cake, that's what," her mother said. "The po' old widow man all by hisself these days. Like me. His children all gone, don't pay him no mind. Like mine. If I don't feed him, the po' man won't eat."

Ladonis walked over to the refrigerator. Okay, Martyr Theresa was in control. She knew her mother's griping would start full blast any minute. Her mother's personality had split around the time her husband did. Ladonis had named the three people her mother had become: Sick Puppy, Pissed Off and Martyr Theresa. Her mother could conjure up one or another to be cynic or victim, whichever it took to get her way.

That capability to become someone else made Ladonis feel jealous sometimes. She had no way of escaping her feelings for her runaway dad. She harbored a deep resentment toward him. Not so much because he'd left, but because her mother had been fun-loving before he had left. She would never forgive her father for taking away her happy mom.

"Seven-Up," Ladonis said, opening the refrigerator. "I need a 7-Up."

Her mother kept the sodas in the bottom bins. Seven-Up in the left bin. Dr. Pepper in the right for HeartTrouble. She rubbed her forehead with the cold can before popping the top.

"You ain't been by here in three days," Mrs. Washington said. She had a way of contorting her face so that the little moles on her cheeks bunched up to look like freckles. "How come you showin' up now?"

"Ma, please," Ladonis said. "I call you every day. I have a job. I cannot be at your beck and call twenty-four seven."

"When I'm dead and buried, you gonna wish you had."

"Let's not talk about your death today," Ladonis said. "Okay, Ma?"

Death was the last thing she wanted to talk about. Tim's death had put her life in a tailspin. She couldn't help wonder though, what would happen if her mama outlived her?

"Like I said, when I'm gone . . ." Mrs. Washington said.

"Keep talking like that," Ladonis said, "and I'm going to leave."

Martyr Theresa was on a roll. Pretty soon she'd quote scriptures from the New Testament. Recite passages from her pastor's last funeral sermon.

"I didn't come here," Ladonis said. "To listen to you plan my life after your death."

Why had she come? It couldn't have been for emotional support. Their mother/daughter powwows were to solve her mother's problems. To do something her mother wanted. Did she need to feel what it's like to be put upon in her own world in order to cope with that feeling outside of it? Did she expect to be reminded of some inner wisdom and strength from her experience of being the conflict go-to person at home to get through her situation at the Floating Palace?

"When my friend Mildred passed on," Mrs. Washington said. "Her daughter practically fell in the ground after her tryin' to 'pologize for not payin' her mama no never mind. You talk to her now and she'll tell you. She'll tell you, you don't miss the water 'til the well is dry."

Ladonis scooped up cake dough with her index finger and licked it off. Mrs. Washington dumped a chunk of margarine into the bundt pan and proceeded to spread it with a paper towel. She sprinkled flour on the greased pan, moved it around until the sides were as white as the bottom, and tipped out the surplus.

Ladonis had enough of Martyr Theresa. Maybe she could convince sniveling Sick Puppy to rear her head. After all, her mom was up and about. How sick could she be?

"How are you feeling, Ma?" Ladonis asked. "Any more pain in your hip?"

"You know how unsteady I been since my stroke. But I'm feelin' pretty good today. No pain. Good enough to go to the nursery to get some potting soil and a coupla them big flower pots."

Ladonis was amazed how her mother's aches and pains disappeared when she wanted to go somewhere. And the nursery was her favorite place to waste her daughter's time. If not there, it was the fabric store out in the East.

"Ma, can this wait a few days? I'm really snowed under at work."

"Never wait for tomorrow for what you can do today," Mrs. Washington said.

She poured the cake batter into the pan. She put the pan in the oven, took hold of her cane standing at her side, hobbled over to the table and sat down.

"Why can't your no-account son go with you?" Ladonis said. "He makes his own hours."

"You always was a smart ass," her mother said. "And more selfish than your brother ever was."

"Me? Selfish? What's that bum ever given you besides heartaches?" Ladonis took a deep breath. "Ma, look, I don't want to fight with you."

"Me neither. But if you didn't come here to see how I was doin' and if I need somethin', then why you come?"

That was a damn good question. She should've known when she walked through the door that her mother was going to get on her last nerve.

"You know what?" she said, moving toward the door. "I don't know why I came. You don't appreciate anything I do anyway."

"Where you think you goin'?" Mrs. Washington lifted her cane and shook it at Ladonis.

"I'm going home," Ladonis said, slamming the door behind her.

Her head hurt so badly, she expected it to explode. And what had she accomplished by coming here? Had she gotten the fight she had come for?

16

Warning Bell

Ladonis hesitated in the hall outside Velcroy's door, nervous as a chicken facing the chopping block. Time had run out on that no-body-no-story shield. The police had found enough of Tim that his death couldn't be hidden from the media any longer. And she'd been summoned by Velcroy. Did he want to fire her himself? Bret walked up behind her as she tried to muster up the courage to go inside.

"Don't look so glum," he said. "I told you I didn't mean it." His breath was warm on the back of her neck. "Let's go in. Everyone's waiting."

Ladonis stepped aside, turned to face him, feigning a smile. Jerk. Between thoughts about losing her job and disrespecting her mom, her head was like a clogged-up drain. And Bret, Mr.-keep-it-quiet-or-you're-fired, was definitely no Drano.

"It's Tim, you know," Bret said. "I can't believe he's gone."

He'd said the same thing to her over and over the night before after apologizing for threatening to fire her. Sure, he was grief-stricken. He was also too distraught to make rational decisions. Empathy aside, she wanted to wring his neck.

Ladonis followed Bret through Velcroy's office on into the adjoining executive meeting room. This was it. The boardroom at Microsoft. The Oval Office. As badly as she wanted to be among the chosen few who met in rooms like this, she wondered why the elusive billionaire, who ruled from afar like God, wanted to see her in person. In her three years at the Floating Palace, he had barely said more than hello to her.

She glanced around the room, struggling to suppress her awe, comforted somewhat by the smell of books on shelves that lined a wall. She'd sought refuge in her school library from the taunts about her homemade gingham dresses and the sugar-and-mayonnaise sandwiches she had to eat for lunch. Books had empowered her. Exposed her to the outside world. Taught her to dream.

She walked in slow motion towards the conference table in the middle of the room, savoring each step. Remington statues decorated the credenza beneath the windows. One wall was covered with lithographs of the steamboats, another with framed awards and pictures of past steamboatin' presidents fraternizing with government officials and financial dignitaries. At least she could say she'd made it through the door.

Bret sat down next to Kasdan, who was examining the morning newspapers. Ladonis took a seat facing Bret. Despite Bret's frazzled look, his scant beard gave him a grungy, sexy appearance. He poured himself a glass of water from the pitcher on the table. Ice rattled in his glass when he took a sip. He loosened his tie. He reminded Ladonis of a freaked-out kid waiting to see the dentist.

Kasdan laid down the *Times Picayune* and picked up the *USA Today*. The *New York Times* and *Wall Street Journal* lay in disarray in front of him on the table.

"Any news?" Bret asked.

"Not a word," Kasdan said.

"What about television?" Bret said looking at Ladonis.

"Nothing so far," she said, thinking there should have been, if he'd had the guts to let her have a news conference. Her morning was off to a bad start. "I stayed up all night waiting for the story to break."

The door swung open. All heads turned. Ladonis looked up. It was Bunnie Sinclair. Cheeks flushed. Head held high. Wide-eyed confidence. Just like Loretta Young on those AMC old black and white movies Ladonis liked to watch. Did Bunnie watch those old movies too?

"Good morning, gentlemen," Bunnie said. "I trust everything is okay in here."

Bunnie glanced from Bret to Kasdan, then pranced over to the credenza near the picture window. She poured herself a cup of hot coffee. Ladonis eyed Bunnie's gray wool-blend pantsuit and maroon blouse. She wanted to say, "That's a nice outfit," but didn't, aware of the K-Mart simplicity of her own two-piece ensemble.

A toilet flushed, the noise loud. Everyone sat up straight in their seats like rowdy kids who heard the teacher approaching. Edward H. Velcroy strode into the room, drying his hands on a paper towel, his shirttail hanging half out. He had to be at least six feet tall and weigh close to three hundred pounds. He dropped the paper towel onto the floor, and took his seat at the head of the table.

"I see we're all here," he said, looking at Ladonis.

Ladonis didn't know whether she should smile, look away, or stare him down. When the Queen of England had visited the *Bayou Queen* last year, Kasdan had instructed her not to look royalty in the eye. Ladonis looked over at Kasdan now, then at Bret, hoping for a cue. They sat stiffly in their seats with their heads lowered. She avoided looking at Bunnie altogether. To get fired in front of her would be the worst humiliation ever.

Velcroy reared his heavy body back into his seat and lifted his legs to place his feet on the table's edge. Ladonis' eyes stretched at this unorthodox behavior. No one else reacted. Velcroy scanned the table, giving each of them a long moment of concentration.

"A terrible thing has happened," he said. "A man has died. One of our own. But, despite our sorrow, we must move on. I commend you for doing just that."

He winked at Ladonis. He hadn't come to fire her. She perked up, like flat hair treated with mousse.

"I've arranged," he continued, "for several members of the Lou–isiana legislature and a few of the Floating Palace's new major stockholders to cruise aboard the *Magnolia Belle* along with all of you tonight on a . . . let's say a one-night shakedown cruise."

Traditionally, the crew called the one-night rehearsal cruise after lay up a shakedown. When all the new and repaired parts were checked out. What was Velcroy checking out?

"Stockholders?" Bunnie asked.

Ladonis saw the sly glint in Bunnie's eyes as she fished for an explanation. Bunnie already knew the answer. She was sure of it.

"As of this morning," Velcroy said, "the Floating Palace Steam–boat Company is no longer a privately owned business, but a public enterprise."

So much for rumors.

"Can we take the *Belle* out?" Bunnie asked. "I mean, isn't there some rule about that, since it's the scene of a . . . a . . . death or something?"

Ladonis frowned. Bunnie's dumb girlie routine not only grated on her nerves, but pissed her off. Women all over the world were working their butts off to eradicate that image of females.

"Not only are we taking her out," Velcroy said, "we're bringing in gambling gear."

Gambling had been illegal since Prohibition. And just like that he could reinstate it on the boat? Who was this guy?

"Our only restriction," Velcroy said, "is that we do not exchange the chips for cash."

He snatched a piece of tissue from the box on the table and stuffed it in his mouth. Ladonis' mouth flew open. Was this guy for real?

"And, yes," he said. "Tim's room and the upper deck have been taped off by the police. However, the authorities agree that there's no reason to put this overnight trip off. Mostly because we won't have a full passenger load."

What authorities? The NOPD? City Hall? Who did he know? Where did he get his clout?

"Besides," Velcroy told them, "many of the passengers are elected officials. Members of the court in one form or another."

NOPD and City Hall. But what was in it for them? Ladonis could only imagine. All that money and sin on the horizon could take the favor-for-pay ideology to new heights even in a compromised systemic bureaucracy like New Orleans.

"The police and their investigation," Velcroy said, "will not be discredited in any way."

Velcroy chewed on the tissue as if it were gum. Leaned forward with both hands on the table. Weird man.

"By the way, Bret" he said. "I spoke to Mayor Bruchard this morning. He sends his apologies to you and, ah, ah, Ladonis for not getting back to you sooner."

Velcroy must have caught himself in a potential slip. Probably wanted to call her the "black one." She'd overheard him once with the Marketing Vice President. "Who can the black one put you in contact with?" he'd asked Kasdan when the company had faced a hotel city zoning crisis. Ladonis turned her face away from Velcroy's gaze. He didn't need to see her vulnerability.

"Mr. Mayor says he looks forward to speaking with you tonight," Velcroy said. "He and his wife will be joining you onboard." Velcroy poured himself a glass of water, took a big swig, then belched. "Now, as you know, we're embarking upon our one-hundred-year anniversary. The problem is that the company has not reached a prime. That is, it has aged, but has not grown for some time. Not since the remodeled *Belle* set sail in '76, I believe."

"Wouldn't you," Kasdan asked, "attribute that to the uniqueness of our product? We do, after all, sell nostalgia."

"That's true," Velcroy said. "What I'm proposing will not alter that, instead taking the company to the next stage of its business lifecycle—which is to a market young enough to learn about its history, not relive it."

Corporate lifecycles? She'd made an "A" in that class. She leaned forward in her chair.

"The stage," Velcroy continued, "that gives us the flexibility of a young company as well as the controllability of the seasoned enterprise we are."

"I see," Ladonis said, before she knew she was speaking. "Gambling is the past. But, if it's reinstated, it can reinvigorate future packages."

"Correct," Velcroy said. "So we've entered the gaming lobby."

Legislators. Stockholders. Gambling. This was a shakedown. If only she had paid more attention to the gaming issue. To the growing clout of politicians and businessmen desperate to get that venture capital into the Crescent City. Hadn't the city's Jesus contingency had a lock on the debate? The Catholics and Baptists, black and white, agreed that organized betting was a sin and fought against it.

Besides, the media had made no mention of Velcroy or the Floating Palace to pique her interest in the publicity. She hadn't made the riverboat connection. However, the financial market had an increasing stake in gambling. Stood to reason why Velcroy would be eager to get on the bandwagon. After all, history proved that riverboat gambling hadn't just offered excitement to sleepy colonies, it had been lucrative. Some historians said that riverboat gambling had proved to be as important to the livelihood of river towns like New Orleans as the steamboat itself had been in transforming river transportation.

That was it. Enthusiasm rose up inside her. That was the promotion connection between her centennial celebration and those other-than-white, nostalgic, baby-boomers with discretionary spending money. She could see the publicity. America's music comes of age where it started—on the rivers, with the slaves. Use the old to bring in the young. Those well-off yuppie music lovers and upper-class, bourgeois blacks who ordinarily distanced themselves from the black-American experience were black as could be when it raised their societal presence. What an appeal. The Floating Palace would celebrate one-hundred-years young. That was it, Tim.

Her excitement died as quickly as the idea had come to her. Tim was dead. And she still didn't have a handle on why Bret was determined to keep his life and death under wraps. But how could she ignore Velcroy's vision for the company? Her own centennial plan could ensure her future. So what if Tim was a scoundrel? What was so bad about that? Was it because the SEC and the gaming commission were involved? Would image carry more weight in those outside agencies? There was always some scandal or another brewing in the city's corporate and political arenas.

Something else more haunting was going on here. Had to be. And Decatur. What about him? Somehow her quest for answers now came back to that dark and scary purchasing director.

"By the way," Kasdan said, interrupting her thoughts, "who owns the controlling stock?" He stared at Velcroy. "You?"

A spark of hope flickered across Kasdan's face. Would the answer "no" make him happy? Velcroy's fuzzy brows drooped like his fleshy cheeks at Kasdan's cynicism.

"If you're asking whether or not there will be any personnel changes," Velcroy said, "the answer is—not at this time. But, if you're asking if I'm still the head of this company, the answer is yes."

Therefore, his friend's young son Bret was still Kasdan's boss. And Kasdan would remain just a VP. Ladonis almost felt sorry for the old guy.

"Does that mean that you'll be along tonight?" Kasdan asked, gathering his newspapers.

"No," Velcroy said. "It means business as usual. You'll be there in my stead. That's why you're paid the big bucks."

She'd regarded Velcroy as the eccentric rich guy who owned the company before this meeting. She'd failed to study him. A mistake. The Floating Palace had been a public company when he'd bought up the stock from Coca-Cola about five years ago. Now he was going public again. Why?

Industry predicted that casino and riverboat gambling attracted dollars that would otherwise buy new clothes or a car. That there was no substitute for the action at the roulette wheel. In order for the Floating Palace to cash in, the law had to be changed. Easier said than done in this ultra-conservative neck of the woods. What did Velcroy think the company would be worth if it got into gambling?

Maybe she could get a handle on Velcroy's corporate modus operandi if she knew more about his past. Tim had told her more than once to learn about the players on and off the team. She had to call Jake Lee at the other news station. She'd ask him to get the 411 on the "big guy," as she'd heard Tim and Bret refer to Velcroy.

Ladonis glanced around the room. Why was she there? A sign of good faith to city officials? That was a laugh. New Orleaneans knew that the black faces at City Hall had nothing to do with tradition. Old money controlled government and its services. To maintain that status quo, outsiders were not accepted and progress often sacrificed.

Velcroy nodded at Bunnie who took the cue and reached for the papers in front of her and passed them around the table. Velcroy stood up, circled his chair, and sat back down.

"That's the guest list," he said. "You'll see that I've outlined tasks for each of you. I have another meeting before I head off to New York. I'll be here around two to answer any questions before I leave."

Chairs rolled and squealed as Bret and Kasdan stood. Ladonis' and Velcroy's eyes met. His grin softened his stare, but she felt no warmth. Not like she did when Tim had smiled at her.

"Tim believed in you," Velcroy said. "I understand why."

Ladonis responded with a simulated grin of her own, proud that she had not allowed the big boss to intimidate her. Even so, she couldn't shake the feeling that she was the cat to whom the rat had given the warning bell.

17

Four One One

"Ladonis," Bret called out. He rushed up behind her, took her by the elbow and escorted her into his office. "I want to meet with the mayor as soon as possible. Arrange it."

What the hell for? Velcroy had everything and everyone under control. Including the mayor.

"Can it wait until tonight?" Ladonis asked.

"No, it cannot." Bret's voice rose and fell reflecting desperation as well as aggravation. "I want to speak with him before tonight."

Then call him yourself. Acting as the middle person between the non-natives and her hometown leaders was getting ridiculous. What did it solve anyway?

"Tell him," Bret said, "that the Floating Palace has laid out quite a bit of money and opportunity in this town and is about to do more."

Of course Velcroy's gambling venture was the impetus behind that remark. That list of stockholders and potential stockholders that Velcroy handed out included some of the country's wealthiest high rollers. No doubt Bret believed that, if that gaming bill passed, the Floating Palace would open some lucrative doors for the city to walk through. Even she was thinking about how the gaming bill could advance her career.

"And what should I tell the Mayor that you want to see him about?" Ladonis said. "The shakedown cruise?"

Bret didn't answer right away. His silence worried her. Was this about Tim's body being found? He couldn't possibly think he could suppress that much longer. She wanted to tell him that the sooner he faced up to Tim's death, the better. But she wouldn't.

"Just do it, Ladonis."

"You'll meet with him anywhere that's convenient, right?" she said. "Lunch someplace? His office?"

"You bet," Bret said. "Anywhere. But it has to be before tonight. Before the cruise."

She headed toward the door. What Bret was up to? A jolt of reality replaced that goose bumpy and fluttery feeling she'd gotten earlier thinking about her own career-advancement prospect. Tim was dead. And Bret was scared as hell.

⌁

Ladonis sifted through a small stack of messages on her desk and brought them into Kasdan's office. She glanced out his window. Several men on the loading dock hauled slot machines from a Tac Amusement Company truck. Getting ready for the big night.

She walked back to her desk, not too thrilled about asking P.J. for another favor. She envisioned her friend re-affixing her fake eyelashes, a nervous habit Ladonis had become accustomed to when they were in college. Oh, well. Better make the call.

"My CEO, Bret Collins, wants a meeting today with the Mayor," she said to P.J. "How does it look?"

"I wish it was possible," P.J. said. "I'd love to see your cute CEO again today. But the mayor's in Baton Rouge until tonight when he and his wife will be taking an overnighter on your boat. Can't this wait until then?"

"Beats me," Ladonis said. "Bret just told me that he'd like to meet with him before the cruise. No way, huh?"

"I'm afraid not," P.J. said. "But I'm going to call his wife to have her meet him there for a seven o'clock departure. I could tell her to let him know Bret wants to speak with him before they get underway."

"That's fine, P.J.," Ladonis said. "I'll tell Bret."

Ladonis laid the phone receiver in its cradle as Kasdan slipped into his office and shut the door. She'd noticed him rushing down the steps to the first level after their meeting with Velcroy. Where had he gone to in such a hurry?

She reached down for the phone and saw Line One light up. Kasdan never dialed the phone for himself. He always had her make his calls, even though that speaker at the efficiency seminar they'd attended had stressed how impolite that practice of power had become.

Ladonis pressed the button to Line Two, then put the receiver down. She didn't want to risk Kasdan overhearing her own conversation. She walked to the end of the hall, made a U-turn and sat at a vacant reservationist desk facing an empty office on Manager's Row and made her call to Jake Lee. Her old friend Jake Lee was the head night maintenance guy at WDSU and a computer junkie. He had gotten hooked when he had worked for Radio Shack and the TRS-80 home computer had hit the market. She thought he'd never answer the phone.

"Hey, Jake, it's me, Ladonis," she said when he finally picked up. She could hear the sleepiness in his voice. Jake Lee worked the late-night shift to play on the television station's sophisticated computer equipment since he wasn't a certified tech. He had had to quit college to support his younger orphan siblings when his father had killed his mother and then himself. He was probably just getting to bed. His siblings off to school.

"Are the reporters at the station," Ladonis asked, "tied into Inter-link yet?"

"Are you kiddin'?" Jake Lee said. "There's the rest of the world and then there's New Orleans, remember?" Jake Lee often complained that Louisiana—and especially New Orleans—was a decade behind in the science of computer technology. "What's on your mind like that, Sistah?"

"Don't the reporters have access to FBI-like data on Fortune 500 people like my company's owner, Edward H. Velcroy?"

"Yeah," Jake Lee said. "They get some information."

"Can you?"

She knew he could. He knew WDSU's system and what was in it better than the hired techs there did. He was that smart and a geek through and through.

"I can try," he said. Ladonis sensed his delight in her challenge to him and thought of Jake Lee's offbeat smile. The man lived to explore the inner space of the computer chip. "What you wanna know like that?"

"Anything," Ladonis said, "that will explain why this guy is keeping a low profile while his privately owned company goes public Also, he's lobbying big time for the gaming legislation, and not once has his name come up in the reporting. I want to know what's up with that. Oh, and find out who owns the controlling stock shares in the Floating Palace now that it has gone public."

"I'll see what I can find out," Jake Lee said.

She knew he would, and he'd keep quiet about it. He'd been keeping her secrets for years. Ever since she had been in second grade and they had met in Sunday school at New Hope Baptist Church.

"Thanks, Jake," Ladonis said. She didn't want anyone to get a whiff of how far she was willing to go to get the upper hand. "Send it on my home email. I'll look for your message when I get in tonight."

When she got back on the other side, Bret was pacing in front of her desk.

"Did you call?" he asked.

"Yes," she said. "But Mayor Bruchard is in Baton Rouge. He won't be back until tonight. P.J. is trying to arrange for you two to get together before departure, though."

"Damn." Bret sighed.

Before he had a chance to say anything further, Decatur walked up in front of Kasdan's closed door and beckoned to Bret. Ladonis picked up a stack of folders and pretended to review them, trying to keep curiosity off her face. Decatur pulled Bret to the side and jumped all over him like an army drill sergeant.

"You'd better find it," he roared, "or I'll start talkin'."

Bret's face was moist with sweat. A delivery man in a gray khaki uniform strode up waving an invoice and a pen at Decatur. Bret took the opportunity to escape.

What the hell had that been about? Tim? The gaming bill? Business as usual? A man was dead and the only thing that seemed to matter was the Floating Palace's bottom line. Her Grandma Lucille had told her that she could be anything she wanted to if she worked hard. But, if she'd learned anything at all in the corporate world, especially today, it was that hard work was the least of it.

18

Soul Mate

Ladonis pulled her Geo into her carport, a loggia on the side of her townhouse. If only she could forget this day. She longed for the familiarity of the loud and lively life in the Magnolia projects. Yet, she was anxious to close up with a cold glass of Chardonnay inside her comfortable new home on this quiet street. If only she didn't have to spend the night on the *Magnolia Belle.*

But she'd come too far to turn around. She was hustling in the big league now. And, as her job became more tenuous, being privy to why Tim had died, especially if his dying in a paddle wheel were tied to the gambling scenario, could make her a player in a way that no degree or contacts could.

She turned off the engine. Would she find her neighbor's ornery alley cat perched in her drive as usual? She hoped so. Better that pesky beast than no one waiting for her to come home. HeartTrouble? She wasn't expecting him. But there he was, sitting with his long legs stretched out on the ground massaging the cat as it lounged on his lap. Ladonis jumped from the car.

The cat looked up at her and took off, proof to Ladonis that the feline despised her as much as she did it. HeartTrouble stood to greet his sister, his loud yellow and black print shirt hugging his lean, though muscle-defined physique. No baggy jeans and big white t-shirts for this street hustler. He was way too into his body for that.

"What are you doing here?" Ladonis said. "I told you I'd call when I wanted the shelves built."

"Tell that to Mama," HeartTrouble said. "She's been on my case all day about your stupid bookshelves."

"Okay, so why did you come?" Ladonis said.

"You know how Mama is," he answered.

Ladonis knew. Mrs. Washington had a way about her that could make you feel on top of the world or guilty as hell. She'd put the guilt hex on Ladonis earlier because Ladonis wouldn't take her flower pot shopping. She could only imagine how her mother had manipulated HeartTrouble into showing up on her doorstep again.

"Mama said you came by her place today actin' like you sick or somethin'," HeartTrouble said. "You sick?"

"Do I look sick?" Ladonis asked.

"Since you ask," HeartTrouble said, "you do looked kinda toed up."

"Boy, please."

Ladonis' eyes narrowed. She didn't need to be reminded of how badly she'd behaved toward her mama. She headed for the door.

"Well, if you ain't sick," Heart Trouble said, "Mama said you must be stone crazy."

"There's nothing wrong, okay?" Ladonis said. "Leave me alone. And you can tell Mama that I'll talk to her tomorrow. Now leave."

First Mama. Now HeartTrouble. Could she tell either one what was really going on with her? Ladonis fumbled with keys until she found the one for her door. HeartTrouble, an inch or two taller than she was, stood to the side watching.

"So," he said, "how's what's his name? You know. Jackson? He live here with you?"

"Jack," Ladonis whispered. "He prefers to be called Jack."

The mention of Jack's name sent a chill through Ladonis' body. With Tim's death and everything else going on, she hadn't dwelt on that particular pain. And now was not the time to unload her feelings, especially on her good-for-nothing brother.

"Why is that?" HeartTrouble asked. "Jack is just as white as Jackson."

"I thought I told you to leave," Ladonis said, turning the key in the front door lock. "Do I ask you about those project hootchies you hang out with? My love life is none of your business."

"Y'all broke up, huh?" HeartTrouble asked.

"Do you have any pride?" she yelled at him. "I don't want you here. Go away. Leave me alone."

She put both hands on his chest and shoved. HeartTrouble didn't move. He just stood there looking at the tears welling up in her eyes. At the aggravation curled around her mouth. No one pushed her buttons the way HeartTrouble did. She threw up her hands.

"The bastard left me," she said.

"You shittin' me?" HeartTrouble said. "I thought you said he was your soul mate."

"Soul mate?" Ladonis said, staring down. "He went off to work in California."

"Couldn't take you, huh?" HeartTrouble said. "Ain't that the way soul mates do things?"

"What do you know about anything?" Ladonis said. "He wanted me to go. Only he wanted me to give up my life to live his."

"Yeah," HeartTrouble said. "Like a soul mate."

Was this her cue to go berserk? She'd never felt anything but disdain for her brother. Each disapproved of the other. She accused him of dragging the family, namely her, down, and he accused her of being a wannabe, as in "want to be white." What other torture could this day bring?

"Shut up," Ladonis said. "Not even a welfare, card-carrying project queen would consider you soul mate material."

The blood drained from her brother's face. His lips pressed together. He made a slight turn to leave, but stopped and turned back around to face her.

"I'll stay out your face and your business," he said, "if you let me crash here awhile. Me and Charlene need to spend a little time apart."

"You still have a room at Mama's," Ladonis said, stepping inside the door. "Crash there."

"I can't live in the same house as Mama," HeartTrouble said, stepping inside and closing the door behind him. "She'd be all in my shit."

"Maybe that's what you need," Ladonis said. "Someone all in your shit."

Ladonis kicked off her shoes and opened the kitchen window to release the stuffy, closed-in smell that greeted them. Then she headed for the refrigerator.

"Look, Donnie," HeartTrouble said. "Me and Charlene havin' a rough time and all, but the truth is, I got trouble with the law. I need to lay low until it blows over. I can't stay with Mama because I don't want her to worry."

"What's with you?" Ladonis said. "You're not going to be satisfied until you're locked up, are you? And you say you don't want to worry Mama? What do you think is going to happen if you're locked up? You're not called HeartTrouble because of your looks, you know."

HeartTrouble had been really sick as a kid. Rheumatic fever that had gone undiagnosed by the doctors at Charity Hospital, the only access poor people had to medical care. The whole thing had left him with a heart murmur. When the neighborhood kids had found out, they had nicknamed him HeartTrouble. Everybody, including Ladonis and Mrs. Washington, had come to call him HeartTrouble, even though his given name was Woodrow.

"So how about it, Donnie?" HeartTrouble said. "Can I hang here for awhile? I won't charge you nothin' to build your bookshelves."

Ladonis fished through the refrigerator for the Chardonnay she'd opened the night before. First, Jack had walked out, then Tim had died, now this. She had a career to escalate and so many unanswered questions. She had to get the power of knowledge on her side.

"You can stay here." Ladonis didn't have enough negative energy and emotion within her to blast her low-life brother when he was down. "Tonight only. I'll be out. I have to work. Business."

"Business?" HeartTrouble said. "All night? Has the slave boat become a brothel?"

She dared not tell her brother what was going on with her. Not only would he give her a hard time, but at this level of high-stake corporate shenanigans, the fewer people in on the details, the better.

"The owner of the company," Ladonis said, "has invited a few lawmakers on board to lobby the gaming bill, and he wants me to be there."

She wanted to sound excited. But how could she express excitement about Tim's passing? Or her plans to get on board to find out why he'd died?

"The gaming bill?" HeartTrouble said. "Donnie, don't you know what gambling will do to this city? Its people? Which just happen to be mostly poor black people?"

"Provide a few jobs, I'd think." Ladonis poured herself a glass of wine and downed it. "Of course that would mean that you and your buddies would have one less excuse for sleeping all day and loitering all night."

"What you talkin' about, Donnie?" HeartTrouble said. "People will spend their rent money, grocery money, insurance money. They'll gamble it all away." HeartTrouble sat on the stool at the kitchen counter. "Girl, why you let them use you to tear down your own kind like that?"

"Bringing your people down is what you do," Ladonis said, pouring another glass of wine. "Your way of thinking is so limited."

HeartTrouble's victimized philosophical air was more than Ladonis could take. How could two people who had grown up learning the same principles and ideals from the same source have such a different context of thought?

"Limited, huh?" HeartTrouble said. "Why you say that? Because I don't believe that, unless black folks are moving in white circles, dreaming white dreams, or in plainer English, kissing white ass, they aren't worth a shit?"

"If you'd open your mind," Ladonis said, "you'd realize that's exactly what you think. And you'd see that dreams and success are not spelled w-h-i-t-e."

Ladonis downed another glass of Chardonnay. She'd never hear the end of it if he knew why she was so keen to get on board tonight. How she planned to use the dirt she could dig up on Tim and Bret to advance her career. HeartTrouble's outlook and stubbornness could be so frustrating.

"Open my mind, huh?" HeartTrouble said.

"That's right," Ladonis said. "Open your mind and listen to yourself."

She mounted the stairs to her split level bedroom. Ladonis' fantasy bedroom. She'd dreamed of this bedroom since she was twelve, when she saw a picture in the *Ladies' Home Journal*. She'd sworn that no matter what, whenever she had a place of her own, she'd have that bedroom. HeartTrouble followed her into the room.

"I don't think you realize," Ladonis said, "how demoralizing it is to have to analyze the content of race in every single life choice you make. Where you live. What school you attend. What sport you can play. What job you can do. Where to shop. The music you like." Her hands splayed. "Dealing with the rights and wrongs of everyday living can be complicated and traumatic enough."

Why couldn't her brother see things her way? Grandma Lucille's way? Grandma Lucille had told her that if anyone had a problem with her skin color, it was their problem, not hers. She'd told HeartTrouble that too.

"I want to move up in my job," Ladonis said. "How I conduct myself on this excursion can help me do that. And, frankly, I don't care if the people are purple."

"If that's true," HeartTrouble said, "then you are in trouble."

"Why?" Ladonis didn't wait for a response. Didn't want one. "I'll be damned if I'm going to run scared just because I want the same things that some white people want. And I don't intend to spend my life justifying my existence to white folk either. Like I'm some sort of black freak of nature."

She hadn't allowed him near any bed of hers since junior high school.

"Turn the air on, Miss Black Corporate America." HeartTrouble threw himself on Ladonis' king-size bed and tossed the decorative pillows to the side. "It's hot as hell in here."

Ladonis clicked the switch to the air conditioner, pulled down the window shade and turned on her bedside lamp. It took only a little light to brighten the off-white room with its antique-white, shirred-lace curtains and white carpet.

"I've got to get packed," Ladonis said. "I want to get onboard before the guests arrive."

She marched into her walk-in closet. HeartTrouble stretched out on the bed. He yawned, long and loud.

"*Leopold's Ghost*," he said. He must have found her book on the nightstand. "What kind of mystery is that?"

"It's not a mystery," Ladonis said. "It's a nonfiction about the Congo."

"The Congo?" HeartTrouble said, yawning again.

"Haven't you heard of the Congo?" she asked. "It's in Africa. You have heard of Africa, haven't you?"

How could black folk in America know so little about Africa? She had a professor who said that was why American blacks had such a hard time figuring out who they were and how they fit in. And her Grandma Lucille had told her often never to forget where she came from or she'd run the risk of never becoming who she was really meant to be.

If she had the guts or the time, she'd tell him about her centennial plans and how her African past was going to help her map out the course of her future. But she didn't have the time. She especially didn't have the courage. Aside from what she wanted from her career, she didn't have a clue who she was supposed to be.

Ladonis tossed her old Reeboks in the overnight bag and came out carrying an overnighter packed with a dress-up dress for dinner and a comfortable sleuthing outfit. She looked over at HeartTrouble, getting situated on her bed, already half asleep. Her bed. She simply didn't like the sight of him there. She wanted to tell him to get out of her bed, to make a pallet on the floor. But looking down at him, she saw the little boy who had followed her around, fallen asleep anywhere she was just to be near her. She pulled the throw at the foot of the bed over her brother's body.

"Donnie," he said, drowsily. "Sounds to me like you headed deep into white-folk shit. Anybody got your back?"

19

Be Like the Sun

Ladonis rushed from the terminal onto the wharf. The *Magnolia Belle* loomed before her in the dusky twilight of the sun fading into an orange haze in the sky. She had to get onboard, visit the boat-house library to find out all she could about the remodel and look around Tim's cabin before the shakedown began. Only she wanted to watch the sunset.

"Nothin' can stop the sun from shinin'," her Grandma Lucille used to say. "Not even a hurricane. Be like the sun and crawl from under the clouds and glow." Could she be like the sun? Could she crawl out from under this mess with her natural goodness intact? Her career on track?

Ladonis bumped into the galley steward on the gangway. The news of Velcroy's impromptu cruise had hit like a tropical thunderstorm on board. Velcroy expected the new board members and potential stockholders to experience every aspect of steamboatin'. Excellent service, fine food and spirits, enjoyable entertainment and gambling. Even if it was with monopoly money. His mandate was to make it all happen without a glitch.

"The man," the galley steward complained, "is making me miss my daughter's dance recital."

"Some people," Ladonis consoled, "were called in from their vacations."

She understood the steward's frustration. The logistics involved in preparing for a regular adventure were harried at best. For a rushed event with a crew working on long-awaited time off, intensity ran on overload. But Tim's untimely death, Bret's particular demands along with Velcroy's edict was the combination that complicated her life. At least the galley steward could gripe to her without consequences. Who did she have?

The boathouse library was located on the boat's bow on the observation deck, tucked away a few feet from the passenger wheel house. Ladonis had embarked on the opposite end of the vessel because the passenger gangway was still hoisted. She walked outside on deck, the long route, to avoid more crew rushing around making preparations.

A maid she didn't recognize blocked her way. The young, brown-skinned woman struggled to get her cart over a raised door sill. Ladonis held the door open to assist her, staring. The words *a lighter shade of brown* from a Latino song came to mind. Was the woman Mexican?

"I'm Ladonis Washington," she said to the maid. "I work in Public Relations. Could I borrow your master key to get into my stateroom?" She really wanted to get into Tim's room.

The woman's eyes bucked. She looked around. Who was she looking for?

"Uh, uh," the woman grumbled.

"You're early," a male voice said.

Ladonis turned and faced another worker she didn't know. That in itself wasn't unusual. She hadn't traveled on the boats in a while. But she'd never seen any Mexican workers on board before.

"We were just on the way," the man said to her, "to make up your room."

"Oh, good," Ladonis said, sounding a little too cheerful. "Would you take my bag there, please?" She put her clothes bag atop the maid's cart. "And you can let me in cabin 219."

"That's the dead guy's cabin, isn't it?" the man asked.

"Yes," Ladonis said, "it is."

"I can't get you in there," the man said. "Nobody can except the captain. The Coast Guard padlocked that door."

Padlocked? How was she going to get inside? And she didn't know these people. Suppose they couldn't be trusted to keep their mouths shut? Ladonis wasn't thinking on her feet.

"Thanks anyway," Ladonis said. "Would you mind still taking my bag? Oh, and could you lay the black dress out for me?"

She rushed off before getting a response. She would go to the library and check out those remodel plans. Who knew? There might be a secret entry way.

She cut through the passenger wheel house, a replica of a steamboat pilot house where passengers could get a hands-on piloting demonstration. She passed through into the library, tossed her purse on a reproduction of a pilot's chair that faced an authentic wooden-spoked ship's wheel, and pulled the plans down from a shelf. She sat in a late eighteenth-century style chair covered in light blue mohair velvet and spread the drawings across her lap.

Velcroy invaded her thoughts. How Louisiana was it to get the Mayor, city council members, state legislators and a few of America's richest all together in a closed environment and throw a party? And why today? Could it be because of Tim and not in spite of him? Would a whiff of scandal kill this bill? Was that the great fear?

⌒

Ladonis reviewed the boat renovation plans. While she didn't find a secret entrance, it became clear to her that she had to find out why Tim hadn't minded sleeping in the heat, hearing the boat's engine roar all night. That answer could be a clue as to why he had died.

She wandered around thinking about how to get into Tim's padlocked cabin and found herself standing in front of 219. She scanned the hall, grateful that the area was a bit off the path of normal everyday traffic.

"What?" she said, looking at the lock. "Did you expect the police to leave it unlocked for you?"

She knelt down to unlatch the lock with a credit card. That didn't work. She lifted the padlock and tried a paper clip. She'd seen it done with a hairpin in the movies hundreds of time, only she didn't use hairpins. Sweat dampened her brow as she tried and tried to get that lock to click.

"Damn," she said.

Lock picking was an art form. More to it than placing a clip into the key hole and jiggling it. She leaned over for a closer look into the key hole. Perhaps, if she could see her mark, she might zero in on it. A hand touched her shoulder. She inhaled and froze into the longest second of her life.

"What you tryin' to do like that, Sistah?" a male voice said.

Ladonis recognized the Magnolia Project twang. She exhaled and looked up at a Herculean man with sandy-colored hair and freckled reddish-brown skin.

"Redboy." She plopped down into a seated position on the floor. "You almost gave me a heart attack."

Redboy was an old family friend who'd gotten into trouble. After his stint in Angola, his common-law wife had dropped off their two daughters with his mother for a visit and never came back. Ladonis had found him a job at the Floating Palace so that he could take care of the two little girls.

"Like I said." Redboy towered over her. "What you up to?"

"I need to look around in there," she said. "I've got to find out what Tim was up to before he passed on."

Redboy's brows lifted. She held out her hands. He pulled her up onto her feet.

"Yeah," Redboy said. "Tim was up to somethin' all right." He stuffed his hands into his pockets. "But don't ask me what. 'Cause I make a point of mindin' my own business 'round here."

Too bad she didn't have sense enough to take that option. She'd be at home nursing her broken heart. Instead, she was out playing detective.

"Redboy," she whispered, like she was waking up from a dream.

Redboy had been sent up for burglary. Maybe he could jimmy the lock. Or he could tell her how it was done.

"I know how you can get in there," Redboy said before she got around to asking him. "I can give you the key."

"The key?" she asked. "To the padlock?" This was too good to be true.

"Yeah," Redboy said. "The captain leave all his keys down by me for safe keepin'. He say he always losin' things. I'm the only one who work on the boat who stay in one place."

"What time should I be there?" Ladonis asked.

"Captain usually drop 'em off around nine, nine thirty. Even on a special cruise like tonight," he said. "You can come anytime after that. But you gotta be done with 'em by midnight. That's when my shift up and when Captain make his rounds."

"Okay," Ladonis said. "I'll see you sometime around ten."

Redboy nodded, turned, and walked back up the hallway. She dusted off her butt and went in the other direction to her cabin. That was too easy. Could something go wrong? Her gut said probably.

⌒

Ladonis entered her stateroom with a fifteen-minute window of time to dress for the night's festivities. She splashed a little soap, water and deodorant under her arms, and applied her makeup. Then she stood on her verandah and watched the less than enthusiastic entertainers dressed like Rhett Butler and Scarlett O'Hara perform the traditional up-beat, African-West-Indian, welcome-aboard dance to the tune of "When the Saints Go Marching In" as if it were a mournful march to a New Orleans jazz funeral.

The dining room seating had been pre-arranged by Velcroy. Ladonis was to sit at the table with Kasdan, his Tammy-Faye looking wife, Barbara, and the bearded New York tycoon known as the Grave Dancer. Ladonis had read in *Business Week* that the businessman had gotten that nickname because he bought troubled corporations, turned them around and sold them to make millions.

Despite the romantic Victorian elegance of the dining room, the glittering chandeliers, the dramatic floral upholstery and women dressed in evening sleek and jewels, negotiations were intense. Documents and flow charts were passed around as often as the butter and bread. The so-called healthy male appetite received satisfaction from talk of gambling and jobs. Districts and re-elections. Stock options and donations. Barbara interrupted to comment on the delicious scallops cooked with white wine and mushrooms and the roasted leg of lamb oozing garlic juice.

"If your company succeeds," Ladonis said, jumping into a conversation, "in securing the Dixieland Hotel for this Vegas-style hotel/casino, how many management jobs will the city get? Or do you intend to bring your own people in from New York?"

"Good question," the Grave Dancer said. "One I'm sure my people will take up with the city's leaders. But I can assure you there will be some management jobs available to this city's citizens. The number, of course, will depend on the capabilities of the workforce here."

The Grave Dancer passed her a sly half grin and lifted his wineglass in a toast to her. Was he mocking her? The New Orleans workforce was service-industry oriented, and so was its dismal public education system.

Kasdan leaned forward to get their guest's attention. Ladonis felt sure this overture was meant to exclude her. She didn't care. It was more important for her to concentrate on her own agenda. She slid her seat over a bit giving Kasdan exclusive access to the Grave Dancer.

Ladonis finished her meal. Observed the faraway look on the Grave Dancer's face as Kasdan poured out details about his brother's upholstery and carpet business. The last thing that man wanted to hear was how he could get a bargain on shag carpet for a hotel he didn't own yet.

"I have a splitting headache," Ladonis said. "I'm afraid I must ask you to excuse me."

Kasdan rose to see her off, stumbled, and knocked over his chair. Still, he had a smile. Would he be so glad to see her go if he suspected what she was up to?

Ladonis spotted Mayor Bruchard near the door sitting at a table with his wife, his councilman colleague, Reverend Whitetower, and the New York money magnate who'd named his youngest daughter after a famous jewelry store. She tried to pass them without being noticed. It was a quarter to ten. She'd hoped she'd have time to change before going to crew quarters, that little town below, to check out Tim's old room.

"What percentage," the Mayor said, "over the gaming commission's limit of gross revenue can the city count on for capital projects?"

Intrigued, Ladonis slowed to listen. A mistake.

"Ladonis," Mayor Bruchard said. "Hello."

She wheeled around to face him. This was not in the plan. She could not afford the time.

"Come join us," the Mayor said, pulling a chair from the empty table beside him.

Ladonis wanted to leave, but remembered her working orders from Velcroy—fraternize with the guests. And this was the Mayor, for God's sake.

"This is Ladonis Washington," the mayor said. "She works for the owners of this establishment, in public relations."

Thank God he hadn't called her a city treasure. Ladonis smiled at the millionaire sitting beside the Mayor. He at her. She couldn't stand people oohing and aahing over her accomplishments as if she were someone's artwork. The gentleman offered her a glass of wine. She refused, but poured herself water instead. She couldn't afford a light head.

"What type of capital projects are we talking about?" The man seemed eager to get on with the conversation he was having with the Mayor.

"There's a group of educators," the Mayor said, "who have been hounding us to put computer labs in all public schools, elementary through high school."

Councilman Whitetower straightened up and nodded his approval. He was on record that education was his passion. That was why Ladonis liked him.

"A costly undertaking," the millionaire said.

"Not nearly as costly," Mayor Bruchard said, "as a casino at the foot of Canal Street will be lucrative." He bit down into a bread stick. "A religious town like this . . . reaching out to its deprived kids. Preachers bound to tell churchgoing voters a company like that can't be all bad."

"I see what you mean." The financier placed his wineglass on the table. Dabbed at his mouth with his napkin.

"Good," Mayor Bruchard said, taking a swallow of his wine. "By the way, I'm thinking five percent."

The bureaucrat, often described in the media as the city's fundraiser, seemed in his glory. The moneyman had been relegated to a mere smile. Mayor Bruchard leaned over closer to the man.

"Now, listen," he said. "My law firm represents a major shipyard. And we'd be . . ."

Ladonis eased her chair away from the table. No need to witness the Mayor hustling this guy. Across the room, the city's usually laid-back officials courted outside ideas and outside money with some of the country's richest financiers. The benefits had to outweigh their concessions, while at the same time, be generous enough to cover their political butts. She could see why journalists entangled the terms "lobby" and "personal gain."

Ladonis sensed the anxiety, felt the excitement. The same adrenaline pumped in her veins. She had to keep ahead in the corporate game she was playing. Otherwise, as her Grandma Lucille would say, her career at the Floating Palace could end up like a ladder in a chicken coop—short and shitty.

20

Nothin' Nice

Ladonis stepped out onto the balcony of the Dixie Deck where it overlooked the cherry-red paddle wheel. A couple of musicians walked behind her lugging their instruments inside to the Majestic Room, the grand ballroom and now the gaming room for this trip, complete with blackjack, roulette, and a live jazz band. She moved to the side, leaned over the rail just above the thirty-five-foot *Magnolia Belle* nameplate and listened to the rhythmic splash of water off the paddle blades. She glanced at her watch. No time to change.

A swift movement above on the Moon Deck gave her a start. Sounded like a chair sliding across the wooden floor. Someone stumbled and fell against the calliope, forcing a chord to cry out.

"Motherfuck," a voice said.

Ladonis pictured Burl Decatur but dismissed the thought. His name wasn't on Velcroy's list of attending employees. She moved back from the rail and bumped into Bunnie Sinclair.

"I swear to God, girl," Ladonis said. "You ain't nothin' nice."

Bunnie's eyes crinkled up mad. Ladonis snatched the door open and headed inside. She rushed through the Majestic Room onto the corridor, down the wide three-story staircase. She stopped dead center, one story down, directly beneath the diamond cut crystal chandelier that hung from a mirrored ceiling. She whirled around to face Bunnie on her tail.

"Is spying a part of your job description?" Ladonis asked. "Or just a part of your ethical makeup?"

"Ethical is a mighty powerful word coming from a parasite."

"Don't you think you should be serving coffee or something?" Ladonis said.

Her jaw clenched. Bunnie's cheeks flushed hot pink. The last thing Ladonis needed was Bunnie breathing down her neck. She had to get the key to 219 from Redboy and still have time to look around before midnight. She'd already lost valuable time.

"I heard something crash on the Moon Deck," Ladonis said. "Didn't Velcroy put you in charge of security and coffee? I would check it out if I were you. Remember, it's your head if that crime tape's disturbed."

The elevator door opened. Ladonis hopped in. Pushed the down button and watched the door remove Bunnie's anguished eyes from her sight. She'd guessed correctly. Bunnie didn't want to risk not checking.

Ladonis got off on the lower deck next to the beauty salon and walked another flight down to the bottom of the boat. The last deck was the employee's home away from home—tiny little dormitory rooms barely large enough to hold a bunk bed and a chest of drawers. The conveniences available to the passengers on the top decks—climate control, lavish furnishings, adequate lighting—could only be enjoyed by the employees while they worked up above.

Ladonis ducked under the low door lintel and stepped over the raised sill into the tight quarters. She made her way through the narrow, semi-darkened hall on through to the cafeteria. Big, empty pots sat on the shiny stainless steel countertops, waiting for the black, rotund, grandmotherly cook, "Mama" to the crew, to fill them with her tasty down-home meals.

Ladonis darted past the opened lounge door, careful not to be seen. She pinched her nose to hold out the harsh aroma of marijuana. She'd discovered in college that she was allergic to the drug. According to her best friend, Evalena, that condition had caused her to miss out on the best times of her life.

A few feet more and she stood at the laundry's door. Redboy worked inside, shirtless. His muscles glistened with sweat. The washing machines and dryers rumbled. Steam from the presser heated the air like a sauna.

"Psst," Ladonis signaled.

Redboy picked up a white towel off the wooden worktable, wiped his face, and ambled towards her. He reached into his pants pocket and handed her a key on an Aries the Ram ring.

"Don't forget," he said. "Get it back here by midnight. I gotta put it back on the captain's hook before my shift is up."

"Don't worry." Ladonis smiled up at him. "Thanks, Redboy."

"No prob, Sistah. I owe you."

Ladonis retraced her steps back to the Beauty Salon, clutching the key ring. Now for Tim's cabin. Two one nine. The numbers pounded on her brain. She approached the door and stepped under the yellow crime tape. She used the key and the door opened, then stepped inside, closing the door behind her.

She stood inside the cabin, trembling from head to toe. What was she doing? She felt like an intruder, no better than a graveyard thief invading a dead man's tomb. She imagined the howls and cries of Tim's ghost in the sounds from the exhaust cylinders, pushing-pulling, the squeaking sliding pistons of the engine pumping steam.

The moon's light funneled in through a crack in the pale green drapes and guided her to a twin bed. Perspiration crawled down her back, and trailed between her small breasts. Her plan? To examine Tim's hard drive. Bret's skin had turned chalk-white when the detective removed the disks from Tim's computer. Beyond that, she just didn't know.

She sat in Tim's chair fumbling for the computer's turn-on switch. The machine booted up. She typed a command for a list of everything on the hard drive and hit return.

Male voices argued outside the door. She recognized Bret's. Her finger sat on the off button, but wouldn't budge.

"I told you," Bret said. "Tim and I didn't speak before he got on board. In fact, I didn't know he was on board."

"Just open the goddamn door," another man said.

Oh, Lord. She knew that voice. Decatur.

"I've been waiting all day to get in here," Decatur said. "The captain was too scared to let me in."

"What?" Bret said, sarcastically. "Didn't you have anything to persuade him with?"

"Not like I do on you," Decatur said.

Ladonis' hand went limp on the switch. The computer clicked off. Her knees shook. But she managed to get over to the bed.

"Fuck off, Decatur," Bret said. "You've got a lot of nerve for a guy who's been caught ripping the company off with phony purchases."

"Is that what your friend Tim told you?"

"Believe it or not," Bret said, "Tim didn't tell me everything."

"That's what you say," Decatur said. "But, like I told you, I go down, so will he. Dead or not. And you too."

"Think, man," Bret said. "The company's gone public. We'll be applying for a gambling license soon. There will be investigation after investigation. Clear out now. It's only a matter of time before you—before we all—are under a microscope."

The doorknob rattled. Ladonis attempted to crawl under the bed but found the box spring encased in wood to the floor. She scanned the dark room. The closet? Her legs were too long for the tiny space. She headed for the bathroom and stopped at the door. Suppose one of them had to go. She tried the verandah door. It was locked. She took the key chain from her little beaded evening purse. The key fell from her trembling fingers onto the carpeted floor. She dropped to her knees. Her fifteen-dollar Donna Karan pantyhose ripped as her hand touched the key ring.

"Watch the tape, you idiot," Bret told Decatur.

The key turned in the cabin lock. The sound of the lock slipping loose boomed in her ears.

"Listen, pretty boy," Decatur said. "I know all about your buddy. And it's like I told you before, you find what I'm looking for and nobody else needs to know."

Know what? Things were getting even more confused. More scary. The sound of Decatur's voice would put fear into Christ. Could he hear her knees knocking? How was she going to get out this mess?

"Just what exactly are you looking for?" Bret asked. "You never did say."

Ladonis held the key with both hands to control her shaking. The door unlocked. She stepped onto the verandah and shivered, chilled to the bone by the night river dampness. She eased the door shut and leaned up against it.

"I told you," Bret said from inside. "Tim didn't tell me anything about you. What are you? Fucking deaf or just stupid?"

"You'd better find it," Decatur said. "I don't care if he told you or not."

Something crashed. A vase? A glass? What were they doing? Tossing the place? What would happen if the cops found out?

"It's got be somewhere in this room," Decatur said.

"What are you talking about?" Bret said.

Was that fear or aggravation she heard in Bret's voice? If he had any sense, he'd be scared. Or did he think he could reason with the devil? Someone knocked on the cabin door.

"Bret," a voice called out. "Are you in there?"

Kasdan? Did he know what was going on between Bret and Decatur? This was more serious than she'd thought. Whatever was going on had to be valuable for her to know.

"Bret, what the hell are you doing in here?" Kasdan asked. "Decatur? What are you doing here?"

"My job," Decatur said.

"How did you find me, Kasdan?" Bret sounded just as irritated as Kasdan did. "Decatur, I think you'd better leave."

Where did Bret's control come from all of a sudden? Footsteps filled the silence. The cabin floors squeaked with each step.

"We'll talk later," Decatur said.

The door latch clicked. Ladonis felt a cramp in her neck. She moved her head from side to side.

"What do you want, Kasdan?" Bret said. "And what made you look for me in here?"

"What the hell are you up to, Bret?" Kasdan said. "Do you know more about Tim's death than you're telling?"

"I don't know what you're talking about," Bret said. "Right now I'm more concerned with Decatur. What a disaster your guy has turned out to be."

Decatur a disaster? That was an understatement. Decatur was not just a bad employee. He was a bad person.

"Why?" Kasdan said. "What's Decatur got to do with this?"

"Pick up that vase," Bret said. "If the police find this mess, we'll have more problems. Did you say why you're here?"

"Trouble," Kasdan said. "A group of the investors wants a rundown on the company's finances for the past five years."

"Tim was working on that," Bret said, sadness in his voice. "Velcroy said he'd explain that to them. Tell them to refer to last year's financial report in their packets. That a more detailed, current report is forthcoming."

"Full disclosure in these matters is an SEC requirement," Kasdan said. "Remember Home Stake? Ivan Boesky? S&L? Equity Funding?"

"Notorious examples of securities fraud," Bret said. "We're not into fraud. Fluff that pillow, will you?"

"What about incomplete financial disclosures?" Kasdan said. "The point I'm making is that these 'notorious examples of securities fraud,' as you call it, have been headlines for almost two decades. We don't need that kind of media scrutiny on our business operations. Not on top of everything else. I suggest you put in a ship-to-shore call to Velcroy. Let him know what's going on."

Kasdan was going at Bret the way he went after Ladonis when she'd made a mistake, that preachy-teachy cockiness that made her feel dumb.

"Look," Kasdan said. "I know Tim was your friend. More like a brother."

Had Kasdan's irritation changed to sympathy? For Bret? That would really be something.

"You're not thinking straight," Kasdan said. "And there are rumors. Look, what I'm trying to say here is, if you know something, anything that will tell us why this happened, you can tell me."

"I don't know what you're talking about," Bret said, a little too anxious.

"I might be able to help," Kasdan said. "I mean, if there's anything you don't want to get out, maybe. Well, you know what I mean."

If only she could see Kasdan's face. She'd learned to read him pretty well. If he wasn't sincere, those two folded lines across his brow were a sure-tell giveaway.

"There's nothing," Bret said. "So drop it, will you?"

Ladonis heard footsteps. Were they leaving? Thank God.

Ladonis leaned up against the wall on the verandah for a long while after Kasdan and Bret had left. Then she paced, moving to the rhythmic slide of the pistons thrusting and pulling back and forth hundreds of pounds of steam. Burl Decatur crashed in on her thoughts. She walked over to the rail and hung her head over. Push. Pull. Push. Pull. The pistons slid backwards and forwards. Her stomach churned. What the hell was Decatur looking for? Whatever it was, Tim had had possession of it last in this cabin. She shivered. The thought of Tim and Decatur in cahoots chilled her.

As far as she knew, the police hadn't taken anything from Tim's room other than the computer disks. She walked to the opposite end of the short verandah, went inside, and sat on the bed. She looked around as if the answer to her confusion would jump out at her. It didn't. She walked over to the bathroom and called up to memory everything she'd learned about the boat's remodel.

Part of the space was the engineer's quarters before the remodel. Without a deep hull, the steam engine was moved to the new second deck just above this space. She walked, measuring her steps across the cabin. The engineers used to come up to this room from below. Below from where? She strolled across the entire floor listening for a hollow spot. Nothing.

Frustration warmed her blood. She needed air and went out on the verandah. Her feet sank into the turf carpet. She looked down and stomped. The wood creaked louder, and her feet sank deeper. She stooped down and pulled at the turf. The turf lifted and revealed a trap door.

"I found it," she shrieked like kid at an Easter egg hunt.

She put her hand over her mouth. Had someone heard her? She pulled at the latch. The door opened upward. This had to be the space left off the remodel plans, the error too involved to rectify.

Ladonis slid down, putting another rip in her pantyhose. The air that greeted her was hot and mildew-musty. Her face flushed, moistened by the steam seeping through the pores of the haphazardly boarded walls. The push and pull of the sliding pistons rang even louder in her ears.

Her eyes took a minute to adjust. When she could focus, she looked around. A turquoise nylon bag lay in a corner. She grabbed the hand strap. She leaned back against the wall, reached up to move the carpet blocking the dim light from the moon, then unzipped the shrimp-smelly bag.

"Sweet Jesus."

21

Knee-Knocking Dance

11:56 P.M. Ladonis rushed into the laundry room in an oh-my-God frame of mind. She moved swiftly, yet careful to look natural. She couldn't afford to arouse anyone's suspicions. Not with that bag in her possession.

She walked up to Redboy staring at but not seeing his shirtless chest. She handed him the Aries key ring. He looked over her shoulder, picked up a couple of towels, thrust them into her chest, turned, and walked off. Ladonis pivoted to see the captain about to enter through the door.

"Thanks for the towels," she said to Redboy, holding them close to her face.

She stared straight ahead, pretending not to see the captain when their paths crossed. Would he recognize the bag? Could he smell it? The hot air had a hard time circulating below deck. She kept moving to maintain her composure as well as to keep her bladder from exploding. The captain didn't notice her. Or he pretended not to.

She bounded down the narrow corridor to her cabin fueled by a full bladder tormenting her insides and an adrenaline rush potent as pure caffeine. She flung the shrimp-smelling turquoise bag across her back out of nose range, away from her throbbing head. No one hid that much money unless it was acquired illegally.

And any illegal activities uncovered on board could prove detrimental to operations.

And now she had a plan. Bret and Velcroy had to be impressed and grateful she'd found the bag before the police did. The company's position on Tim's death could be established, his reputation protected and, more importantly, her professional standing enhanced. That was the plan.

Her fingers got stuck around the cabin key. One by one she unwound them to unlock her door. Pain sent another signal to her bladder. Was this the feeling her mother had described when her arthritis flared up? The lock slipped. Ladonis sighed.

"Thank God," she said.

Just as she was about to close the door behind her, Burl Decatur cruised up the hall. Was this bag what he'd been looking for in Tim's cabin? Had to be. His haunting eyes found hers. Did he recognize the bag? She felt dampness between her legs.

Decatur didn't stop. Didn't say anything either. Ladonis took a deep breath, stepped up into her cabin. The fright from Decatur's mean-spirited stare lingered. She closed the door, threw the bag and towels onto the floor and did a knee-knocking dance to the bathroom.

Ladonis picked up the bag and dumped everything out onto the blue velvet bed cover. Bundles of hundred-dollar bills fell into a pile along with a thin piece of aluminum about the size of a cookie sheet. She'd never seen that much money in one heaping before. Her fingers went limp. The turquoise bag fell up against the cookie sheet. She heard a clanking noise. Was something else in the bag? She pulled out two brown clasp envelopes and a mini cassette tape.

The flowers on the wallpaper started to move. The room got

smaller. Her mouth went dry. She opened the little refrigerator for a 7-Up but opened a can of orange juice instead. She mixed it with the welcome-aboard champagne that sat on the nightstand. All through college, P.J. had drunk this stuff. Mimosa. Called it a relaxer.

She took a big gulp of the champagne mix as if she were drinking just the orange juice. The alcohol stung her throat. She stared at the contents from the bag on the bed and took another swallow, a smaller one this time.

Whatever all of this meant, finding the bag in Tim's space was not a good thing. Had Tim found out about Decatur and stumbled onto all of this? Or was it his? She drank more, opened one of the envelopes, and pulled out a couple of pages of paper.

"It's in Spanish," she declared.

Another envelope contained a deed, an airline ticket to Tahiti, an un-addressed letter and a Kodak photo pack filled with negatives. She picked up the off-colored, pinkish piece of aluminum. The apparatus looked like the ink transfer plate for the ditto machine her fifth-grade teacher used to write test and homework questions before running off copies. Had she uncovered a counterfeit money plate? Her imagination was all over the place.

She held the aluminum sheet up to the light. The image imprinted on the center of the sheet was the size of a business card. The yellow lettering read: "Department of Immigration," and there was a government seal. The sheet slipped from her sweaty hands. She picked up the pages. Spanish names, addresses, social security numbers were listed on the pages. She glanced at the property deed. An address on a street in the East. She examined the photograph negatives but didn't recognize anyone. If only she had a recorder to listen to the tape.

She drank more of the mimosa and paced. A printing plate. A shitload of money. Mexicans. An airline ticket. What the hell was going on? People smuggling? According to an article she'd read in the *New York Times*, corporate types were bringing in workers from financially devastated countries. Could the Floating Palace's fabulous tourist vessels be transporting illegal laborers?

She plopped down on the bed and took several deep breaths. Mayberry's Barney Fife couldn't misread these clues. But clues could be misconstrued. She had to get the facts. Answer the big questions. The who, what, when, why and how. Then what? Would the facts make her dreams come true?

Ladonis checked her watch, pulled off her little black cocktail number, and grabbed the sweats from her bag. She had to get to the employee's lounge. The crew would know what was going on. They would have the answers.

She fell to her knees and scrabbled around her Reeboks. A cellophane packet on the floor lay caught in the corner of the bedspread's drag. It must've fallen when she had dumped the stuff from the bag. She examined the packet and its brown powdery contents. Could only be one thing.

"Lord help me," she cried. "What in the world have I gotten myself into?"

22

Spades

Ladonis entered the employee lounge and scanned the room for familiar faces. Bill Greenville and a few others were playing cards at a table behind the sofa facing the television. How was she going to extract information from these workers without instigating panic? Suppose they didn't know anything? Could she play detective without being detected? Ladonis cleared her throat. Bill raised his head.

"Hey, y'all," Bill said. "Look who came down to chill."

Ladonis eased further into the room and waved at Trina, the Floating Palace's first black maid. A short, stocky woman with two gold front teeth. Joe, a stately looking older white gentleman, sat next to Trina. Joe looked up and smiled.

"What's up, everybody?" Ladonis said.

"Spades," Bill said. "That's what."

"The black man's version of bid whisk," Ladonis said.

She winked at Trina. Living and working together in such a confined space had changed attitudes, had evoked a spirit for sharing. A long way, Ladonis knew, from Trina's first day on the job.

"Yeah," Trina said, "and I got these white boys by the balls." She focused a look on Ladonis. "Okay, Miss Tightass. What you really doin' down here this time of night?"

Ladonis' eyes rolled with surprise. Her mouth opened, but nothing came out. Bill and Joe passed Trina a disapproving, though teasing look.

"What y'all lookin' at me like that for?" Trina said. "You know that's what we call her behind her back."

Tightass, huh? Ladonis had to smile. P.J. had called her that the first time they went out to dinner together at Arnaud's. Ladonis had never even heard of Arnaud's. From her vantage point in this great eating city, the soul-food restaurant, Chez Helene, on North Robertson Street with its red-checkered tablecloths, was the showcase for fine cuisine and elegant dining in her world. P.J. had leaned over and whispered, "Relax, Tightass. The KKK's not here."

"Don't worry, Ladonis," Bill said. "It's a term of endearment."

Bill rubbed his balding head leaving strands of hair on his head standing up like teeth in a comb. Joe laid down his cards and pulled his long, thick reddish-brown hair back into a rubber band. He was still wearing his waiter's uniform. Black trousers. A red bow tie hung off the collar of the white shirt.

"Trina's right," Ladonis said. "I need information."

No one could accuse Trina of not calling a spade a spade. Of not speaking her mind. Made sense for Ladonis to do the same. Besides, she had the feeling that this crew had discussed how to handle inquiries about Tim. The question was did they know what Tim had been into. And would they tell her.

"Bret sent you down here to find out what we know about Tim?" Bill said. "Didn't he?"

"Well," Ladonis said. "Yes, in a way, but this is more about . . . I mean . . . I found a . . . a . . ."

What was she doing? She couldn't tell them about that bag. She had come down to get information, not give it. Too bad she hadn't thought beforehand about how to broach the issue.

"I saw a woman," Ladonis said. "A Mexican woman, I believe, when I came on board. I could've sworn she was wearing a housekeeping uniform. But, when I approached her, she acted as if she didn't understand me. As if she couldn't talk."

Bill and Joe's eyes flashed on Trina. Trina slammed down her cards. She sat up straight. Her body stiffened.

"Say no more," Bill said. "Don't get Trina started."

"What do you mean?" Ladonis said.

"We're the ones," Trina said, her voice rising through clenched teeth. "We're the ones that got beat up, lynched, hosed down, burned up. And, as soon as things change, foreigners come in, work for pennies and we shit again."

Ladonis understood Trina. Ladonis had learned through conversations with some of the old timers, including Trina, that it had been only twenty or so years ago that the Floating Palace had began hiring blacks as maids and waiters. Before then and after slavery, blacks had been hired to tend the non-tip jobs, such as dishwasher. Away from passengers. Out of sight.

"Are there Mexican maids working onboard?" Ladonis asked.

"Maybe a few second or third generation Mexican-Americans," Joe said. "But not the non-English speaking Mexicans that Trina is all bent out of shape about. Not anyone needing a green card."

Ladonis heard the concern in Joe's tone. Concern for his friend Trina's state of mind. But could that be doubt lurking behind his dancing eyes?

"We've noticed more and more Mexicans hanging around the ports," Bill said. "And, like you, Trina claims she saw one on board wearing housekeeper digs. She's been in an uproar, afraid for her job ever since."

"This ain't Morgan City," Trina said, "where Mexicans seem to be breeding these days. So can you tell me why a no-English-talkin' foreigner in a maid uniform would be on this boat?"

"Maybe she's a stowaway," Joe said.

"She could be a passenger," Ladonis said.

"No," Bill said. "I checked to see if any of them big wigs on board had a Mexican wife or girlfriend. No one does."

Three things rushed to Ladonis' attention. The contraband in her cabin. Bret's anxiety. And why Tim died. But how did one affect another?

"You know how much they make in Mexico for an hour's work?" Trina asked. "Not even a dollar. Can you believe that? They work cheap, and the Floating Palace is as cheap as they come. They're gonna take over our jobs, I tell you."

Could Trina be right? Would Velcroy and Bret stoop that low? That would explain a lot, but still left the specifics—the who, what, when and how, all the main questions—unanswered.

"Trina," Joe said. "You've straightened us out about a lot of stuff. I know how you feel, but you're over the top on this one."

"I don't know about that," Bill said. "Like I said before, them Mexicans been hanging around the ports more and more."

"Why are you encouraging her?" Joe asked.

"I know you say paranoia is part of my black legacy or some shit like that," Trina said to Joe. "But, when you wake up one morning and the captain say it's your last ride, you're gonna wish you'd been paranoid too."

"If she's not a passenger," Ladonis said, "and not an employee, why is she on board? And where is she now?"

"Can't tell you," Bill said.

Can't or won't? The more pressing question was how did she get onboard? If these guys didn't know that, they wouldn't know about the money and printing plate in that bag Ladonis had found. Or would they?

"There was this man, too," Ladonis said. "He came out of nowhere. I've never seen him before. He told me the woman was going to make up my room. Joe, you get any new people in housekeeping?"

"Nobody new," Joe said. "Beats me who they are."

"Until you said you saw this woman," Bill said, "we'd practically convinced Trina . . ." He looked over at Joe. "And ourselves that Trina was seeing things."

"Now you know," Trina said. "And that means we've got trouble."

"I don't know shit," Joe said. "And that's the way I like it. This place is full of crap and if you want to keep out of it, and keep your job, keep your eyes, ears and mouth shut."

That was the second time Ladonis had heard those words. What had everyone so uptight? That kind of foreboding indicated insight as well as fear. Should she press for answers? Why not?

"Is that why nobody ever gets nailed," Ladonis said, "for drugs around here?"

Rumor had it that half the crew did coke. Ladonis knew for a fact that the other half smoked weed. Chances were that whoever was behind the drug thing, knew about the Mexican thing.

"It's no secret," Bill said, "where to score a joint on board."

"I'm talking about coke," Ladonis said, though the stuff in her cabin was brown.

"Look, girlfriend," Trina said. "Joe's right. Some things go on around here ain't for us to know about, let alone talk about."

"What do you mean?" Ladonis said.

"I mean we've got responsibilities at home," Trina said. "That's what. We need our jobs."

Trina's tone was tough. Like a sistah who'd been pushed too far.

But why was it okay for her to bitch about illegal immigrants and not about illegal drugs?

"Listen, Ladonis," Joe added, "we know you're trying to do your job. We always say how hardworking you are. That's why we do our best to help you out. But, take it from me, somebody who has been around here for a long time. Stay out of this."

Ladonis had to know. How could she shut the media out if she didn't know what to shut out? On the other hand, she didn't want to alienate these guys. A successful administrator was only as good as the people doing the actual work. And she planned to be a good administrator. Besides, she was ninety-eight percent certain that Decatur was behind whatever was going on. That being the case, she could see how a person would be afraid. Decatur certainly scared her.

"What if?" Ladonis said. "What if I ask how you think drugs can be smuggled onboard? Not who's doing the smuggling. You don't have to name anyone. Just give me a scenario. How would someone, anyone, smuggle coke from Mexico on board?"

The Mexicans. The printing plate. The drugs. Crimes were being committed. Somebody or everyone had to know something. Joe's flat expression was just like the look on Trina's and Bill's faces.

"The way y'all looking at me," Ladonis said, "you'd think I'd asked you to count to a trillion."

"They'd have to cross the Gulf," Joe said. "And come through the bayous."

"Can boats travel through those marshes?" Ladonis asked.

"Shrimp boats do," Bill said.

Shrimp boats? A shrimper was involved. Tim was last seen checking in a shrimp delivery. There was the shrimp smell on the turquoise bag. But this was also where her doubt crept in.

"Would shrimpers cross the Gulf to get to Mexico?" Ladonis said. "Those waters are peppered with offshore oil rigs and oil derricks."

"That's right," Bill said, a stubborn know-it-all tone in his voice. "And don't forget the weather. Storms and hurricanes can turn that Gulf into a killer in a hot minute."

"Yeah," Joe said, "but you're forgetting that a pusher will do anything, go anywhere, to transport cargo."

Ladonis experienced a fleeting moment of déjà vu. Somewhere she'd heard those words before. Probably something HeartTrouble had said.

"There's another possibility," Joe said. "Maybe they fly the drugs over the Gulf and drop them in the swamps."

"Fly?" Bill said. "It's hard even for helicopters to fly that low over those swamps."

"They can on a pontoon," Joe said. "My uncle is a fish spotter and he says they copter over the Gulf two, sometimes three times a day."

"A pontoon?" Ladonis said.

"You know," Joe said. "A sea plane. It's a little plane with a balloon-like bottom that can land on water. They're used to take people on swamp tours. And to spot fish in the Gulf."

Tour planes? She'd heard of them. That was it.

"How many people can ride a sea plane at one time?" Ladonis asked.

"Six. Eight," Joe said. "Depends how small they are."

"And these sea planes can land on the Gulf's beaches?" Ladonis asked.

"Yeah," Joe said. "Especially in the summertime when the weather is good and the skies are clear."

"Are we playing spades or what?" Trina said. "You've told her enough." She looked at Ladonis. "Girlfriend, I'm gonna be pissed off if you come down here just so you could pump us and then go upstairs to snitch on us."

"Who is she going to snitch to?" Joe's quiet tone hinted sarcasm. "The president?"

"We didn't say anything about anybody," Bill said. "Just like she said. We didn't name any names."

"I'd never repeat anything," Ladonis said. "Unless you say I can. I won't tell anyone what you've told me. I promise."

The wary look the three co-workers shared put Ladonis on notice. Perhaps she was wrong to pursue this with them. After all, Bret had issued an ultimatum. Spread rumors and be dismissed, he'd said. But what about that woman she had seen? She had to be somewhere. And what about that crack about the President? About Bret? Was it because he used the dope or smuggled it in?

"Are you havin' a good time?" Trina said. "Down here slummin'? Did you get the information you came down here for?"

No, she hadn't gotten the information she had come here to get. She still had no idea why Tim had had to die. Trina's brazen expression switched to sullen. Why couldn't she trust Ladonis enough to explain why she felt so threatened?

"Tell me, Trina," Ladonis said. "Tell me what's going on."

Bill, Joe and Trina shared a look, lowered their heads. Were they sending each other signals? Bill and Joe stood up.

"I'm out of here," Bill said.

"Me, too," Joe countered.

Joe leaned down and kissed Trina on the forehead. Bill squeezed her hand. Trina rose from her seat. She gave Ladonis a strained, joyless look.

"Good night, Ladonis," she said. "Good to see you." She turned to walk away.

"What's the deal, Trina?" Ladonis said, stepping in front of Trina.

"You gotta learn," Trina said. "You don't go 'round tellin' people about things that ain't your business."

"Okay," Ladonis said. "I can live with that. But can you please tell me how Bret, I mean, the President figures into whatever it is?"

Trina shifted her body weight. Her thick lips compressed. And there was this unpleasant glint in her eyes.

"All I know," Trina said, "is that Tim and the president was close. I can't say nothin' about Tim and drugs or nothin' like that because I don't know about that. And it ain't my business anyway. But Tim, nice as he was, wasn't who everybody thought he was. I hate to say this, but Tim was an abomination."

An abomination? What the hell did that mean? Trina pushed past Ladonis before she had a chance to question her further.

23

Pusher Dude

Detective Travers tossed the white wrapping from the Italian muf-fuletta sandwich. The paper landed at Wellsburg's feet near a uni-formed cop standing in front of the Coke machine inches away from a trash can.

"Sorry," Travers said.

Wellsburg pressed a button on the vending machine, a Diet Coke tumbled to the pick-up bin. He grabbed his Coke, picked up Travers' soppy wrapper and dropped the paper into the trash can. If only Travers could get rid of his partner that easily, he'd be all in that CEO's face right now.

"How can you eat all that grease and cheese?" Wellsburg said.

Travers sucked and picked salami from his teeth. Damned if he'd miss the opportunity to let the bane of his existence know what he thought of his well-heeled ways. Besides, the olive oil and dairy were what he liked most. Wellsburg turned away, a look of distaste on his face.

"Any night you want a nice home-cooked meal," a uniformed cop said, "you're welcome at my house. My wife is related to Betty Crocker."

Laughter erupted. The other officers, sitting and moving about, including Wellsburg gave each other high fives. Travers and his wife, FeeFee, had been married for sixteen years, and, for sixteen years, his fellow officers had teased him because his southern-belle bride couldn't boil water.

"Yeah," Travers said. "But according to the whores on Bourbon Street, your wife gave up screwing. You put out for snatch. I put out for food. I like my deal better."

The building shook from the howls and whistles. Not much consolation to Travers, though. He would have loved to go home to a nice hot, cooked meal once in awhile. But he'd married up. Up into the Glassier Steel family. FeeFee had married down. The family fortune and all that went with it were off-limits. Part of FeeFee's adjustment to life as a cop's wife was her never-ending griping about what she'd given up for him. Cooking, she'd made clear, was taking the sacrifice thing over the top. So every night before he went home, Travers ordered out and ate his supper at his desk.

"I've been wondering about that Honey Man," Travers said to his partner.

"Why?" Detective Wellsburg asked. "Honey Man is not a priority. He has nothing to do with the case we are working on."

Wellsburg took a big gulp of Coke and picked up a file. Travers placed both hands on the flat surface in front of him and pushed his chair-on-wheels back from the desk.

"I'm not so sure," Travers said.

"Have it your way," Wellsburg said. "Just don't screw up this case."

Travers got up and headed toward the bathroom. He dialed a number into his cell phone. He was determined to see Honey Man.

"Say, Cliff," Travers said into the earpiece. Cliff was the sheriff in charge of prisoner transports and visitations at the jail. He and Travers had grown up together. And Travers had helped him clear up a few police matters that could've lost Cliff his job. "I'm calling in a favor. Get me in to see Honey Man."

"Honey Man?" Cliff asked. "That pusher dude who sold to the young DA?"

"Yeah," Travers said. "Him."

"He still in holding," Cliff said.

"What?" Travers said. "You mean he's still in court?"

"A late-night show," Cliff said. "You know the warden and the boys on the cellblock. Nobody goes back until they're all done. And those two young assholes who raped and killed that black girl after her birthday party still in court."

"Cruel punishment," Travers said. The holding cell in Judge Dugar's courtroom was a fenced-in stairwell in the back hall of the court. Prisoners had to sit there until it was their turn to face the music. "Even for a junkie criminal. Sitting on a stairwell for twelve hours."

"Why are you interested in Honey Man?" Cliff asked.

"I have this hunch," Travers said, "that he might be able to clear something up for me that can help me solve another case. That's all."

What Travers wouldn't do for the old days. No one had questioned methods back then, and everybody had played along. None of this cover-my-ass bullshit. No one had feared facing a review board.

"Well," Cliff said. "You better get your ass on over here. The guard told me that the judge told that defense lawyer ten minutes ago that he had twenty minutes to finish up for the day."

"I'm on my way," Travers said.

Travers flipped his phone shut and went back to his desk. A uniformed officer walked up and handed a message slip to Wellsburg.

"A call for you," the officer said. "Said he has some information on the murder."

"Who called?" Travers asked.

"Reverend Sweeney," the officer said. "You know, the preacher who fornicated with a hooker and got caught."

"Yeah, okay," Wellsburg said. "So what did he want?"

"He says he has information about the dead guy," the officer said.

"Which dead guy?" Travers asked. "It's not like we got just one, you know."

"The paddle wheel dead guy." The young officer glared at Travers through his gray-green eyes.

"Did he say anything else?" Wellsburg asked. "Like where he is? How he came across this information?"

"That's it," the officer said, annoyance in his voice. "That's the message and the number I found in dispatch when I came on duty."

"That was when?" Travers looked at his watch. "Two hours ago?"

The officer walked away. Travers wanted to walk away, too. To get to the courthouse and talk to Honey Man before he was carted back to the jail. It would be nice if he could avoid all that rigmarole at the prison in the morning by seeing Honey Man tonight.

"What's his problem?" Travers said to Wellsburg. "I can't help it if he finished last in his class and got assigned crap work."

Wellsburg frowned his disapproval. Dialed the number on the message slip. Travers put the cover on his old Remington. The only one left in the precinct.

"A machine," Wellsburg said, hanging up. "I'll call back in the morning. I promised to take Mary Jane to a movie tonight."

Wellsburg picked up his jacket off the back of his chair. Travers did the same. At least he and the partner from hell would walk out together.

"I'm outta here," Wellsburg said, stuffing the message slip into his pocket.

The uniformed officer came back. This time he handed Wellsburg a brown, clasp envelope. The detective stared at the officer.

"From forensics," the officer said.

"Look," Travers said, checking his watch. "Tell me later what's in it. I've got to run."

"Yeah," Wellsburg said. "Me too." He took another long look at the envelope. "It'll keep. Mary Jane won't." He laid the envelope on his desk, tossed his jacket over his shoulder and headed home. "Tomorrow."

"Yeah," Travers said. "Tomorrow."

Only he was going to solve the case tonight.

⌒

Travers eased through the courtroom doors. The crowd inside was small. Family for the two young white inmates on trial. He looked straight ahead at the judge. Ernest Dugar reminded him of Baby Huey. A tall, broad man, with a small head and a kid's face. A gentle giant sitting behind the high bench. At thirty-four, Dugar was the youngest criminal judge sitting. And, as Travers and the guys often teased, the only one with all of his own hair.

Travers moved all the way into the courtroom. The public defender, Larry Frank, whose craftiness Travers respected, was on his feet, involved in a heated debate with the DA about the relevance of something or the other.

Travers walked up to the sheriff's deputy who stood guard at the door to the stairwell, past the judge's bench. He identified himself and was allowed to enter to the stairwell holding cell closed in by a barred gate. Honey Man, black as tar, sat in the half-dark space with two other brothers sporting prison orange and uncombed mini Afros.

"Honey Man, get over here," Travers said. He lit up two cigarettes and handed them to the other two inmates, signaling them to go to the bottom of the stairs. "I want to ask you a few questions."

"Say what?" Honey Man said. "Man, I ain't got nothin' to say to you." He stood off in a corner. His lanky and weary-looking body twitched as if he was doing a dance gyration. "Talkin' to you could get me killed."

"Need a hit, don't you, man?" Travers said.

Honey Man crept over to the iron bars. His eyes were dark pools swimming in red, his blue-black skin aflame with a bumpy rash. He pulled at his crotch.

"You got somethin', man?" Honey Man said.

"Maybe," Travers teased.

"Ah, shit, man," Honey Man whined. "Don't be like that."

"You said something about a seafood restaurant in your statement."

Honey Man twitched and scratched. Travers had a fleeting moment of conscience, wished he could wrap this clown up and take him to a doctor.

"All I said," Honey Man told him, "was that I picked up the stuff from this restaurant 'cross the lake. That's all I said."

"Who did you pick it up from?" Travers said.

"Say, man, no name, no blame," Honey Man said. "That's the way I play the game. But I called the dude Popeye."

"Okay, genius," Travers said. "Why did you call him Popeye?"

"'Cause he wore a Popeye hat, that's why." Honey Man leaned closer to the bars. "I know you got somethin', man. You took some good smack off me. Be stand-up, man. Get me a hit. I'm about to bust open in here."

"This Popeye," Travers said. "Did he chew tobacco?"

"Yeah," Honey Man said. "I mean . . ."

Honey Man lifted his shoulders and looked down at the guys sitting on the bottom steps. He backed away from where Travers stood.

"I don't know, man," he said, raising his voice. "I ain't sayin' nothin'. You hear me? I ain't sayin' nothin'."

Travers reached into his pocket, pulled out a pill and handed it to Honey Man. Then he smiled and left.

24

Ace in the Hole

Ladonis made her way from crew quarters to her cabin with even more questions. More theories. More doubt. "Nice as he was," Trina had said, "Tim wasn't who everybody thought he was." What in God's name had she been talking about? Had Tim been a dope dealer or a drug addict? Had he been a people smuggler or a whistle blower? Maybe the answers were in the bag after all

She read the typewritten letter first. From Tim to Bret. Tim had written about a plan to relocate. But he hadn't said anything about drugs, or Decatur, or the Mexican woman. The letter simply read as a goodbye note. Next she picked up a ticket envelope from United Airlines. One way to Tahiti. Tim was going to Tahiti? A business card fell from the folded itinerary page. Ladonis replaced it inside the ticket envelope without reading it.

Had Tim suspected that an SEC investigation would expose him? She could see the media coverage. The Floating Palace Steam–boat Company, owners and operators of the only two paddle wheel-ers traveling America's rivers, transport illegal immigrants and killer drugs to the heartland. Heaven forbid.

The other envelope contained escrow papers on a house in east New Orleans deeded to Bret and to Tim. Apartments in New Orleans East were fast becoming the new projects for the poor. Why would Bret or Tim want to live in the east? Or even own property there?

The land on which the St. Thomas Housing Project had been built was a different story. It was prime real estate, a port expressway close to the Convention Center, to upcoming gentrified downtown neighborhood shops and restaurants. That land had been leased to the city, and the ninety-nine-year lease was coming to an end. The owners wanted the land back. And why not? People with money and jobs in the city wanted to get into that loop. "Urban pioneers" was how realtors labeled these mostly white yuppies. Urban invaders was more like it. However, to move a new population into the city proper, the project's poor had to be cast out. And they were. To New Orleans East, more below sea level than any area other than Chalmette. If a level-three hurricane or a Betsy-like storm were to come through, the entire area could end up under water.

Ladonis checked the envelope with the escrow papers again to make sure she'd emptied it. Two photos of the same image tipped out. She recognized the ex-governor, also the Mayor's right-hand man, Louis Delair, right away. The third man wasn't so recognizable. And the camera had picked up only a hand on the fourth man.

She turned her attention to the cassette tape. That tape might explain why Tim had these pictures. What if the tape was all the police needed to close this case out? She couldn't just hand it over to them. They'd want to know how she'd gotten hold of the damn thing. Should she give it to Bret? Sure. Eventually. First she'd listen to the cassette.

She gathered up all the papers, placed the photographs and the tape in another envelope and put that envelope in her purse. There was a cassette player in the conference room. She'd listen to it there. This tape could very well be her ace in the hole. But she'd have to wait until she was ashore again.

The *Magnolia Belle* rolled under the Mississippi River Bridge near the Pelican Street Wharf. Ladonis felt the boat stop and rock on the low waves. She heard the purr of the dying engine and listened to the muffled voices of the workers as they went about their chores. She got up, dressed in a pair of tan slacks and a pink tunic blouse, in a hurry to get outside. Maybe she'd see the Mexican woman.

Ladonis made her way to the gangway as the moon crested and the sky lightened. The air was warm and damp. The decks were empty. So she watched the deckhands tie the boat to the pier.

Nate Blenner stood at the boat's bow. He threw a heavy rope to a deckhand standing on the dock. The same thing happened at the same time at the other end of the boat. The deckhands tied the ropes around the fat pole. Ladonis felt a little jar as the boat touched the dock.

A man from the pier tossed up two stacks of newspapers—the *USA Today* and the *Times Picayune*. Nate Blenner pried a copy from one of the bundles. A wide-eyed look of astonishment exploded on Nate Blenner's face. What was he reading? Ladonis rushed over to Nate Blenner and pulled another copy loose from the stack. "Murder on the Mississippi," the headline read.

"Sweet Jesus," Ladonis said.

The mutilated body of Tim Ganen, Vice President of Finance for the Floating Palace Steamboat Company, was found in the Mississippi River two days ago. Initially, authorities believed Mr. Ganen's death might be an accident, but police officials issued a statement last night stating there had been foul play.

They also reported that they haven't uncovered any evidence that can provide a motive or direct them to a suspect at this time.

"Foul play," Ladonis whispered.

Images of Burl Decatur throwing her overboard and of the contents of that bag appeared before her. She lifted her eyes, aware of someone else's presence. Bunnie Sinclair watched her through the window of the Observatory.

"God," Ladonis said. She met Nate Blenner's shocked gaze with her own. "Somebody killed Tim."

Nate Blenner shook his head from side to side. Corked eyebrows and colorless skin painted disbelief on his face.

"Sin against God," Nate Blenner groaned. "Praise the Lord."

Ladonis picked up two more copies of the *Times Picayune* and ran for the elevator. She dropped one at Kasdan's door and knocked loud enough to wake him and Barbara. Then on to Bret's room. She pounded on his door. No answer. She tried the knob, but the door wouldn't open. Bunnie Sinclair materialized in front of Ladonis like somebody on Star Trek.

"Funny," Bunnie said. "You don't look like Nancy Drew."

"What?" Ladonis said.

Her brain was too busy to entertain any thought of insulting Bunnie. She had to return that bag where she'd found it. Nothing was important enough for her to get caught in the middle of a murder. She brushed past Bunnie as if the woman were a spider web.

⌒

Ladonis paced her cabin floor. She couldn't get the key from Redboy now. Too many people were moving about. And, if the police found out that she'd been in that room, her life could be ruined. She picked up her purse, her luggage and Tim's bag. Her new plan? She didn't have one.

When she stepped off the boat, she saw that the wharf had been transformed into a scene from *NYPD Blue*. Cops were everywhere. Plastic gloves snapped noisily as the officers touched and picked up and bagged everything from cigarette butts to what looked like someone's spit.

Detective Travers approached her. Her heartbeat accelerated. The sight of this one made her nervous. She clasped her fingers around the strap of Tim's bag so tight, the thread cut her skin.

"We're looking for Bret Collins," Detective Travers said.

"He's on board," Ladonis told him. "Is there something I can help you with?"

She prayed she sounded calm. Not suspicious. She recognized that "gotcha" look in Detective Travers' beady eyes. That cocksure expression she had seen imitated in cop movies all the time.

Detective Wellsburg approached them. A uniformed police-woman walked up from the other direction and handed Detective Wellsburg a Ziploc bag. Ladonis craned her neck to see the contents but was unsuccessful.

"Where'd you get this?" Detective Wellsburg asked the police-woman.

"Over there," the policewoman said, pointing towards the pad-dle wheel. Detective Wellsburg glanced down at the bag in his hand. He fingered the small item through the plastic, then handed it to his partner, Detective Travers.

"Looks like somebody got his clothes ripped off," Detective Wellsburg said.

"Yeah," Detective Travers said. He looked at Ladonis. "Tell Mr. CEO . . . I mean that Collins fellow, to meet us in his office in ten."

Ladonis nodded and rushed off. Things were happening way too fast. How could she keep a step ahead? She had to get to her car. She unlocked the trunk and tossed her purse, luggage and Tim's bag inside. What in the world was she going to do?

Ladonis found Bret and Kasdan having coffee in the dining hall, moping over the headlines. Bret looked glassy-eyed and dazed. Kasdan, with lowered eyelids and long creased cheeks, appeared more furtive. Ladonis had hoped to find Bret alone. Maybe tell him about Tim's bag. Perhaps get him to worry about what to do with it. But she didn't say anything. Bret wouldn't appreciate her blabbing about that bag in front of Kasdan. It was just the sort of thing that the old guy would find a way to use to discredit Bret. Her, too, for that matter.

"The detectives are here," Ladonis said to Bret. "That Detective Travers wants to see you in your office right away."

"Fuck," Bret said.

He slapped the newspaper down on the table and rose to leave. Kasdan continued to read. Ladonis started after Bret.

"Ladonis," Kasdan said. Cool as ever, the old guy stood up. He picked up his cup and took a sip. "I want you to start working up the publicity itinerary for that Democratic campaign river cruise. I left the information on your desk back at the office."

"What about the meeting with the police?" Ladonis said. "Shouldn't I be there?"

"Right now," Kasdan said, "the Democrats' cruise is more important."

She sensed Kasdan's eagerness to get rid of her. But he no longer had that power over her. Right now, she had more important tasks to accomplish. She had to find out what the cops were up to.

The office was abuzz with chatter. Gossip. About Tim. About what the police were looking for. And Ladonis knew what the police were looking for. It was in her car. Lord, when and how was she going to put that bag back? And the tape. How could she listen to that tape with the cops lurking about? She couldn't chance trying anytime soon. Tonight. She'd come back tonight when everyone was gone.

She approached Tim's office and heard movement and voices inside. She leaned up against the wall outside Tim's open office door to listen.

"Not a picture anywhere in sight," Detective Wellsburg said. "You think this guy might've done himself in after all?"

"He planned to jump ship, that's for sure," Detective Travers said. "He took great pains to clean this place up. But I'm not sold on him diving in those paddle blades."

Ladonis peeked in. Detective Wellsburg sat behind Tim's desk tinkering with the computer. Travers rummaged through the files.

"Look at this wall," Detective Travers said. "Nothing personal. No diplomas, no mementos."

What about his mom's picture on the desk? His degree on the bookshelf? And what about the festival posters? The Chicago Blues Festival had been Tim and Bret's first real gig. Tim had plastered the walls with those posters. Ladonis walked past the door, slow enough to get a good look inside. The Chicago festival posters were gone. Wellsburg lifted his head up from the computer. She skipped by so he wouldn't notice her.

"I stopped by this guy's apartment," Detective Wellsburg said, "on my way into the station this morning. He lives on Burgundy. Not too far from my place."

"Find anything?" Detective Travers said.

"Same thing as here," Detective Wellsburg said. "Nothing."

Ladonis tried to picture Tim's home on that row of square-built houses on Burgundy Street that travel guides described as hall-less dwellings called Creole cottages. Did Tim live in a Creole cottage? The close knit houses didn't have porches or front yards. A narrow sidewalk separated the front doors from busy street traffic. As close as she and Tim had been, they'd never visited each other's homes. Why?

"You know what's pissing me off?" Detective Travers said. A metal file cabinet drawer slammed.

"Are we going to go through this every time we get a high profile case?" Detective Wellsburg said.

"I hate Ivy League guys," Detective Travers said. "They act like their degrees are vaccines to ward off the rest of the human race. Like that fucking Mr. CEO Bret What's-His-Name."

"Yeah, right," his partner said. "You hate the money he gets for sitting on his ass ordering people around."

Tap, tap, tap. Computer keys continued to click. File cabinet drawers opened and closed. Ladonis inched over to the side of the door's opening closest to her cubicle a few feet down the hall.

"Damn straight," Detective Travers said. "We bust our asses to find a fucking criminal. But, if the investigation leads to one of them, it ends up on some assistant DA's hold pile. The next thing I know that junior DA from nowhere is a big shot."

Sally, the pretty almond-brown Indian girl, from personnel, rounded the corner facing Ladonis. Ladonis moved to the other side of the hall, stooped down as if she'd dropped something. Sally nodded but didn't stop. Ladonis didn't move either. She looked up and saw Bret making his way down the hall. He passed her without a glance, but stopped when he saw the detectives in Tim's office. Ladonis made her way back close to Tim's door.

"If you would tell me what you're looking for," Bret said, "perhaps I can help you find it."

"We can't do that," Detective Wellsburg said.

"Why not?" Bret asked.

"Because, Mr. CEO," Detective Travers said, "we're looking for clues, and we won't know what they are until we find them."

The loose springs in Tim's chair cried the way they used to whenever Tim stood up. A flutter went through Ladonis' chest. She expected Tim to walk through the door.

"What can you tell us," Detective Wellsburg said, "about the million-dollar insurance policy your friend took out on himself recently?"

"What insurance policy?" Bret said.

"The one that names you the beneficiary," Detective Travers said.

The detective's voice got closer to Ladonis at the door. She began a slow walk in the direction of her desk. The volume of the man's voice faded. Detective Travers was apparently pacing. She eased back again toward the office doorway.

"What are you talking about?" Bret said.

His voice had a shaky intonation. Surprise? Fear? Ladonis couldn't tell.

"So," Detective Travers asked. "Are you trying to say you didn't know about the policy?"

"That's what I'm saying," Bret said, sounding more assured. "Yes."

"Mr. Ganen," Detective Wellsburg said, "went through your company's broker."

"So what?" Bret said. "Several of our executives have used that broker to get additional coverage. He's a good guy, works for a fine outfit. There's no crime in that, is there?"

"Maybe," Detective Travers said. "A million dollars is a lot of money."

"Are you suggesting," Bret said, "that I had something to do with Tim's death because of this . . . this . . . insurance policy?"

"That's exactly what I'm saying, Mr. CEO," Travers told him.

Lord, lord. First the letter. Now a million-dollar insurance policy. No wonder Bret was nervous.

"Gentlemen, gentlemen," Detective Wellsburg said.

"Why don't you tell us all about your friend and that insurance policy downtown?" Detective Travers said.

"You're taking me in?" Bret asked.

"That's right," Detective Travers said. "Let's go."

Ladonis heard their feet shuffling towards the door. She turned and moved away, trying to appear as if she'd arrived near Tim's office doorway just in time to witness the face-off between Bret and Detective Travers.

"I'll have your job for this," Bret said to Detective Travers.

Travers gave Bret a nudge and a wide smirk-smile. Bret strutted down the hall, Travers and Wellsburg in procession behind him. Ladonis walked behind them like a gawking voyeur. Bret and the detectives passed the open doors of the grand river-view offices. Bunnie Sinclair sat at her desk. Bret beckoned to her, glancing back at Detective Travers, his expression defiant. He stopped and whispered something to Bunnie. She nodded and flipped through the cards in her Rolodex.

One by one Bret's fellow executives came to see what was happening. They stood in the doorways, their expressions as intense as the inmates watching Sean Penn take his last stroll in the movie *Dead Man Walking*. All but Kasdan. Where was Kasdan?

Ladonis went downstairs to the first level and stopped at the glass wall facing the parking lot. She watched Bret get into the police car. She was in a bad situation. She had Tim's bag and that tape. Exactly what evidence did she have? Could she clear or condemn Bret?

When the car disappeared around the curve, Burl Decatur's beefy profile rounded the corner from the food warehouse. His mere presence removed all other life forms from Ladonis' sight. She turned to go back upstairs and hurled smack dab into Bunnie Sinclair posed on the stairwell like a statue. Jesus. They were closing in on her.

She spun around and headed to the receptionist desk. The young black girl sitting there was struggling to quiet the buzzing, lit-up switchboard.

"Tell Mr. Kasdan," Ladonis said, "that I am not feeling well. Tell him I'll be back in the morning."

25

You Got My Back, Right?

Ladonis slipped into her car. Her abrupt departure from her job wouldn't rid her of Decatur's menace, not as long as she had Tim's bag. Not only could her life be in danger, as Tim's must have been when he had possession of the bag, she could be jeopardizing everything she'd worked for. Her only option was to return the bag to its original hiding place on the *Belle*.

Could she still come out on top? If she didn't panic. First, she had to get rid of the dope and money—and listen to that tape. Then talk to Bret. Innocent or guilty, he had to know what she'd learned. And she had to know how he played into all of this. She started her engine, checked her mirrors, and headed home.

"No matter what you do in this town," she said, "good or bad, some part of it always ends up being against the law."

She pulled into her driveway, emptied the trunk including Tim's bag and trudged up to her door. She glanced around looking for her neighbor's cat and saw a blue Toyota drive by. What? No way would Bunnie follow her. In her inattentiveness, her handbag fell and sent its contents flying to the ground.

"Shit."

She knelt down to pick up her lipstick, comb, a couple of crushed tampons, and that tape. That was when she noticed the business card and the reservation confirmation in Tim's name at the New Haven Hotel, 224 David Street in Key West. "Premiere Guest House for Gay and Lesbian Travelers." Gays and lesbians? Had Tim been gay? She'd never suspected. How had he kept a secret like that?

The only homosexual she knew was L'il Wolf, a little brown man who strutted through the streets of the Magnolia wearing tight shorts and flip-flops, with his dyed fire-red hair under a stocking cap. Nobody talked to L'il Wolf, so he talked to himself. She'd felt sorry for him, but she'd never said anything to him either, not even hello. She thought she'd become sophisticated. That she'd outgrown her grandmother's belief that homosexuality was an abomination.

An abomination. That was what Trina had said—and meant. That was why she had said Tim wasn't who everyone thought he was. And Decatur must have known Tim had been gay. That was what he had used to threaten Bret. Potent ammunition, keeping that information secret.

Who else knew? Certainly not Velcroy. She had read Kasdan's copy of a memo from Velcroy to all the Vice Presidents: "I implore you to bring more blacks and women professionals on board to work in administration. However, despite their large presence in the travel and entertainment industries, there is no room for homosexuals in this organization." Keeping Velcroy in the dark about Tim's sexuality would explain why Bret had sent that memo about gossip and innuendo, especially since he and Tim were such close friends.

Had that been why Bret had wanted her to handle the investigation? Bret had known the nature of her relationship with Tim. He also knew how badly she wanted to get ahead. Better for her to uncover Tim's secret than Kasdan or the police. Shit. Bret had played her, confident that if she came up with the goods, she'd bring it to him, and he'd have a chance to file it away. Keep the police and the media from thinking—more importantly, from broadcasting—that he and Tim were maybe more than close friends. What nerve. No wonder Bunnie called her the company's fool.

Gay or not, it didn't change the fact that she had to put that bag back. Nor did it affect her dilemma on how to do that without being noticed. Particularly by Decatur. And what about Bunnie Sinclair? She hung around like a foot fungus and was just as aggravating.

Ladonis went into her quiet living room and closed the blinds.

"HeartTrouble," she called out.

No answer.

Should she tell her brother about the bag she'd found? Better not. Too much rode on her current state of mind. She clicked on the CD player. Motown always soothed her tensions. Marvin Gaye's "What's Going On" tuned in. She called out to HeartTrouble again. He must've gone out. Thank God.

She placed Tim's bag inside three green garbage sacks to trap the odor. Upstairs in her bedroom, she probed her walk-in closet for a place to hide the contraband until she figured out how to get it back on the boat. She placed the garbage bag on the top shelf next to the box containing her gray suede pumps and purse.

She stripped down to her underwear, looking forward to a long, hot bath. A damp breeze crept in through the open window and hit her naked skin. She shivered, hugged her shoulders and closed the window, cursing HeartTrouble for leaving it open. Then she scurried off to the bathroom for her robe.

Her computer sat on the left corner of a walnut French antique desk. She clicked it on. The IBM clone didn't boot-up in a heartbeat like the Dell at work did. She clicked CONNECT to get to her e-mail to retrieve Jake Lee's message, though Velcroy's past had lost its urgency. Still, Ladonis wanted to know what Jake Lee had found out about him. Sure enough, Jake Lee had come through.

Seems the FBI kept watch over Edward H. all during the sixties and seventies. Velcroy was eventually charged with insider trading. It's on record that he turned state's evidence to avoid prosecution. Don't know who against. No names were mentioned.

Velcroy's motives became clearer. If the gambling bill passed, the company still had to get a license in order to operate. Since Iowa had passed its strict gambling law, the news had been filled with stories about developers seeking licenses, and the hard time that the state's gaming commission put them through. The gaming commission's practices could be just as arbitrary as a Senate Committee hearing. Velcroy wanted to rid the Floating Palace of its weaknesses, previous legal infractions, before it got in the game.

She trashed Jake Lee's message and went downstairs for a glass of wine. She had more pressing concerns now. A page from a yellow pad hung from a magnet on the fridge, a message from HeartTrouble. Seemed her houseguest had hooked up with the girl next door, and they were off to the dollar matinee to see an old movie.

The girl next door? Ladonis only knew that damn cat. She popped the cork on the half-bottle of California Chardonnay from the refrigerator and took a long swallow. She envisioned Burl Decatur. His surly expression mirrored the fearsome and pleasurable look on Robert DeNiro's face when he tried to kill Nick Nolte in the movie *Cape Fear*. Now fright captured her. All she could think about was death, Tim's and the possibility of hers.

The doorbell rang.

"Donnie, you in there?" HeartTrouble said.

"Shit."

She opened the door. HeartTrouble ignored her pinched lips and walked inside, an expectant look on his face. The musky odor of beer scented his colorful pimp wear. Shit. Ladonis took a swig of wine straight from the bottle.

"You better not let Mama walk 'round here and see you drinkin' like that." HeartTrouble passed her a mocking grin.

"I don't have to take this shit." She put the wine bottle on the kitchen counter. "You're in my house." She stumped towards the door. "I refuse to entertain your insults in my house. Now get out."

A car backfired. Her breath caught in her throat. She practically jumped into HeartTrouble's arms.

"What's wrong with you, Dooda?" HeartTrouble said.

Dooda. She experienced a fleeting moment of warmth. He'd called her Dooda since he was two years old, following her around like a pet dog. Especially when she had gone to the ice-cream truck. She had loved the cute look on his face when she'd let him lick ice cream from her Nutty-Buddy cone.

"Nothing," Ladonis said. "I just found out that a good friend—I mean a co-worker—died."

Tim was no longer her "good friend." Keeping a secret about one's sexuality did not suggest a "good friend."

"Oh, yeah," HeartTrouble said. "How?"

"What does it matter?" she said.

"It don't," HeartTrouble said.

Ladonis went back to the refrigerator and took out a cold 7-Up. She held the cool can to her moist forehead.

"You look like you scared or somethin'," HeartTrouble said. "You scared about somethin'? You in trouble?"

"That's your role in life," she said. "Remember?"

The green specks in her brother's hazel eyes dimmed. She looked away. It wasn't his fault she was in all this trouble.

"I stole a bag full of money," Ladonis said. Her heart rate sped up.

She backed onto the wooden bar stool behind her. "And some kind of street drug. And a printing plate to make counterfeit green cards."

The words spilled from her lips. Why had she let go like that? She didn't know. Only that she felt like a weight had been lifted. But what could HeartTrouble do?

"Yeah, right." HeartTrouble leaned on the counter. "And I'm goin' on tour for Billy Graham."

"Well, not stole, not exactly," Ladonis said. "Removed evidence from the scene of the crime is more accurate."

"What the fuck?" HeartTrouble lifted up his body and stared at her.

"I was just doing my job," Ladonis said, her hands splaying.

In college she'd listened to hours and hours of lectures on work ethics and business savvy. Now she realized how far apart the business class and business world actually were.

"I was following the rules according to corporate America," she said. "Grabbing my chance wherever and however I could."

Those had been Tim's words. Now her grandmother's voice rang in her ears, "Excuses. Excuses. Excuses ain't nothin' but high-class lies."

"They used me," Ladonis said.

She attempted to rouse her brother's them-against-us bias. His knowing glare said he was having none of it. That he'd warned her.

"They used me, and I let them." Ladonis felt shame confessing to HeartTrouble. She was shamed admitting that she'd made a mistake. A error in judgement that could chip away at her self-esteem for the rest of her life. "Just once I wanted to be in a position to get what I wanted," she said.

"I ain't hearin' right." HeartTrouble covered his ears with his hands. "Can't be. You always get what you want."

"But I was doing my job," Ladonis said.

"Your job?" HeartTrouble moved toward the door. He shot her a hateful look. "Forget it. I don't want to hear this."

"I found a bag full of money," she cried, "and illegal drugs that could . . . Where are you going?"

"I'm going where I belong," HeartTrouble said.

"You can't go," Ladonis yelled at him. How could he leave her in such a bad way? "You've got to help me."

HeartTrouble turned to face her. The horror—or whatever it was he was feeling—threw darts at her through his eyes. She retreated.

"Me?" he said, thumping his chest. "Help you? How can a low-life like me help the likes of you?"

"I don't know," she said. "You're the criminal. I'm sure you can think of something."

She leaned her body against a wall. How dare he speak to her that way? How dare she expect him not to? Nothing like a dose of truth to pit sister against brother. There wasn't a living soul who could get Ladonis more riled than HeartTrouble. He had to feel the same way about her. They'd been pushing each other's buttons since they were children. Trouble and misunderstanding were to her and HeartTrouble's youth what measles and mumps were to childhood. The trouble she avoided, her brother found. The trouble she strove to rise above, he stooped to. Now she was the one in trouble. Real trouble. Stupid trouble.

"This between you and your white folks," HeartTrouble said. "The way I figure, this black man better off out of it. And you can forget usin' that sad look you get. I could wind up in the pen if I get in your white folk shit."

Ladonis stood, dazed. She'd spilled her guts, asked for his help, and he was leaving. How could he just walk away like that? She picked up the 7-Up can and threw it at him. The can hit HeartTrouble on the shoulder and nipped his right ear. He wheeled around, his temple veins pulsating.

"You bastard," she said.

"You never needed my help before," he yelled at her. "You call me the no-good nigger that drag decent black people like you down."

"If the shoe fits . . ." She shouldn't have said that.

"See ya." HeartTrouble walked to the door waving at her.

Her breaths came long and heavy. She wanted him to go but needed him to stay. What if Decatur was on the boat when she got there? The police? HeartTrouble knew people like Decatur. He had dealings with the police. He'd know what to do. He could help her.

"Wait," she said.

HeartTrouble stopped walking. Her body slumped with relief. She was afraid. Afraid of the trouble she was in. And more afraid that she'd alienated her brother for good.

"All I wanted was a chance to show what I can do." She started to cry. "Before this happened, I had it all planned. Then Tim gets killed. And I find the dope in his room and . . . and . . ." Hearing herself made her want to cry more. "Then the police picked up the one man who I'd convinced to give me a chance, and now . . . You've got to help me."

"What you want me to do?" HeartTrouble said. "I ain't no lawyer."

"I'm sure Decatur," she said, wiping her eyes with the back of her hand, "the redneck who's looking for the stuff, killed Tim. Pretty soon he's going to figure out that I found it and come after me."

"You mean you've got dope and money that some dude got killed for?" HeartTrouble shouted. "Well, you figure right. Ain't nobody more desperate or more dangerous than a junkie except a dealer." "

"And a printing plate for green cards," she said. "I'm sure of it."

"Dooda." HeartTrouble punched the palm of his hand. "Dooda, how you get yourself in this mess?"

Dooda again. She'd baited the hook despite the circumstances, despite their differences. Now she had to reel him in. She really did need him.

"I thought if I got rid of the drugs and everything," she said, "that I'd be helping my friend who died. At first I thought Tim's death was an accident. Then I believed that maybe he'd killed himself. Either way, I wanted to keep his memory from being tarnished."

Ladonis looked into her brother's eyes and into a questioning stare. He either thought she was the most naïve person in the world or a crazy who should be herded off to the loony bin.

"But then I found out that somebody killed him," she said. "And I'm betting on Burl Decatur."

"What?" HeartTrouble said. "Who?"

"No one knows I have that bag," she said. "I don't think any-body but Decatur even knows it exists."

Well, maybe Bret knew about the bag. Then again, maybe he didn't. But she'd kept that tidbit to herself. Helping a dead white guy was one thing. Protecting a live one could just be too much for her brother deal with.

"Decatur the redneck, right?" HeartTrouble asked.

"Yes," Ladonis said.

Was HeartTrouble warming up to the idea of helping her? The thought didn't make her gloat. In fact, she felt some other emotion. One she wasn't used to. She felt connected. Safe, even.

"What you think I can do?" HeartTrouble said.

"Maybe you could take it back," Ladonis said. "That way nobody will ever have to know that I found it."

Was that selfish? She didn't mean it to be. She just wanted the nightmare to end.

"Back where?" HeartTrouble asked. "Where you find this stuff anyway?"

"On the boat," she said.

"You mean the slave boat," HeartTrouble said.

Considering the alleged people-smuggling operation she'd uncovered, he could be right. Slave labor had always been about someone's personal wealth. And Velcroy, his stockholders and every other corporate exec she could think of, were definitely into their personal wealth.

"Look, Donnie," HeartTrouble said. "Right now ain't the time for me and the law to be hookin' up."

"But nobody's on the boat," she pleaded. "And I know security. Nobody has to know you were there."

"Then you do it," HeartTrouble said. "Take it back yourself."

"I'm scared," she said. "Everywhere I turn, I see Burl Decatur. The man's a killer. But he doesn't know you."

"You don't understand nothin' that ain't about you, do you?" HeartTrouble said. "I can't go mixin' up in no police shit."

"Your life is police shit," she yelled at him.

"That attitude you got," HeartTrouble said, "can stress a dude out. You too busy bein' a big shot to have any feelings?"

She stared at her brother, the lines folded around his eyes. For a second she thought she saw her mother looking up at her from her hospital bed after her stroke. The same expression of fear and concern that had shrouded Mrs. Washington's face showed now on his.

"I've never been in police shit like I'm in right now," Heart-Trouble said, throwing up his hands. "What the hell. I don't know why I feel I have to explain things to you. You ain't about nobody but you."

"What do you mean?" Ladonis asked. "Explain what?"

"A whilst back," HeartTrouble said, "I scalped this ticket, see. Got a hundred big ones from some rich tourist dying to see the Niners whip up on the Saints." He picked up the 7-Up can. "Anyway, after I scored, see, this dude he went his way and I went mine. So I'm struttin' down Perdido Street. Right? Mindin' my own business, when I see the dude again. This time he got his hands in the air, pissin' on hisself 'cause some other dude got a gun stickin' in his chest."

HeartTrouble talked with his hands. And he wasn't looking at her. More like he was talking to himself out loud.

"But it's a cop, see." HeartTrouble smacked his lips. "So I'm thinkin' to myself, what this dude done? I'm wonderin' if the cops been watchin' him and saw us dealin'. I'm sayin' to myself, nigger, you better get your black ass on away from here."

"Boy," Ladonis said, "why are you lying to me?"

"So I split, right." HeartTrouble ignored her contemptuous tone. "Then I hear the gun go 'pop.' I turn around and see the rich dude lyin' on the ground. I done seen a dead man before. But I ain't never seen nobody whiles they dying. I tell you it ain't nothin' nice. Blood comin' out the side of his mouth. Him tryin' to talk. His eyes open. Man, I almost shit on myself."

"What did the policeman do?" Ladonis asked.

"That motherfucker went for the guy's wallet," HeartTrouble said.

"The cop robbed him?" Ladonis said. "Right there?"

"Fuckin' A. Took his money and left."

"How do you know it was a cop?" Ladonis said. "Was he in uniform?"

"It was a cop." HeartTrouble looked right at her, right into her eyes. "I know the dude."

He coughed, something he did a lot when he was excited or nervous. His hands were spread out in front of him, as if to stop someone or something. The he coughed again.

"Turns out the dead dude was some big-time millionaire from out West somewhere. He came here to see some people about building a gambling casino."

Ladonis remembered watching that story on the news. "Another mindless killing," the reporter had called it. When the man's face had flashed across the television screen that day, she recalled seeing him tour the Floating Palace with Bret the day before.

"Why would a cop kill a tourist?" Ladonis asked.

"A hit, probably."

"A hit?" she said in disbelief.

"Yeah, a hit," HeartTrouble said. "In this town, cops are hit men, you know. Just the other day, one got sent up for killin' a dope dealer. Shot him in the head when he stopped at a red light."

"So why is this cop after you?" she asked.

"Why you think?" HeartTrouble said. "I tried to milk him. To sell my silence. But the scam backfired. The murderin' suit jammed me up. Had me arrested and shit for shootin' that tourist so the city could get some real ugly press about us thievin', murderin' black folk."

"That was you?" Ladonis said. "The news said they were questioning someone, but the evidence didn't pan out."

"If he could," HeartTrouble said, "that cop would pin that one on me. Especially since the new Mayor got the Feds investigatin' crooked cops."

HeartTrouble's nasal voice drifted. What had happened to his

I'll-show-them tone? To that I'll-be-just-as-gangster-as-they-think-I-am. Ladonis hated that attitude. Aspired to do just the opposite. He complied, and she defied.

"But my podnas backed me up," he said. "Even Charlene. Swore up and down we was altogether chillin' at the Melody Lane. And me and the DA tight, you know. On account I go through the system every now and then. Anyway, he believed the fellas. But that white boy on Tulane and Broad still looking to lock me up. If he ever get me inside, I'm a dead man. Case closed."

Yesterday she would've told him that was the breaks for good-for-nothings. You hang out with losers, you lose too. Today she had a different perspective.

"I'm sorry," she whispered.

"Yeah," HeartTrouble said. "Me too."

A silence stretched out like a year. Was HeartTrouble willing to see that he was responsible for the course of his life? Was she willing to dig deep inside her soul to figure out who she really was? Ladonis couldn't begin to understand the many feelings she was experiencing. It was as though she was meeting her brother for the first time. And seeing herself from the inside out.

"Where the stuff at?" HeartTrouble whispered.

Hallelujah. He was going to take the bag back to the boat. She rushed off to her bedroom to pull the package down from the closet shelf.

"What's that noise?" HeartTrouble shouted from the living room.

"Shoe boxes," she called out. "They fell off the shelf."

She ran back down the stairs. HeartTrouble moved toward the window. He peered outside.

"Didn't sound like no shoe boxes to me," HeartTrouble said. "Sound like it came from your driveway."

She laid Tim's bag on the kitchen counter. He walked over to see. She showed him the printing plate.

"Where's the dope?" he asked.

She pulled the packet from the bag and placed the cellophane packet with the brown powder on the counter in front of him. HeartTrouble picked it up.

"It's brown," she said. "Why is it brown?"

"It's H, that's why," HeartTrouble told her.

"What's H?"

"Junk," he said. "Heroin."

"Heroin?"

"Yep," he said. "H. The brown kind. From Mexico. Not enough to make a killin' on the street, though. This dude must be a user."

HeartTrouble dug his hand around in the bag, making the opening big enough to show the contents. He scoped out the money and stepped back. His expression was serious and thoughtful when he raised his eyes to hers.

"Lots of cash. Maybe you right. Maybe this dude is sellin' the Mexicans. If not them, the green cards for sure."

"Why is the heroin brown?" Ladonis asked. "It always looks white on TV."

"They didn't do whatever they do to the morphine that's in it to make it white."

"Morphine?" she said. "You mean like the pain killer the doctors gave Auntie when she was dying? That's what's in this stuff?" When HeartTrouble nodded, Ladonis shivered. "Drug dealers will sell anything to junkie brothers."

"All brothers ain't junkies, you know," HeartTrouble said.

"I know that," she said with a touch of a whine.

Ladonis didn't want to goad him into an argument, especially about being black and proud. To her being black and proud meant not just surviving but thriving against all odds. Looking at her brother in front of her, she realized that maybe it meant that to her brother as well. Only how she went about surviving and thriving differed from the way he did. That was the problem.

"Seems to me, Miss MBA," HeartTrouble said, "you up shit creek without a paddle."

"So," she asked, her voice as direct and strong as his. "You got my back, right?"

26

Up the Creek

Ladonis stepped onto the gangway guided by a bright moonlight, HeartTrouble close behind. She tiptoed through the purser's office headed for the stairs. The elevator would've alerted the deckhands. The yellow tape stopped her movement when she arrived at Tim's cabin. This had to work. Putting the bag back onboard where she had found it had to get her out of the devil's clutches. And she was sure the devil was Decatur.

"You got a key?" HeartTrouble asked.

"No." She glanced around at him. "You remember Redboy, don't you?" She slipped under the tape. "Be careful."

"Yeah, I know the dude," HeartTrouble said. "So what?"

"Well, he works in the laundry room on board. The captain keeps all his spare keys there. That was the call I made before we left. I asked Redboy to open the door for me." She tried the knob, and the door opened. "Thank you, Redboy."

"Damn, it's hot in here," HeartTrouble complained when he entered the stateroom. "And what's that noise?"

"The engine." Ladonis caught herself before she called him "stupid."

She and HeartTrouble were a team. Real brother and sister on a mission. Unless she wanted to risk running into Decatur alone, she'd better refrain from giving out insults.

"But the boat ain't movin'," HeartTrouble said and checked out the stateroom.

"No," she said, "but the staff living onboard needs the power."

"So," he asked. "How did you beat the cops to the H?"

"I told you." Her breaths came out shallow. "It sort of fell into my lap while I was trying to figure out what happened to my friend."

HeartTrouble picked up Tim's leather jacket from the back of a chair. He held open the jacket as if to try it on. Ladonis slowed her brother with a hand on his arm.

"Don't. Do you want to explain your fingerprints to the police when they ask you what you were doing prowling around a dead man's room like a snake in the grass?"

"Do you?" he asked.

Ladonis huffed up but didn't retort. Instead, she moved toward the verandah, her brother in tow. She spotted a couple of house-keeper pink dresses lying on the bed. She halted. That Mexican woman hid in here. Had Tim hidden her? Or had Decatur? And where was that woman now?

"What's the matter?" HeartTrouble asked. "Is this where you found the bag?"

"No. I found it outside." She walked out onto the veranda and stomped around listening for the spot where the trapdoor was. "Out here." She sighed, annoyed. "Turn on the flashlight."

Lucky she had remembered how dark it had been when she'd found the bag. Tonight she'd made HeartTrouble stop at the Claiborne Street 7-Eleven to buy the light and batteries on the way to the dock. She wasn't going to delay her task because she couldn't see.

"Here it is," Ladonis said.

HeartTrouble helped her pull back the turf-like carpet. He lifted the door. Ladonis felt a surge of adrenaline. Much as she hated to admit it, she felt safe knowing he was with her.

"Here," she said, handing him the garbage bag, "take this down and put it next to that stack of wood."

"No way," HeartTrouble said. "This is your gig. You do it. I'm the lookout. Remember?"

Ladonis responded with a wordless glare. Then she shrugged and went to the space below. No time to waste arguing. Decatur or that Bunnie Sinclair might show up any second. She was too close to the end of this misery to make a fuss.

Ladonis opened the garbage bag, held her nose, and dumped out Tim's sack on the floor. HeartTrouble ducked his head inside the hatch above her and clicked off the flashlight.

"Have you lost it?" Ladonis called up to him. "It's dark down here. Turn that light back on."

"Keep quiet, somebody's up there," he whispered, pointing upward.

"What?" she asked.

She poked her head up, grumbling about the dark and the shrimp odor. HeartTrouble pressed a finger across his lips and pointed to the deck.

"It's probably Decatur," Nate Blenner said. "He been hangin' around down there a lot since that . . . Mr. Tim died. Praise the Lord."

"I seen that black gal nosin' 'round down there too," the other male voice said.

"Oh, yeah?" Nate Blenner said. "When you seen her?"

"Come to think of it," the man said, "it was the night of that cruise. I seen her down there tryin' to open the door with a hairpin or somethin'. A cop saw her too."

A cop? Another unexpected development. Her hands shook and her breathing became labored.

"A cop?" Nate Blenner said. "How you know he was a cop?"

"I know he was a cop," the other man said, "because of the way he kept circling the area. Leaving and comin' back ever so often."

"A cop saw you?" HeartTrouble whispered.

"Not with the bag," Ladonis whispered back, praying she was right. "That was much earlier. I didn't get the bag until late that night, when I had a key. I'm sure he would've stopped me if he'd seen me come out with something I didn't go in with."

"Well," Nate Blenner said. "I don't hear nothin' down there now. I'm gonna catch a few winks. Night. Praise the Lord."

"I'm gonna turn in too," the man said. "Long day tomorrow. Got behind with the cops hangin' round all day."

Feet moved across the deck. Ladonis came up, breathing hard. She hung her head over the boat's rail, inhaling and exhaling until her breathing caught up with her.

"Thank God that's over," Ladonis said and tossed the garbage bags into the river.

HeartTrouble covered up the trap door with the turf. He slapped his hands together. The job was done. He headed back into the stateroom.

"I'm gonna stop by Tim's old room." Nate Blenner's voice again grabbed Ladonis' attention. "Just in case. No tellin' who that she-man had down there. The abomination of it all. Praise the Lord."

She-man. Abomination. Nate Blenner knew Tim was gay. And he didn't like gays. So why hadn't he told the police? Hadn't Preacher

Man been the last person to see Tim alive? No. There was that drunken passenger. But, what if . . . Could Preacher Man have committed murder in the name of the Lord?

"Praise the Lord my ass." Ladonis made her way to the stateroom door. "Check the hall," she whispered to HeartTrouble. "Make sure nobody's out there."

She bumped into a chair that overturned and sent whatever was on it, sailing across the floor. And, as if the crash hadn't been loud enough, HeartTrouble dropped the flashlight and stumbled over to the door. Ladonis froze as the flashlight rolled in slow motion. Her life flashed through her head until a leg on Tim's desk halted its journey. Then HeartTrouble eased out onto the hall, looked around, and waved to Ladonis.

A breeze swept up to the gangway from the river that chilled Ladonis to the bone. She felt exhausted, relieved and exhilarated, like she'd just stepped off a roller-coaster ride. All she needed now was a hot bath and a good night's sleep. But, first things first. She had to ditch HeartTrouble, listen to the tape, and go see Bret.

⌣

"You got a minute?" Ladonis said as she and HeartTrouble walked off the gangway. "I want to go inside to my office to check my messages."

"What?" HeartTrouble said. "You ain't scared no more? You ought to be. Suppose a cop did see you with the bag. You know how much trouble we in?"

She motioned with her hand for him to follow and headed for the terminal building. Her thoughts were already on that tape and what secrets it might hold. There was a tape machine in the conference room. She wanted more information before she went to see

Bret. She wanted some leverage. No one would notice if she borrowed that tape machine for the night.

Ladonis tapped on the terminal door to arouse the guard as if they'd just arrived. She signed them in and headed for her workstation, HeartTrouble mumbling various complaints but still following her.

"So," he said, observing the office surroundings as if he'd just entered Oz. "This is where you act like a big shot."

"This is where I work," Ladonis said.

"Same difference," HeartTrouble told her.

"Get a life, HeartTrouble," she said, "so you can stop beating up on mine."

Why did she say things she didn't mean? Minutes ago, she couldn't imagine life without him around. Was she so relieved, she wanted to get things back to normal?

"Mess with me," HeartTrouble said, "and I'll sic the cops on you."

HeartTrouble stopped to stare at the lights on the Mississippi River Bridge shining through the picture window in Tim's office. Ladonis couldn't help but notice the look on his face. Like he was looking at something beautiful for the first time.

"Where is it?"

The voice was male and familiar. And threatening. Ladonis whirled around to face Burl Decatur.

"Where is it?" Decatur repeated.

He reached his hand around his back. HeartTrouble jumped in front of his sister. Ladonis grabbed the tail of her brother's shirt.

"Where's what, you ugly motherfucker?" HeartTrouble said.

Street life gave new meaning to the word *attitude*. It could be a weapon to fight aggression and a mask to disguise fear all at the same time. No matter what the context, it was almost always unnerving to encounter. But Decatur remained unfazed and moved closer.

"Who you supposed to be?" Decatur said. "Chris Rock?"

Decatur pulled a revolver from behind him and placed the muzzle on Ladonis' ear. His broad forehead and icy glare conveyed evil. Ladonis crossed her legs and squeezed her thighs to hold back her pee.

"I'm gonna be the joke up your ass," HeartTrouble said. "If you don't move that gun, dude."

"She knows what I want," Decatur said. "Either I get it, or you're both dead. Got that, dude?"

"No," Ladonis said. "I don't know what you want. I don't know what you're talking about."

"Don't give me that dumb-nigger routine." Decatur cocked the pistol with a slow, exaggerated motion.

"Who you callin' nigger, motherfucker?" HeartTrouble said. "You hurt her, you might as well put that thing to your own fat head."

He gave Decatur what had become known in the projects as the Kunte Kinte wild-man look. A look that said, "I can end it for you right here, right now. I don't have a thing to lose."

"I have no idea what you're talking about," Ladonis said. She inched away from Decatur. "Does it have anything to do with the investigation into Tim's death?"

"It does," Decatur imitated the fake calmness in her tone. "You've found what I've been looking for. And I want it."

"What have you been looking for?" she whispered.

Decatur took a deep breath. Ladonis trembled. HeartTrouble grabbed Ladonis' hand and yanked her closer to him.

"Get lost, white boy," HeartTrouble said. "You picked the wrong sistah to fuck with."

Decatur grunted. Then he slammed his fist into HeartTrouble's stomach. HeartTrouble's torso slumped over. Ladonis lunged forward.

"What're you trying to do?" she yelled. "Kill him?"

Decatur took her wrist and squeezed it back. She squealed in pain. How could this be happening?

"That's exactly what I'm going to do," Decatur said. "If I don't get that bag."

"What bag?" Ladonis repeated and tried to twist her arm free.

"Don't act innocent with me," Decatur said. "I know you have it. You were seen snooping around Tim's cabin. And Sinclair saw you with the bag."

Decatur reinforced his grip on her arm. Pushed it hard up her back. Ladonis pulled and tugged, trying to get free.

"Sinclair?" Ladonis said. "Bunnie Sinclair?"

"Who's Bunnie Sinclair?" HeartTrouble groaned.

"A throwed-off white girl from Vermont or someplace," Ladonis said. "She can't stand me."

"Don't you know how to watch your back," HeartTrouble said, "out here in wannabe land?"

"Listen, Decatur," Ladonis said. "I don't know what Little Miss Busybody told you, but I don't have a bag or anything else that belongs to you, for that matter."

"I'll say it one more time." Decatur grabbed her by the hair and pulled her head so far back, she couldn't breathe. "I want that bag."

HeartTrouble lurched forward. Decatur backhanded him across the face with butt of the gun. The blow drew blood from Heart–Trouble's lip.

"Oh, God," Ladonis cried.

She made a step towards her brother. HeartTrouble held his arm out, telling her without words to keep away. Decatur took another swing at him. HeartTrouble ducked. Decatur went after him again, loosening his grip on her. She twisted loose. Time to get help. Ladonis bolted for the double-swing door. She punched it open so hard she bruised her hand.

"Guard, guard," she yelled.

The guard came rushing up the stairs, followed by Detectives Travers and Wellsburg. Travers bounded up to where she stood, gun drawn.

"What's going on?" Detective Wellsburg asked.

Oh, God. The police. The bag. That goddamned Bunnie. She'd told Decatur about the bag. She must have told the police too. It wouldn't matter that she didn't have the bag. Only that she had had it. She was trapped. HeartTrouble was trapped. And he was wanted by the police. What had she gotten him into? She looked from detective to detective. She couldn't think.

"Nothing, officers." Decatur appeared next to her. "Evidently, Ladonis, here, mistook me for a prowler." He looked at Ladonis, a slight smile on his lips. "There she was. Working at her desk. And I appeared. I guess she hadn't heard me walk up, because, before I had a chance to say anything, she was on her feet, running down the hall. Isn't that right, Ladonis?"

Ladonis didn't trust herself to speak. She stepped into Detective Travers' range of protection, made a quick search for any sign of her brother, then nodded. Decatur wanted to kill her, and the detectives probably wanted to arrest her. And she still had to protect HeartTrouble.

"Yes," she whispered and nodded again to the officers and Decatur.

Detective Wellsburg seemed satisfied and nodded back at her. Detective Travers pointed his pistol up, the barrel grazing her arm. Chill bumps spread over her like measles.

"Do you put in overtime often?" Detective Wellsburg asked her.

She peered down the hall and caught a glimpse of HeartTrouble. His body leaned backward and moved toward Kasdan's open office. HeartTrouble couldn't confront these boys in blue. She had to protect him. That meant she had to keep quiet about Decatur.

"Well, do you?" Detective Travers said.

"Sometimes," she said. She glanced back again, but didn't see HeartTrouble. "Sometimes. Yes."

"We all do," Decatur added. "It's the nature of this business. What are you fellows doing here?"

"Actually," Detective Wellsburg said, "we're here looking for you."

"Me?" Decatur asked. "What do you want with me?"

"We understand you've set up your own business," Detective Travers said. "With company assets."

Travers had a mocking way about him. A police tactic, perhaps. But obviously an aspect of the work that gave him great pleasure.

"Is that what Bret Collins told you?" Decatur couldn't rid his voice of his trademark condescending tone.

"He mentioned it," Detective Wellsburg said.

"Well, I'm not saying anything until I talk to my attorney."

"All right by us," Detective Travers said, looking at his partner. His eyebrows lifted, a half-grin on his face. "In fact, you can make the call from our phone downtown."

The four men headed for the stairwell, Decatur sandwiched between Detective Wellsburg and the guard. Detective Travers held up the rear. The white detective turned at the door and glanced back at Ladonis.

"Don't work too hard," he said, still in smirk mode.

Ladonis watched them leave. The cops were gone. They hadn't come for her and knew nothing about him. She rushed back to Kasdan's office to find HeartTrouble.

"You can come out now," she called out to HeartTrouble.

The cops hadn't nabbed him. She felt like doing a dance. She called out to her brother again.

Had he gone down the back stairs? Then he'd be at her car. She headed for the door. But HeartTrouble wasn't at the car on the wharf. She waited and waited. After an hour and fifteen minutes, she left. Shit. He'd left her up the creek.

27

Piece of Work

Ladonis was pissed. At HeartTrouble and at Bret. More at Bret. After feeling the cool metal of Decatur's gun on her skin, she was ready to confront Tim's best friend. She hightailed over to Bret's Garden District condo on St. Charles Place. For sure he'd been set free, or at worst, posted bail.

Bret answered Ladonis' knock in his bare feet, black silk boxer shorts and a white oversized New Orleans Saints t-shirt. Her eyes bore into him. His dark hair was wet and slicked back. She avoided thinking how sexy he looked and reminded herself how he'd roped her into this huge mess.

"What the hell are you doing here?" Bret said.

"Tim sent me," Ladonis answered.

She wanted to sock him one in the nose. Bret knew she'd want to protect Tim. Tim had been her mentor, even if he hadn't trusted her with his personal truth, and Bret's best friend, maybe his lover. How could Bret use her to cover his ass?

"What did you say?" Bret asked.

"May I come in?" Ladonis said.

Bret unlocked the knob-operated bar latches on the shutter door and stepped to the side to let her in. She'd been to his place before to taxi Tim when his antique Plymouth had conked out. She'd marveled at how much the town houses resembled the 1800 French

Quarter mansion, Bosque House, on Chartres Street. Her long-range plan included trading in her Gentilly home for a house in this happening part of town one day. But today she had to concentrate on the beast inside. She wouldn't allow the outside beauty of the surroundings get her off track.

"Can I offer you something to drink?" Bret said, walking to his wet bar.

"No, thanks," Ladonis said.

Her feet left the wooden porch and touched down on thickly padded carpet. She eyed the length of the exquisite light fixture hanging from the ceiling. She eased through the foyer into the living room with its down-home country décor. The clutter, magazines, papers, books, glasses, beer and wine bottles, all added to the room's sex appeal.

"I know you and Tim were friends." Bret poured himself a glass of Johnny Walker Red Label over ice. "But this has been a trying day. And, frankly, I'm too exhausted to reminisce."

Ladonis held her purse to her chest. She didn't appreciate the look he gave her. As if she were a pauper wearing a rented suit, an annoyance to be ignored.

"So am I," Ladonis said.

"Are you here," Bret asked, "about producing the centennial shows we discussed?"

"That's exactly why I'm here," Ladonis said.

If he wanted to begin there, she would. She had planned to chew him out for setting her up to fail, no matter what. The words *down and dirty* came to mind. Tim had told her once not to run scared if the game got down and dirty, but to get down and dirty too. "The opposite of down is up," he'd said. "And the winner will be whoever gets up and throws the first punch."

"I can't focus on that now," Bret said.

He leaned down to the wood-top coffee table and placed his drink on a stack of *Sports Illustrated* magazines. He picked up a pack of Kool cigarettes and a gold lighter shaped like a football, patted out a cigarette and put it in his mouth.

"Yes, you can," Ladonis said.

"I beg your pardon?" Bret said, his brows lifting.

"You can focus on this." Ladonis spoke in a deliberate, cynical tone. "I got into this mess expecting to get something in return. I'll be damned if I'm going out empty-handed."

"Why?" Bret said. "I didn't get what I wanted."

"You got everything you wanted. And more," Ladonis said. "Tim died two days ago, and the story just hit the press. That was not by accident."

"Listen, Ladonis." Bret lit the cigarette, inhaled and blew out a ring of smoke. "I think you'd better leave before I decide it's best to fire you after all."

"You don't want to do that," Ladonis said, fanning away his smoke. "Not unless you want the police to get proof of your motive."

"Excuse me?" Bret said.

Ladonis closed her eyes, reining in her inner strength. She needed to stay the course. What was it some philosopher had written? Sometimes an evil deed can lead to something worthwhile. Like the city ordinance that legalized gambling in nineteenth-century New Orleans. If that so-called evil deed hadn't occurred, the world wouldn't have jazz.

"I've wondered," she said, "why you were anxious to keep Tim's death a secret. Came up with all sorts of theories. Then I found this."

She reached into her bag and pulled out the deed. She waved the folded document in front of his face. He stared at her.

"What's that supposed to be?" Bret said.

"Proof that you used me."

"Well, now, Ladonis," Bret said, "welcome to the real world."

"I wonder," she told him, "what will happen if I bring this proof in black and white to the police."

Bret bent over the coffee table, put down his cigarette, and picked up his drink. He took a swallow, then placed the glass on the mantel above the fireplace. He gripped the shelf's edge and stared at her through the mirror hanging over it. Ladonis watched him watching her, saw that infuriated glint in his eyes. She couldn't let him scare her. She had to see this through.

"I'm sure," she said, "you don't want people to find out that Tim was gay. And that the two of you were—"

"Friends," Bret said. "Best friends."

"That's not the way Tim felt," Ladonis said.

Bret's cheekbones slacked. He was as apprehensive as he was angry. A feeling of isolation swept over her. But her Grandma Lucille came to mind, reminding her that, if the road she'd chosen was rocky, and even though God wouldn't carry her, she wasn't walking it alone.

"What about the property the two of you purchased?" Ladonis said. "Try explaining that to that Detective What's-His-Face. You know, the one who hates CEOs."

"How do you know about the property?" Color drained from Bret's skin.

"I found this deed, that's how I know." Ladonis dangled the paper in front of him again.

"Investment," Bret said. "It's an investment."

"Is that all? Isn't that what you were stalling for?" Ladonis said. "Time to get hold of this and more before the police? Isn't this why you put me in harm's way?"

"What are you talking about?" Bret said. "In harm's way? I offered you an opportunity."

"That's right," Ladonis said. "You did. And I intend to take it."

"Give that to me." Bret reached for the deed.

"No way," Ladonis said, leaning back. "Not until we make a deal."

Bret let out a snide grunt, his glare condescending. Ladonis inhaled, then blew out her anger.

"By the way," she said. "I also found heroin and a sack of money."

"What?" Bret said.

"You heard me," Ladonis said. "And, if the police find it before that thug Decatur, the Floating Palace will have some explaining to do to the Securities Exchange Commission. You'll have to explain the same to your new stockholders."

"Was there anything else in that bag?" It was as if he hadn't heard a word she'd said. "Another package perhaps?"

"Are you talking about this?" Her eyelids rose. She pulled out the metal printing plate and waved it in front of him.

"What is this?" Bret asked.

"A printing plate. For a green card," Ladonis said. "You know, that document immigrants have to have in order to work legally in this country."

"You found this in Tim's cabin?"

"I found it all in a turquoise bag hidden in an obscure spot off Tim's veranda," Ladonis told him. "Tim had a special hiding place for all this. But I bet you knew about that, didn't you?"

"What else did you find?"

"Well, let me see," she said, putting her finger to her chin. "There's this plate, a packet of heroin, too much money to count, and—oh, yes—a Mexican woman who made good use of Tim's facilities."

"Come on, Ladonis," Bret said. "Don't play that way. Was there something more?"

"Like what?" she said. "A little black book with the names of your suppliers and dealers? No wonder you're about to blow a gasket."

If he knew about the picture and the tape, he'd have to come out and admit it. She wasn't going to give him any breaks. She needed some for herself.

"This is no game, Ladonis," Bret said. "The day before Tim got on board that boat, he called to tell me that things could get ugly for the company if we pressed on to get a gambling license."

"I bet he did," Ladonis scoffed.

Bret rushed her. He stood so close, her nose almost touched his. She backed up, not sure what he might do. Or what she should do. But she wasn't going to give in just because he was standing there. He wasn't Decatur.

"There has to be something more," he said. "A photo. Something. Tim said that what he'd found out could dry-dock the boats forever if the SEC got wind of it."

"More than illegal Mexicans and drugs?" Ladonis said. "If there was anything more, I didn't find it."

"Are you sure?" Bret said. "If you're holding back—"

"Don't you threaten me," Ladonis said. "Believe you me, I can give you as much grief as you can give me."

Bret threw up his hands and wheeled around to get more whiskey. Ladonis watched, forcing herself to react like his equal.

"How in the world did we get here?" he said.

"Don't make me laugh," Ladonis said. "Like you don't know."

"I don't know." He gulped down a swig of liquor.

Could he be telling the truth? Should she trust him? Tell him about the tape and the picture? Maybe . . .

"Drugs," Bret said. "Counterfeit green cards. If Mexicans are being smuggled on our boats, why didn't someone notice? Why didn't the captain?"

"You're a piece of work," Ladonis said. "Do you think the police are going to believe you weren't in on this when they read what Tim wrote. 'You'll never know what our relationship means to me, the closeness we've shared. I don't have the words to express how much I love you.'"

"You read that all wrong," Bret said, pain in his voice. His hand swept over his face. "And you can't really believe that Tim pushed drugs? That I would smuggle in Mexicans? Where are they? Where do I hide them?"

Reality plagued her thoughts. She'd seen only one Mexican on board. Then she remembered what Bill and the others had said. That more and more Mexicans were hanging around the ports. And Joe had told her about the pontoons and shrimp boats.

"Stranger things have happened," she said. "There's lots of press these days about corporate honchos who shoot up and take all sorts of risks to make sure they stay drug-connected."

"You can't believe that about Tim. Or me," Bret said. "Tim must've caught Decatur."

"That's what I wanted to believe, too," Ladonis said. "But, let's face it, if Tim wasn't in on it, why did he meet that tug? Why did he hide everything that way?"

"That proves nothing." Bret lowered his head. His voice wavered between angry, sad and doubtful. "He could've just stumbled onto things same as you did. And he was going to tell me about it. I know he was."

"Even if Tim wasn't in cahoots with Decatur," Ladonis said, "he certainly planned to benefit from his criminal exploits. According to his letter, he quit his job. Had to leave town. He'd bought a one-way ticket to Tahiti. Why did he do that, if he was so innocent?"

"But then he was murdered," Bret said. "And Decatur's looking high and low for something Tim's left that was his. Get it? His, Decatur's. Don't you see? Tim was not Decatur's partner. He was his nemesis."

Would Tim lie to his best friend? Tim had always been the good guy, hadn't he? He'd always looked out for her, hadn't he? He had gone to bat for her, advised her, helped her, liked her. This couldn't be about Tim being the bad guy.

"And tonight," she whispered in a sad, faraway tone. "Decatur came after me with a gun."

"Decatur did what?" Bret asked. "Oh, Ladonis . . ."

"I knew he'd figure out I was up to something sooner or later," Ladonis said. "Every step I made, I ended up bumping into him. Thank God the police picked him up."

"The police?"

"Yes," Ladonis said. "They took Decatur in for questioning just in time to prevent him from blowing ou—my brains out."

Oops. She'd almost said *our*. HeartTrouble was out of this now. For good. Dooda. She'd keep him out despite the way he'd left her on the dock.

"I don't believe this." Bret looked over at Ladonis.

"Hey, chill out," Ladonis said, straightening back. "You're in the clear. I cleared you when I removed Tim's stuff."

"I swear before God this is the first I've heard about any of this," Bret said. "I knew from Tim that he'd uncovered something. But he died before he had a chance to tell me what. No way Tim was hooked up with Decatur. I swear."

"I can't get over you, you know that?" she said. "Acting like all of this is a surprise to you. I knew Tim too, remember? Apparently not as well as you." She let the thought of him and Tim together trail off. "He told me all the time never to let an opportunity pass by. Even if it meant compromising a principle or two."

"A lesson right out the how-to-succeed handbook," Bret said, staring at her, his eyes clear and focused.

"Yeah," she said, "and looks like he learned it well." Ladonis turned away, unnerved by his gaze. "I'd say he compromised a principle or two. Wouldn't you?"

"Where's the other stuff?" Bret asked, his voice low and husky. "The money and heroin?"

"Oh, no, you don't," Ladonis said. "As of this moment, I don't know what you're talking about. By the time the police get through with Decatur, they'll be looking for it too. I don't want to be anywhere near it. I'm doing you and me a favor by forgetting it ever existed."

"Weren't you and Tim friends?" Bret said. "He surely thought so. He spoke highly of you to me, to Velcroy. Are you going to prove him wrong? Show your ingratitude and allow police to tie him to Decatur and this . . . this . . . smuggling thing?"

"Wait a minute," she said. "Don't try to lay some guilt trip on me. Part of the reason I let myself be used by you is to keep Tim's name clear."

"Then do it." Bret's voice rose with excitement. "Tell me where the heroin is."

Ladonis shifted her weight to one hip. What if that heroin was Bret's? What if Bret was a user? A pusher? Wouldn't he say and do anything to get that stuff?

"So you can do what with it?" she asked. "Shoot it up or sell it to black kids in the projects?"

"You're not listening," he said. "I swear I'm not in on this. I just want to keep the law off Tim's case."

"Do I look Hollywood dumb to you or what?"

"Okay, okay," Bret said, holding up both hands. "So I don't want people to get the wrong impression about Tim and me. That doesn't change the fact that Tim was a closet homosexual as well as my best friend. Our friend. Believe me, Ladonis, I'm not just thinking of myself here. Can't you see? Tim didn't want anybody to know. He knew the damage it would do to his father, his career at the Floating Palace. Can't you let this thing die with him?"

"I'm sorry Tim has to go down this way," Ladonis said. "But he's dead, and I like living. Screwing around with drug deals, especially one that's gone bad, is suicide, plain and simple."

"If I give you what you want," Bret said, "will you tell me where the stuff is?"

"No," Ladonis told him. She closed her hands into tight fists. "But you will give me what I want. You'll give me what I want because you don't want Velcroy to find out about Tim. To wonder about your relationship. He's as homophobic as he is rich. A weird man, if you ask me, but when you're that loaded, you can be any way you want to be."

"It wasn't like that." Bret lowered his eyes.

"You'll have a hard time explaining that," Ladonis said, "when Tim's letter becomes public, won't you?"

"You don't want to do that," Bret said.

"You're right," she said. "I don't. But my friend Tim would. And, let's face it, you would too."

"That's where you're wrong." Bret took a large breath, then a sip of whiskey. "Tim had AIDS. Full-blown. That's why he was leaving."

AIDS? She knew about AIDS. Her mother's younger sister, her favorite aunt, had had sickle cell anemia. She'd died from AIDS late last year. She'd become infected from a blood transfusion years before. There'd been no real treatment. In fact she hadn't lasted very long after the diagnosis, after getting sick.

"AIDS?" Ladonis couldn't believe it.

Bret walked over to the coffee table and picked up a sage green envelope. He held it out to Ladonis. She recognized the color and the texture. Tim's favorite stationery.

"The police found out about an insurance policy that Tim left me," he said. "Motive, they tried to call it. Well, I received my instructions in the mail this evening. It's all right here. Read it. Tim told me he was sick. Dying. But he didn't want to die here. He felt that the people he cared about wouldn't understand."

Ladonis took the paper from his outstretched hand. How wrong had she been? As wrong as Tim? She unfolded the paper.

"Say, buddy . . ." the note read. "Here's an insurance policy I took out on myself. Looks like you gonna make it big just like we planned. I would leave this to my dad, but he'd just donate it to his favorite religious militia group. So take care of him, will you. And get out of the river business. Those waters are full of more than mud."

"Tim's dying wish," Ladonis whispered.

It took a magnitude of emotion to watch someone live and die with the stigma of AIDS and the physical deterioration the disease caused. The memory of her aunt's decline and death reduced Tim's alleged crimes to a mere indiscretions. She needed to honor Tim. Some way, some how.

"If I tell you where the drugs and money are," she whispered, "what are you going to do with them?"

"Plant them in Decatur's apartment," Bret said.

28

One More Stunt

Travers came out of the men's room and spotted Detective Wells-burg charging toward him from the sergeant's processing table. The guy was an albatross around his neck. Travers could find out who tossed that Ganen guy into that paddle wheel a lot quicker if he were on his own.

"What gives?" Wellsburg said, rushing his partner. "Why did you let that Decatur fellow leave?"

"We didn't have anything to hold the guy on," Travers said.

Couldn't this do-good cop see that that CEO had implicated Decatur to take the heat off him? By the book. Sissy policing. That was what gave police a bum rap. Not so-called renegade officers. Travers started walking.

"Didn't have anything to hold him on?" Wellsburg said. "That's not what you told me when you insisted we pick him up."

Ringing telephones, sighing copy machines, crying chair springs, ceiling fans running on high, choking window air-conditioning units, conversations, arguments—this was the best NOPD had for hard-working cops. Why did he want to be here? It sure wasn't to work with this partner.

"And then he lawyered up," Travers added.

"I know the dude lawyered up," Wellsburg said, skipping behind to keep up with Travers. "But couldn't you at least have waited until his counsel got here before cutting him loose?"

"His lawyer, Clermond Ferrand, sent a representative." Travers said. "Why prolong the inevitable?"

"You saw his record," Wellsburg said. "Don't you want to know how a convicted felon landed a purchasing director position in a corporation four months after he's let out of prison?" He touched Travers' shoulder, rough enough that Travers stopped and turned around to face him. "How a small time crook," Wellsburg said, "can afford a big time lawyer like Ferrand? Doesn't that strike you as a little peculiar?"

"About as peculiar as the CEO's million-dollar insurance policy," Travers said.

He resumed his trot to his desk and bumped into a uniformed cop directing a suspect to the wire-fence holding cell a few feet away. So what if the guy was up to no good? That wasn't the issue. No way that CEO didn't have that under control, despite what he said. Now that CEO, that was the guy to get. And he wasn't convinced that Decatur was the magnet.

"The guy's a thief," Wellsburg said.

"So says the CEO," Travers said.

"Says the FBI," Wellsburg said. "And for your information, the CEO's story checks out."

Travers led the single file line to two disorderly desks. He stopped at the coffee table against the wall and poured himself a cup of coffee.

"That doesn't mean he didn't order a hit," Travers said.

"No, it doesn't," Wellsburg said. "We also don't have any evidence that indicates he did. But we can prove that Decatur is a thief."

"Was," Travers grumbled. He took a sip of coffee, frowned, then tossed the cup in the trash.

"What?" Wellsburg said.

"Decatur was a thief." Travers took his seat.

"I'm not so sure about that," Wellsburg told him and sat down too. "Remember the FBI report on the company's books isn't in yet. When we sent them off, we were looking for evidence to prove that this Ganen guy wasn't on the level. What we'll probably get back is proof that Decatur is up to his eyeballs in stolen goods—like the CEO said. Did you have to let him walk before we had all the facts?"

"His lawyer sent a fired-up clerk," Travers said, "spouting off about false arrest, holding without cause. And he was right." He threw up his hands. "What was I supposed to do?"

"I'm the primary," Wellsburg said. "You were supposed to check with me. You knew I'd want to lean on him a little before his real lawyer arrived."

Travers shrugged his shoulders. Maybe he shouldn't have let Decatur leave. He probably should have waited until the illustrious Clermond Ferrand made an appearance. Even waited for Wellsburg.

"Look," Travers said. "Why are you getting so bent out of shape over this? It's not like we can't go get the man, if we uncover something concrete and relevant to hold against him."

"I don't get it," Wellsburg said. "You're the one hot to catch that CEO or some other big shot. Suppose Decatur is a front man? How in the hell do you think we're going to get to the head guy without bringing Decatur down first?" He picked up a file and slammed it down on the desk. "You deliberately sabotaged my authority on this, Travers."

"So I screwed up," Travers said. The last thing Travers needed was another citation that could land him in one of those sensitivity workshops for two weeks. Or have him spend another month spilling his guts to that schizophrenic shrink. "So sue me."

Wellsburg leaned on his desk and got in Travers' face. The room went quiet except for a ringing telephone. Travers could feel heat from all the people staring at him.

"You just let our first break in this case walk away," Wellsburg said. "That's sloppy work, man." Wellsburg pulled back. "From here on in, you play this one my way, by the book."

"By the fucking book," Travers said.

Travers reared back, cradling his head between his palms. He knew what he was doing. He didn't need Mr. Straight-Up to tell him how to snag a bad guy. He'd goddamn prove he was right. He had no intention of letting this one get away. Primary or not, that CEO was going down.

"Don't fuck with me, Travers," Wellsburg said. "I don't know what your game is, but I'm not taking the fall with you. Pull another stunt like that, and I'll have the Captain take you off the case."

One more stunt like this, and Travers would have solved the case.

"Fine," Travers said.

29

Just Friends

Ladonis sat scrunched down in the passenger seat of Bret's red Trans Am as he raced down the dark riverbank to the Floating Palace. If only she'd taken a hot bath. Done something for herself and by herself. She couldn't believe she'd allowed him to sucker her into doing his dirty work. Again.

"Listen to me," Bret pleaded. "It will be a lot easier to separate the company from the criminal exploits of Burl Decatur than from Tim. It's the only way we can protect Tim as well as the company."

Bret didn't have anything to do with Tim's death, but she wasn't so sure about his participation in the crimes she'd uncovered. No matter. Her situation couldn't be altered. She'd obstructed justice. Nothing would change that in a court of law. So she'd hang onto the tape and the photos. Leverage in case her crimes became an even bigger issue to tackle.

"Stop talking to me like I'm stupid," she said. "If anyone has to get caught, you want it to be Decatur. You know as well as I do that it'll be difficult to explain how Tim did anything on board without your knowledge, considering your relationship."

Bret burned tire rubber wheeling into the parking lot at #20 Pelican Street Wharf. His car came to a squealing halt in front of the office building. He exited the vehicle like a missile, leaving Ladonis to turn off the ignition.

"I'm going to get my master key," he said. "Meet me at the boat."

Ladonis watched him run toward his office. He wore white high-top, untied sneakers without socks and his black sweats were inside out. He'd dressed as fast he was moving. If he'd been on dirt instead of concrete, he would've left dust in his wake.

She walked to where the boats were docked. So far she'd tried to manipulate the system, gotten too deeply involved in a murder investigation, and had ended up agreeing to help Bret set up Decatur. Had she ventured across the line of her natural goodness to that field of dreams based on egocentricity and lust for power? Was this the place HeartTrouble resisted? Was his identity more genuine than hers?

Headlights blinded her. In the second it took Ladonis to focus, Bunnie Sinclair stepped out of her Toyota. The humidity that made Ladonis' hair limp and straight frizzed Bunnie's into a mop over her frowning face.

"Bunnie Sinclair," Ladonis said, moving toward her. "Girl, you worse than bad weather, you know that? Sooner or later you bound to show up."

"What are you doing here?" Bunnie asked, hanging back behind the car door.

"What are you doing here?" Ladonis countered. "Come to make sure I was dead?"

"Dead?" Bunnie said. "You've been watching too many episodes of *Law and Order*." She looked around. "Where's Bret?"

"Bret?" Ladonis said, glaring at Bunnie. "Bret?"

Hadn't HeartTrouble said he'd heard a noise outside her living-room window? And what about the blue Toyota she had seen driving by her place when she'd arrived home. Had that been Bunnie?

"Why are you here, now?" Ladonis said. "Have you been following me?"

"No," Bunnie said, glancing around. "Why would I be following you?"

"Why?" Ladonis said. "Because you're a snake, that's why."

"Didn't anyone teach you how impolite name-calling is?" Bunnie said, crossing her arms over her chest. "Have you seen Bret?"

"I'll tell you what I've seen," Ladonis said, lunging forward. "I've seen a gun pointed at my head with that hateful ass Burl Decatur's finger on the trigger. That's what I've seen, thanks to you."

"It's not my fault you're some sort of klepto, picking up other people's belongings."

"What did you say?" Ladonis asked. A resurgence of adrenaline pumped new anger into her.

"I saw you, Ladonis," Bunnie said, stepping back away from the car door. "I saw you throw that bag into your trunk. And, when I overheard Decatur asking the crew if anyone had found a bag lying around, I told him."

Bunnie had been around a long time. Didn't she know about Decatur's gangster reputation? Or did she have so little regard for Ladonis that she didn't care?

"Don't you know you can't believe everything you see?" Ladonis said, pushing the car door shut. "Haven't you heard of Rodney King? What makes you think it's Decatur's bag? Did it occur to you that he might be after my bag?"

"Why would he be?" Bunnie said.

Bunnie made a step back. Ladonis took a step forward. She was about to explode on Bunnie. But was that such a good idea? Her whole life she'd run into brick walls disguised as people. Grandma Lucille told her that getting mad didn't tear down walls, but built them up.

"Why would I want his bag?" Ladonis said. "Or is that relevant to your warped, WASP thinking?" She couldn't resist taking another giant step forward.

"Ladonis," Bret called out, holding up a piece of scrap iron. "I heard voices. Thought it might be Decatur."

"Not Decatur," Ladonis said. "Just his stoolie."

"I knew you two didn't get along," Bret said. "But not now, not here, ok?"

"She spied on me," Ladonis said. "Almost got me killed. She told Decatur about the bag."

"Is Decatur really trying to kill her?" Bunnie's eyes bucked.

"Why are you here, Bunnie?" Bret asked. "Never mind." He waved the key at Ladonis and turned to the *Magnolia Belle*. "Let's go."

"Go where?" Bunnie asked.

"None of your business," Ladonis said. "Go home."

"What's going on?" Bunnie ran up behind Bret. "Maybe I can help."

"I'll explain everything later," Bret replied.

"Who's got time to waste explaining life to an imbecile?" Ladonis said.

"Lock yourself in your car," Bret told Bunnie. "Turn off the lights. If you see anyone coming on board, lay on your horn."

Bunnie started to speak. Bret put his finger over her lips. Too kind a gesture for Ladonis. She wanted to smack the woman.

"Shut up for now, will you?" Bret ordered. "And do as I ask."

Ladonis took pleasure in seeing Bunnie left out. Yet, that had to be the worst feeling in the world. Having a man— any man—order you around in front of your enemy.

⌒

Once again the boat's décor stirred up fantasies. This time Ladonis thought of Oscar Wilde and what he'd said about absinthe. "After the first glass, you see things as you wish they were," he'd said. "After the second, you see things as they are not. Finally, you see things as they really are, and that's the most horrible thing in the world." Ladonis glanced around the lobby, the picture of a magnificent vessel. A picture that depicted with nineteenth-century splendor, the drama between wealthy whites in search of the exotic and the blacks who catered to that desire. Even in her imaginary picture, she saw the slave/master relationship. That was pretty much things as they still were.

She hopped onto the elevator with Bret, pooh-poohing the image of herself as a slave girl serving her master. Bret pressed the down button. The elevator made a loud, clanking start-up sound before its slow descent. The tiny lift stopped to another loud clank on the bottom deck, and the door opened.

"I think," Ladonis said, leading the way to Tim's cabin. "If we're going to go to all this trouble, we ought to just throw the bag in the river."

"That won't get rid of Decatur," Bret said.

"Will anything?" she asked. "Would jail? I'm not so sure."

"You're right," Bret said. "If the police can't prove wrongdoing, they have to let him go. When they do, he could come back here and put a gun to both our heads."

The thought chilled Ladonis. She looked out onto the Mississippi, listening to the soft waves and breathing in the humid river air. What if she'd had the presence of mind to throw the bag over-board when she had first found it?

"This way," Bret said, "whether Decatur or the police find the bag, Decatur's off our backs and Tim's rep is in the clear."

"Maybe we should make sure the police find it," Ladonis said. "You know, an anonymous tip or something."

"Too risky," Bret said. "We can only hope that, because of his other activities, the police search Decatur's space and find the stuff before he does."

"Suppose they don't," Ladonis said. "We can't just let Decatur get away."

"Sooner or later, he'll get his," Bret said. "He's got to."

"And what about us?" Ladonis asked. "Will we get ours? Just because we tell ourselves we're doing wrong for the right reason doesn't make it so."

"You want out?" Bret said. "You want to leave and let the chips fall where they may?" He pivoted, pointed to the elevator. "Go on. Leave. And, if you do, look for another job. I don't care about your little blackmailing scheme either. Tell people what you want. Show them the letter. I'll fire you anyway and take my chances. Tim's friendship meant a lot to me, and I know that's how he felt about his friendship with you."

"You know what?" Ladonis said, walking faster. "Decatur told the detectives he wanted a lawyer before he left the building. He'll be out before we get the stuff to his place if we don't hurry."

Bret eased under the yellow tape. She stood close behind him while he unlocked the door. Bret sighed when he entered his dead friend's cabin, taking slow, cautious steps. Tim's brown leather jacket was on the bed where HeartTrouble had dropped it. Bret picked the jacket up.

"We both bought one like this in Mexico after our first year in college," he said. "Tim said it was worth the plane ticket just to pay thirty dollars for a nine-hundred-dollar jacket. He was the brother I never had."

Bret lowered his head, closed his eyes and pinched the top of his nose. Ladonis looked away. She didn't want to give in to his sadness. Career moves and corporate income should be the only binders between him and her. She no longer worked with the people who mattered to her. Ladonis moved to the verandah.

Bret followed her onto the verandah. She lifted the green turf carpet and opened the trap door. She had to take back control of the situation. She didn't want to get too close to that shrimp odor again.

"You go get it," Ladonis said.

"Remind me to study the plans on this boat," Bret said as he lowered his body down the chute-like area. "I never knew this space existed." After a short while, he called up to her. "There's nothing here, Ladonis. Where did you put it?"

"Come up," Ladonis said. "I'll get it."

She switched places with him, once more entering the tight space. Dread surged through her body. Her head throbbed.

"It's gone," she cried.

30

Black Man's Collateral

Ladonis was satisfied Bunnie hadn't taken the bag to embarrass her. Bret figured Decatur must've found it after all. Ladonis wasn't so sure. To be certain, she had to locate HeartTrouble. She left Bret outside his condo where she'd parked her car and headed to her old neighborhood.

The Snugglin' Inn was a bar located across the street from Flint Goodridge Hospital, once a revered black-owned and operated medical institution now all boarded up. The place reminded her of how a community, a way of life, had evolved during the short period after civil rights, when the government's conscience was the black man's collateral. Then all that disintegrated. Black-owned stores and restaurants, gone. Shut down to make way for freeways, discount big-box retail stores and drug pushers.

Ladonis screeched into the no-parking spot in front of the bar. She jumped from her car and rushed inside. Bobby Blue Bland's 1950's hit, "St. James Infirmary," blasted from the jukebox. A little honky-tonk action was going on the dance floor. A middle-aged couple bumping and grinding as if they were in bed. Four other men and two women, all over forty, probably under sixty, sat at various tables. But no HeartTrouble. And none of his pals either.

The Snugglin' Inn wasn't the seedy hole-in-the wall joint Ladonis had pictured either. The banner across the bar explained why: Owned by a Zulu Social and Pleasure Club Member. Translation: The owner belonged to a club for New Orleans black bourgeois, whose original working class members had organized as a benevolent society. The first black insurance company where the dues were used to help out when sickness and death occurred.

Ladonis walked over to the bar. The smell of red beans and hot sausage got stronger as the sound of smacking lips got louder. Several men sat there digging their way through the piled-high plates in front of them. Single men. Motherless men. Had to be. Every black man with a living mother in New Orleans went home to his mother on Mondays for red beans and rice.

Ladonis stood at the edge of the bar feeling out of place. Now what? Where else would HeartTrouble go? Charlene's. About five blocks away, in the Magnolia.

She opened the door to leave when JockStrap, a burly mulatto with a tiny cross tattooed on his forehead, strode in. HeartTrouble's longtime running buddy had gotten his nickname when his junior-high school physical education teacher discovered he'd stolen the personal item from one of his classmates.

"Hey, Ladonis?" JockStrap said. "What's up? You and your brother both out slummin' tonight, huh?"

"What do you mean?" Ladonis said. "Where's my brother?"

"I picked him up in front of that warehouse," JockStrap said. "You know, where they keep them Mardi Gras floats."

Blaine Kerns, the dock and warehouse, two football fields away from Pelican Street Wharf. HeartTrouble must've called JockStrap from Kasdan's office and told him to meet him there.

"Then I had to go to the Chicken Mart," JockStrap said. "Me and L'il Boy left Trouble there by the Chicken Mart."

L'il Boy limped into the bar at that point. A twin, L'il Boy was born two days after his brother, Big Boy, with one leg way shorter than the other. He nodded to Ladonis.

"The Chicken Mart?" Ladonis said. "Which one?"

"The one on LaSalle and Jackson," Jockstrap said.

LaSalle and Jackson. She knew the place. Across from Jumbo Peanuts. She'd attended Jumbo's grand opening with Jack. His friend, a Muslim brother, had his farmer grandfather plant a crop of peanuts for him to sell at events in town. The young entrepreneur said selling peanuts was a way for blacks to tap into the city's entertainment and tourist industry. Jumbo Peanuts were everywhere now, at the Superdome, the Jazz Fest, Mardi Gras parades, college football games.

"He said," L'il Boy told her, "he gotta meet some white dude by the river later on.

"Accordin' to him," JockStrap said, "he's lookin' out for you."

"Me?" Ladonis said. "He said he's looking out for me?"

Suspicions confirmed. HeartTrouble needed to be found. Ladonis needed to find him right now.

31

Tunnel Vision

Ladonis pulled up in front of the Chicken Mart on LaSalle Street. She squinted to see the sign. HICKEN MART, she read. The "c" missing. The area was quiet tonight. But that peacefulness could transform at any time into a battle zone of gang warfare or an illegal drug flea market.

A black Morrison Cab drove across LaSalle onto Jackson Avenue. The Monte Carlo behind it got caught by the red light. Ladonis recognized the black fist painted on the door of the rusty, powder blue Chevrolet. JockStrap's car. Had he followed her? She leaned forward to get a closer look at the driver. Not Jockstrap. HeartTrouble.

Ladonis rolled down the window to yell out. But the light changed, and HeartTrouble made a right turn. The car headed full speed up the street. Ladonis drove off in pursuit. She followed HeartTrouble along Simon Bolivar past the Greyhound Bus Station to the foot of Canal Street, in front of Harrah's, the last turn before the Mississippi River. HeartTrouble made a U-turn, just like he was driving a city bus. Then the car turned onto St. Peter Street, torn up to bring back the rail tracks for the environmentally safe and tourist-popular streetcars.

HeartTrouble driving that Monte Carlo chugged into the heart of the French Quarter and parked the car in front of Jax Brewery, a beer refinery turned tourist gift-shop mall. HeartTrouble was headed for the levee. Ladonis opted to park in the first legitimate available parking spot on the side of the Jax Brewery building. She followed HeartTrouble on foot along the levee that led to Woldenberg Park, a platform raised several feet over the Mississippi River. A mini urban playground where tourists and natives could sit and watch the tugs and riverboats crawl up and down the Mississippi. Or take a stroll along the pier soaking up river air.

Ladonis spotted HeartTrouble up ahead. He was making his way up the concrete walkway, same as a pier on the Port's end of the river. Tim's bag, or some bag, swung at his hip. What was he up to? At the office, she had thought he had run away to humiliate her. Or get away from the police. Could he have hidden out instead, because he saw a way to make a quick buck?

HeartTrouble cut over onto the lawn near John Scott's polished, stainless-steel abstract sculpture. His stride slowed in front of the Aquarium. Ladonis slowed too, winded, and with a little pain in her shin. She stopped altogether when she saw a woman straddling a man on a bench right under a street lantern.

She caught up to HeartTrouble at an opening between the beams that held the park over the muddy river waters, wooden beams on one side and steel beams on the other. The opening allowed viewers to see the river flowing under the Woldenberg. An unplanned attraction that had come about because the two sets of beams represented an unresolved boundary squabble between the Vieux Carré Commission, set up to preserve history on the French Quarter side of the park, and the Audubon Society, organized to protect nature on the zoo side. Ladonis had dubbed the opening the "Impasse" after she'd read about the controversy. A paragon of compromise, the article had reported, New Orleans style. That separate-but-unequal mentality that just wouldn't go away.

HeartTrouble leaned over the railing looking down at the river. A rush of heat flowed throughout her body. After all those years of struggle to prepare herself to succeed in the world outside the Magnolia Project, her two worlds had come together. Here on the Woldenberg. Here at the Impasse. Did she really think she could leave? Leave what? Her brother? Her past? Not with him standing there in front of her now with Tim's bag swinging at his hip.

"You lowlife piece of shit," she said, rushing up to HeartTrouble. "You had to steal it. You had to humiliate me. You had to make this part of your lowlife world." Each word hung in the air like an ax ready to drop. "What are you trying to do to me?"

"Get out of here, Donnie," HeartTrouble said, peering over her shoulder. "Get out of here now."

"Why did you do it? Why did you take that bag?" She felt breathless. "I should've told the police you were in the office building earlier. They'd have your ass strung up by now. And that bag would be where it should be."

"Show you how much you know," HeartTrouble said. "I'm meetin' that cracker ass Decatur. He's comin' to get his junk."

"So now you're making deals with Decatur?" Ladonis said.

"Better him than the mob," HeartTrouble said.

His eyes widened with wisdom. With caution. And with fear. His body slumped too, punctuating that attitude.

"The mob?" Ladonis could hardly breathe, let alone speak.

"What?" HeartTrouble said. "You think Decatur in charge? Well, I've got news for you, Sister Kate, he ain't. The more I thought about it, the more I know he workin' for somebody. Probably the mob."

The mob? HeartTrouble's observation was like a flash cue card. That photograph. The restaurant. In every mob story she'd ever read, the mobster either planned or executed the hit in a restaurant.

A fresh wave of fear rippled through her. If she just knew who those people were.

"That's why I made the deal," HeartTrouble said.

"What deal?" Ladonis asked.

"When that redneck, Decatur, got outta jail," HeartTrouble said, "I was waitin' on him. I told him he could have his damn bag if he left you alone."

"Why didn't you just tell him where to find it and let him go get it himself?" Ladonis said.

"What?" HeartTrouble said. "You think he would let bygones be bygones?" Water beads like raindrops rolled from his brow onto his cheeks. "I know how these wise guys think. They want assurances."

"What kind of assurances?"

"He threatened to kill you and me both if he didn't get this shit back," HeartTrouble said. "I figured he'd say somethin' like that." He lifted his hand to wipe away the perspiration with the tail of his shirt. "I said, if anythin' happen to my sister, man, the police gonna know where to look. I knew he wasn't gonna kill me then 'cause we was on the jailhouse steps. And I wanted him to think I had something on him for the police. The best I could come up with then."

He wiped his brow again. The end of his shirt shifted to show his belly. Ladonis saw the handle of a gun sticking up from his waistband. Who in the world did he think he was? Walter Mosley's Mouse?

"You've got a gun?" she said. "What are you going to do with that?"

"Look," HeartTrouble said. "I don't know how your friend, the one you so gung ho to protect, got the cash and the dope. But you better believe that whoever he ripped off is gonna be plenty pissed. Somebody a lot scarier than that Decatur gonna be lookin' for this stuff."

HeartTrouble paced up and down, looked around, then checked his watch. Ladonis was dumbfounded. Just when she thought she was getting somewhere with her brother, he did something like this. Sprung all her feelings every which way. Nothing going in a good direction.

"The way I see it," he said, "if the redneck think you got it, he bound to give you up if you don't hand it over. And the heat go up on him 'cause he can't deliver. So I made a deal to keep you out the picture. And the gun, well, I need it to make sure I'm protected."

Her brother was a fool. The bag, Decatur and a gun? Ladonis pulled the gun from his waistband. HeartTrouble dropped the bag and swung around in her face. Ladonis stretched to keep the gun out of his reach. HeartTrouble reached up and knocked his shoulder into her. The gun slipped from her grasp, tumbled in the air and fell over the railing. A dull splash and HeartTrouble glared at her.

"You shoulda left, Dooda," HeartTrouble said in a low voice. He peered over her shoulder. "Now it's too late."

Ladonis turned. Decatur walked up to her waving a hand gun. HeartTrouble shook his head, then lifted up the turquoise bag so that Decatur could see it.

"You should learn to listen, girlie," Decatur said. "Your punk brother is right."

Ladonis moved closer to HeartTrouble, weighted down with every emotion in her soul. HeartTrouble responded with a lingering, icy obstinate stare.

"Drop the bag," Decatur ordered HeartTrouble. "You know," he said to Ladonis, "I really am glad to see you. Now I can kill two birds with one stone, so to speak."

Decatur picked up the bag, glanced around at the quiet street. Ladonis did a survey of her own. Not a single tourist wandering around. Not even that couple making out on the bench. Just the three of them, the bridge and the river.

"I wonder what's down there?" Decatur pointed beyond the railing.

"The Mississippi is down there, that's what," Ladonis responded, expressing more fear than she wanted to.

"You're right," Decatur said. "X gets the square." He drew in the air with the butt of the gun.

Ladonis stared down past the railing at the small marsh between the opening left by the separated beams. If a boat docked, the platform where she stood would be like the roof of a basement. A basement under the park walled in by the Mississippi River. Dead bodies had been found buried in basements. Her knees went limp. She held onto the railing.

"Climb over," Decatur said to HeartTrouble. He poked Heart–Trouble with the gun.

Her eyes shifted to Decatur. His gun stared back. Anger rose up inside her.

"Are you nuts?" Ladonis said.

"Climb over." Decatur looked down at the water, then smiled up at her brother. "Now."

Ladonis looked at HeartTrouble, begging him without words to do something. But what could he do with a gun stuck to his ribs?

"The tide's low," Decatur said. "You'll hardly get your feet wet before you die." He shoved HeartTrouble, forcing him to climb over the rail. "Now you," he said, pointing the gun at Ladonis.

Ladonis didn't move, her legs like lead. Decatur held the gun right in her face. She felt the wet metal on her cheek. He cocked the trigger. A detonating bomb couldn't have sounded louder. She climbed over the rail. Decatur followed.

The river crested against a willow-tree buttress, splashing water over her shoes. Decatur ordered her and HeartTrouble to go further under the platform out of sight from the street. Toward Canal Street and the World Trade Center. The streetlights didn't filter much down through the opening.

"I can hardly see," Ladonis said.

"Good," Decatur told her.

It was so quiet, Ladonis could hear the pitter-patter of rodent feet scurrying along the walkway up above.

"I hear the rats down here are as big as cats." Decatur looked around. "This place is perfect. I doubt if the cops will ever find you."

"If it's all the same to you," HeartTrouble said, "I planned on dyin' from cancer, or somethin' else I catch from breathin' Good Hope Refinery air."

"Shut up and keep walkin'," Decatur urged. He sniffed. "Smell that? Dead rats." He laughed. "Dead rats. Get it?"

She'd gotten it, all right. At what point would her whole life flash before her eyes?

"What you gonna do now, Miss Know-It-All?" HeartTrouble said. "How you gonna get us out this mess? While you at it, genius, think on the meal your super-human brain gonna make for the fishes and rats down here."

"Shut the fuck up," Decatur growled, pushing the revolver into HeartTrouble's back.

They were deep under the park now. No longer right on the river's edge. The moonlight had grown dimmer. A strong wave came and pushed the water up past Ladonis' ankles.

"Jesus Christ," Ladonis said. "A boat must be coming."

"Stop here," Decatur said.

"I can hardly breathe," HeartTrouble said.

"Don't worry." Decatur lifted the gun and pointed it at Heart-Trouble's head. "You won't need to."

Ladonis felt something crawling up her leg. She jumped back screaming and shaking. A shadow lunged near her. Too big to be a rat. Another person. No. HeartTrouble. He was kicking at Decatur, aiming for his groin. But he hit the devil man's thigh.

Still Decatur stumbled back, and HeartTrouble was upon him, struggling. Ladonis could see hands and arms hitting and connecting. Grunts followed. But where was the gun? Who had it? Then the gun went off. A loud, dense sound, kind of like a thud. Ladonis struggled to distinguish one man from then other. Then she could see HeartTrouble. He had fallen to his knees. Ladonis closed her eyes.

"No," she cried. "You killed my brother."

She opened her eyes and balled up her fists, prepared to strike out too at Decatur. But instead she saw HeartTrouble leaning over Decatur, his head to Decatur's chest.

"Don't let him be dead," HeartTrouble said. "Please, Jesus. Don't let him be dead. I don't need to have killed no white man, evil or not."

Ladonis dropped down next to her brother. HeartTrouble was listening to hear him breathe. But the white man wasn't breathing. He was dead with a big splotch of blood across his belly.

"Jesus, Donnie." HeartTrouble lifted his torso, bawling like a hungry baby. "Look what you made me do."

"Oh, God. Oh, God," Ladonis moaned. "He's dead?" Words caught in her throat. "I didn't mean to do it." She stared down at Decatur's body. "I didn't mean to. You didn't mean to do it."

HeartTrouble swayed over the body. Ladonis wanted to help him, reach out to him. A dead man was big trouble.

"You got to think on this right," she said, with as steady a voice as she could. "He was an evil man. He was going to kill us. He had the gun. It was self-defense."

"Self-defense, huh? You can say that? After all the trouble you made for yourself and for me?"

"HeartTrouble, you have to think of this in the right way. Self-defense. It's true."

For the longest time, a dazed Ladonis and HeartTrouble knelt beside Decatur's body. She fought to hush the screaming voice in her head. She wanted to yell at her brother. To tell him that he'd been right. That his fears had proven to be higher than her stakes. But how could she? Here they were knee-deep in Mississippi mud, leaning over a dead white man with the river water washing at them. Bigger and bigger waves coming in. She gagged. Another big wave came in, lifted Decatur's body up, pushed him forward, and laid him down again. HeartTrouble got to his feet. He walked over to the edge of the pier roof, closer to the riverbank, wading through the waves.

"That paddle wheeler's real close," he said. "The wash from that boat is gonna drown us, if we don't find our way outta here. We gonna drown for sure."

Focus. Focus. On what? Decatur? He was dead. On Heart–Trouble? Ladonis stood up. Inched backwards, away from Decatur's body.

"We can't just leave," she said, looking around, hoping something, anything would give her some answers. "We've got to do something."

"That's a dead white man," HeartTrouble told her. "The only somethin' we got to do is get the fuck on away from here."

"What about the heroin? The money?"

"You heard what I said? I ain't takin' no more chances for you."

"Don't you see?" She picked up the bag. "We're taking a chance if we leave it."

"Woman," HeartTrouble said, "you really got it in for me, don't you? You don't know what drug dealers can do to people who fuck them over. You ain't read about this kinda shit in them books you're always readin'." He sighed, exasperated. "Do what you want. I'm gettin' outta here." He spun around trying to find an exit. "How we gonna get outta here?"

A fog horn blared. A paddle wheel boat approached the dock. That boat would pull up, full force, to the pier, bringing a wave of water over them. Already the waves and water blocked their way out from under the bridge. They'd hopped the railing. No way to hop back up there.

Water surged with the moving boat. The wake was so strong, it knocked Ladonis down. When she stood up, the water was just below her knees. Ladonis couldn't see. The paddle wheel inching up to the pier was shutting out light of night.

"Woodrow," she said. "Woodrow."

"I'm right here," HeartTrouble said.

He sloshed through the water up to where she was. She grabbed his shirttail.

"How in the hell we gonna get out of here?" HeartTrouble said. He slapped his neck. "Goddamn, the flyin' cockroaches big as bats down here."

"As long as we don't walk toward that boat," Ladonis said, "we can get out, without anyone seeing us. Nobody to connect us to this dead man. No one to explain anything to."

She started walking. HeartTrouble didn't follow. She wasn't sure where she was going anyway, only what she was moving away from.

"Remember Tick?" HeartTrouble said.

"Tick?" Ladonis pivoted to face him. "Who the hell is Tick? Don't you know anyone with a real name?"

"JockStrap's uncle Tick, that's who," he said. "Remember him?"

"No. Why should I remember JockStrap's uncle of all people, when I'm about to be washed out into the river and drowned?"

"Because Tick used to work for the Sewage and Water Board, that's why."

The water moved. Her feet lifted off the ground. She reached out for HeartTrouble and grabbed his arm.

"You gotta remember Tick," HeartTrouble said. "He was always talkin' about the tunnel him and Juney and them dug. From that federal government buildin'." He turned his body as if to get his bearings. "All the way to the Rivergate." He pointed, then walked in that direction.

"The Rivergate?" Ladonis followed him. "Harrah's bought that building. It's going to be a casino when the gaming bill passes."

"Tick said they used to put all kinds of stuff under there, so it could flow out to the river. He said they throwed away concrete and everythin' under there."

"A tunnel, huh?" Ladonis said. "Used as a dumping ground? That I can believe. This city is not known for its environmental consciousness."

"Yeah, yeah," HeartTrouble said. "Tick said them Rivergate folks built them a elevator. All the way down to the underground tunnel."

"So," Ladonis said. "If we get to the Rivergate, we can find a way out?"

A loud squeal from the rats sounded off like a whistle. Ladonis, then HeartTrouble, stopped and stood silent to listen, to let the rats pass by.

"Remember that movie, *Ben*?" Ladonis asked when it was quiet again. "When the rats took over?"

HeartTrouble didn't respond. Ladonis heard him wading through the water and rushed up after him. When she caught up, she grabbed his hand and held tight. HeartTrouble picked up his pace. She didn't. He jerked her forward.

"Slow down," Ladonis said. "Didn't you say Tick told you they dumped construction debris down here? No telling what we could run into."

"If we don't get out of here," HeartTrouble scolded, "we won't be runnin' into nothin'."

"Why doesn't anyone know about this tunnel?" Ladonis asked.

"Anybody like who?" HeartTrouble said. "People like you? Who gotta know everythin' about everythin' even if it ain't their business? Look, Tick said the city and the state was always fightin' over the tunnel. Tick said the city paid them to dig that tunnel with the state's money."

He wasn't just reminding her, he wanted her to understand. Now she understood. Same old, same old. Probably a dispute over who was going to be in charge. Couldn't agree on who owned it, or who should use it. Let alone who should be responsible for it. She laid odds that Harrah's had no idea about the tunnel. Full disclosure would have meant environmental issues and cleanup costs for the sellers. How did HeartTrouble put it? "The projects may be the bowels of the city, but New Orleans is a shithouse through and through."

The water was lower now. Ladonis' eyes adjusted to the darkness. But the embankment was built up. Even though she and Heart–Trouble were beyond where the boat had docked, she couldn't see if she was any closer to getting out. Still she understood where they were going and why it could be an escape route for them.

"Ouch," HeartTrouble said. He dropped her hand. "Feel like a damn bird plucked me."

"Probably a mosquito," she said.

Ladonis stumbled. Her leg rammed into something. She heard a tearing sound, like paper being ripped. Was that her skin?

"What's the matter?" HeartTrouble said.

"I think I ripped my leg open," she wailed.

"Ripped your leg? On what?"

"On a piece of cement. A big giant nail. I don't know. I can't see any better than you can. Remember, they dump construction garbage down here. You said so." She touched her leg. "I feel something warm. Oh, Jesus, it must be my blood."

"Here." HeartTrouble peeled off his top shirt and slipped his undershirt over his head. "Tie this around your leg as tight as you can."

"You do it," Ladonis said.

"Woman, you mo' trouble than you worth." He knelt down to tend to her wound. "With this river stink on an open cut, you gonna need a tetanus shot,"

HeartTrouble tied the shirt tourniquet tight around her leg, patting her leg when the knot was snug. A shot wouldn't be any big deal after what they had been through. And were still going through. She just need to know they would get out. Both of them together.

"We almost there?" she asked.

"I believe so."

"How do you know for sure there's a tunnel down here, anyway?" Ladonis asked. "Because some ditch digger told you? Who says he knows what he's talking about?"

Her voice went all soft and whispery. HeartTrouble sighed. Ladonis gasped.

"Now what?" HeartTrouble said.

"The water," she said. "The water is gone."

HeartTrouble looked down. She followed his gaze to his feet. His hundred-dollar Nikes were sopping wet and screechy. But there wasn't any water or waves or anything like that.

"Just keep going straight," he said. "We must be near dry land. The Rivergate comin' up."

"How do you know?" Ladonis asked.

"Because Tick and his boys dug the tunnel right under the Rivergate," HeartTrouble said. "And there's supposed to be an elevator that leads to the basement."

How scary was that? Even if the elevator still existed, the Rivergate was shut down. How would they get out? A rat scurried across her foot. Her body pulled back. She cringed in pain.

"Wait," she said. "What's that noise?"

"I'd know that sound anywhere," HeartTrouble said, a bit of triumph in his voice. "A truck hit a pothole."

She looked ahead. Dim street lighting filtered down. HeartTrouble ran ahead to check out the sound.

"We made it," he shouted back to her, blinking at the light in his eyes, walking up the sloping path. His voice carried the tremble of relief as well as surprise. "I'll be damned. I told you we'd find a way out."

Ladonis stopped walking and looked around. No more water, just mud and small hills of broken cement covering a stone wall in which she could see the imprint of what could've been a door.

"Isn't that something," Ladonis said. "The elevator has been closed up. So that no one would know this was the city's underground dump."

"Woman, please," HeartTrouble said. "We almost died down here. Don't start carryin' on like some full-of-shit politician."

"Over there." Ladonis pointed to an opening about ten feet away.

Ladonis hopped up to the opening. She spotted the arm of a crane, part of a scaffold, and a short row of pilings. She leaned against the tunnel wall, her leg throbbing.

"Can you see the street?" HeartTrouble asked.

"Looks like they're tearing something down," she said. "But I can see the street."

HeartTrouble pulled up on the side of the opening as if he were doing pull-ups on a bar. He made a single jump up.

"The city's workin' on the street again," he said. "Can you get up here? Come on, Donnie. It's not that high. I'll help you up."

Ladonis didn't care how high it was. She wanted to get out from down under before the workers showed up. And she couldn't help but wonder how far under the park the waves had pushed Decatur's dead body. Whether or not he'd stay buried forever. No way she wanted to draw attention to this place. She wanted all of this done with. No loose ends. Everything finished and ended.

"I know where I'm at now," HeartTrouble said, looking over at the River Walk. He held onto Ladonis. "I'll drive you to Charity Hospital."

"Charity?" Ladonis said. "I can't go there."

"Why not?" HeartTrouble said. "You too good for Charity?"

"No, I can't go see a doctor," Ladonis said. "We've got more important things to do. We've got to finish this. Really and finally."

"You need a tetanus shot," HeartTrouble said. "Your leg could rot off if you don't get one."

"No, this first," she said. "Suppose you're right about the mob. Whatever it takes to get you—and me—out of trouble. We have to put this bag someplace where the right people can find it. Or we might as well have stayed under water with Decatur."

32

From Down Under

The night air was warm, moist. The sky clear and full of stars. The empty street a blessing as well as a disappointment. Ladonis longed to see life stirring about. And no one to bear witness to her and HeartTrouble crawling from down under like a couple of snakes.

She sat on a bus bench in front of a drug store on Canal Street across from Saks Fifth Avenue while HeartTrouble went for Jock–Strap's car. Thank God. She'd just escaped death. Relief was like a hundredweight lifted from her, but so was sadness a hundredweight added. She closed her eyes. Decatur, lying still, stared up at her, dead. She broke out into a sweat. Would she ever shake that image when she closed her eyes? Self-defense or not, HeartTrouble was right. That dead devil was an ugly memory.

HeartTrouble pulled the Monte Carlo up alongside the bench. Ladonis' leg felt numb until she stood up. Then pain shot up to her brain so fast she lost her balance and tripped. HeartTrouble hopped out to help her.

"Where your ride?" HeartTrouble asked

"On the other side of Jax Brewery."

"Can you drive?" HeartTrouble said.

"I have to," Ladonis said. "I can't leave my car there."

"I could drop you at your place," HeartTrouble said driving off. "Pick up JockStrap and come back for your car."

"JockStrap? I don't trust JockStrap."

"Cool it, Donnie," HeartTrouble said. "I'm gettin' tired of your bossin'." He pulled up behind her car. "How I'm supposed to drive two cars at the same time?"

"You're not." She opened the car's door, picked up the bag from the seat beside her and set it her lap. "We have to get rid of this."

"Thanks to you and that bag," he said, lowering his head, "it's a lot about tonight I ain't never gonna be able to get rid of."

"You're right." Ladonis sighed and reared back in the passenger seat. "I never imagined we'd end up in this kind of trouble."

"Do what you want," HeartTrouble said. "I'm goin' fishin' out on the bayou. Getting' away from all this for a while."

"You can't go," Ladonis said. "Not yet. You've got to help me."

"What's your problem, Donnie? I'm done. It's over for me. Get rid of that damn bag and it might be over for you too."

"I did. I put it back," she said. "Remember? You're the one who moved it. This is all your fault."

She started to cry. It was as if her soul was a computer and someone pressed ENTER. All of her emotions downloaded.

"Shit, Donnie," HeartTrouble said slapping the steering wheel. "Dump this stuff in the river. The redneck was right. The cops won't ever find it."

"What about the mob?" she asked.

"Everybody tied to them is probably dead," HeartTrouble said. "Your friend. Decatur. I lay odds they don't know nothin' about you."

"Wait here a sec," she said.

"Hurry up," HeartTrouble said. "Even if a homeless drunk reported two black folks chillin' down here, the cops would come."

Ladonis hobbled over to her car. She reached over into the glove compartment and pulled out the cassette tape. Then she hopped on one leg back to HeartTrouble.

"You were right the first time," she said. "We can't assume anything about the mob, or whoever Decatur worked for. I found this in the bag too. I haven't listened to it yet."

She laid the cassette on the seat next to HeartTrouble. But not the pictures. Even now, after all she and her brother had been through, she still felt the need to secure an ace in the hole. Something left to bargain with, if necessary.

"We need to know what's on this cassette." She held up the tape. "That's why we can't throw the bag into the river. We have to make sure somebody else finds it. Somebody else can find out about the Mexicans and the green cards and that stuff."

"Donnie, I swear to God, woman. How come you just tellin' me about this?"

"Something else," she said. "There's Bret."

"Bret? Who the hell is Bret?"

"The CEO of the company," Ladonis said. "I told him about the bag and he was with me when I discovered you'd taken it."

"What?" HeartTrouble said. "Why you have to tell him anythin'?" He glowered at her. "You was suckin' up, huh? Jesus, Donnie, this make everythin' worse."

"Not really," she said.

"Suppose that white boy went to the cops? They probably lookin' for you right now."

"He didn't and he won't."

A sharp pain shot through her leg. She gritted her teeth and leaned her head back against the car's seat.

"You sound like you one hundred percent sure about that," HeartTrouble said.

"I am," Ladonis said. "He doesn't want the publicity."

"You still on that kick?" HeartTrouble said. "We deep in white-folk shit. If we get caught either by the good guys or the bad, we dead meat. And you still worried about some white boy's good name?"

"You just don't get it, do you?" she said.

"I get it all right," HeartTrouble said. "I see you lappin' up behind these people, hopin' their crumbs can turn you into somebody." He gave her a disapproving glare. "Look at you. You so worried about some guy who don't just steal and push dope, but might be selling people. You done laid your life on the line—and mine too—to keep a dude like that from lookin' bad. A dead dude at that. And what about that redneck, Decatur?" He rolled his eyes heavenward. "God knows if the law finds out I had anythin' to do with him, I might as well have stayed down there in water hell."

"You don't get it." Ladonis shook her head. "You never have."

He didn't get that she wanted to belong. She was black and grew up poor. Did that mean she had to live outside the dignity of human-ity? And she had dreams. Dreams that made her an outside child of the projects. Of the corporate world. Should her dreams be limited to what she could get inside a tract of land designated for her?

"Get what, Donnie? You act like you the only one with sense. It don't take no genius to see you ain't nobody, Donnie. You ain't nothin' but a flunky."

"And you're better?" she said, her anger flaring. "A parasite too scared to figure out his own self worth?"

"At least I ain't givin' up my soul for no handout of somebody else's life," her brother said.

"What do you call ripping people off? Killing?"

"You're cold-blooded, you know that?" HeartTrouble said, his voice low with emotion. "It was either him or us down there. I didn't set out to kill nobody. To steal from nobody. You yourself called it self-defense. If you woulda minded your own business in the first place, none of this woulda happened."

Her guilt was instant. Strong. Too strong to conceal.

"I'm sorry," she said. "Really I am. I know you didn't kill Decatur. I know you wouldn't have gotten involved if it hadn't been for me. But just like you, I'm not the bad guy. And I don't want this to end my life. Right or wrong, whatever opportunity I can get out of all this, I'll have earned. And I want it. Whatever I give up is mine to give."

"I guess that includes me," HeartTrouble said.

"No, no," she said. "It doesn't. There has to be a way out of this that will keep us out of trouble."

HeartTrouble stared her down. She stared back. His resolve was waning.

"The only way," she said, "we can be left out of this is, if someone finds this stuff. The mob. The police. It doesn't matter. That's the only way no one will know we're involved."

Except for Bret. And Bunnie Sinclair. Lord help her, she'd have to find a way to deal with them.

"What about the man on the boat?" HeartTrouble said. "The one who said he saw you snoopin' around Tim's cabin?"

"I could say I had to be there," she said. "That I was doing my job."

"Your fuckin' job gonna get me killed," HeartTrouble said.

"What about the mob?" Ladonis tossed her head. "You said they have more eyes than the CIA and the FBI put together. Do you think that, when Decatur is a no-show, they'll figure out that he never had the bag?"

"If you wanna know the truth," HeartTrouble said, "that's what really scares me. And now, with this tape thing, we can't be sure about nothin'. The police is one thing, but the mob ain't no joke."

"Then maybe we ought to put the bag in Decatur's place." That had been Bret's suggestion. "That way the mob can find it. But even if the cops find it first, the mob will know what happened to it, and they won't come looking."

"And, if the cops find it," HeartTrouble said, "they get hip to that green-card scam. That's a good thing, nailing the assholes who makin' money from sellin' other people."

Yeah, well. That wasn't exactly how it was going to play out. The printing plate was not in the bag. Bret had it. If push came to shove, she'd find a way to steer Monique onto that story. That would put the Floating Palace in the headlines, and she wouldn't go to her grave knowing she, the descendant of slaves, aided and abetted a green-card scam.

"It's scary," HeartTrouble said. "But it could work. Especially if they got a cop or two on the payroll. And more than likely, they do."

"Another lesson from Con Art 101?" Ladonis asked.

"No," HeartTrouble said. "I witness that shit day in and day out with my own two eyes."

"Meet me at my place," Ladonis said, stepping out of his car. "To clean up. Then let's go make this right."

Make this shit right? She'd have to live her life trying. Thanks to her, so would her brother. How right was that?

33

Clean and Simple

Had she been to hell? Either that or she'd had an out-of-body experience. She looked around for HeartTrouble making his way up the walk behind her. How could he, anyone, live through a day like the one she'd put him through? She stepped inside her home and squeezed her eyes shut. She prayed that, when she opened them, she would have that oh-wow feeling, like Dorothy after her trip to Oz. Instead she felt the pain in her leg, smelled the stench of the river on her clothes, and saw the look of despair on her brother's face. She had indeed been to hell and back. Could she live with what she'd done? She had to. It wasn't just about her anymore. She had her brother's freedom to protect.

The blinking light on the message machine caught her eye. Was it Bret?

"Donnie," her mother's voice said. "Where you been, child? Call me."

Ladonis' heart did a flip-flop. What would happen to Mrs. Washington if Ladonis and HeartTrouble were locked up? She stood frozen before the message machine.

"I'm goin' to Mama's." HeartTrouble started for the door. "You know how Mama gets when she can't reach either one of us."

"No," Ladonis said. She felt a little short on natural goodness when she looked at him. But she needed his help. "You can't. That'll take too much time. We agreed."

Ladonis examined her pant leg ripped up to her crotch. Heart-Trouble's bloody undershirt was still tied around her lower shin. She limped up to her brother.

"You go upstairs," she said. "Look in my bottom bureau drawer. Jack left a few things including a pair of jeans. They might be a little big, but you can still wear them."

"I don't wear jeans," HeartTrouble said, walking up the stairs.

"Maybe you should," Ladonis said, thinking about the polyester he did wear. "Use the shower down the hall."

Ladonis grabbed the bag and noticed the blood stains on the fabric. Suppose her blood was on the bag along with Decatur's? Without Decatur or his body, the police would do a blood test. She had to think. What she did or didn't do from here on in could land her in jail. HeartTrouble too.

In her room, Ladonis ripped off her clothes and jumped into the shower. Time for truth and reconciliation. Grandma Lucille used to say it was never good to lie to yourself and owning up to unflattering self-truth hurt the worse. But was it truth or guilt clamoring inside her soul right now?

Certainly she felt guilty about HeartTrouble. About the risks he'd taken and was going to take. Did she feel guilty about her aspirations? Should she feel guilty for wanting to get ahead? Heart-Trouble would argue that her unyielding desire to become this high-society black American businesswoman was what complicated her life. What put her in the middle of white-folk shit. But what she wanted—needed, in fact—was fulfillment. The sense that she'd accomplished something. That what she did made a difference.

When she was clean, Ladonis mustered up the nerve to look at her leg. The cut wasn't that long, only about two inches. The wound still bled a little, but she hadn't passed out at the sight of it. She located a bottle of peroxide in an open packing box and doused the cut. It stung, but not enough to draw tears. Then she put way too many Curad bandages over the wound and tied them in place with white gauze. She dressed in an all-black, two-piece Liz Claiborne casual sweat-suit to look nice but not dressed up.

She stood, and her leg throbbed like crazy. She'd have to get a tetanus shot as soon as possible. But that wasn't the problem. That cut represented more than some tear in her skin. And, no matter what, the eventual scar would hurt too. That scar a painful reminder of Decatur dying under the Woldenberg. Ugly.

Downstairs, she found HeartTrouble sitting on a stool cradling his head. She gathered up her torn, bloody clothes as well as Heart-Trouble's clothes laying in a heap at the foot of the stairwell. She'd have to destroy them, as well as the bag.

"We have to finish what we started," she said, "or end up in jail."

"Too bad you didn't think about that upfront," HeartTrouble said. "No job is worth another man's life. Even a piece of shit like that redneck Decatur."

"You think I don't know that?" she said. "You think this is part of a master plan? I know this is all my fault. That's why I've got to make it right. I don't want you gone."

Tears crawled down her cheeks. She walked around the counter to face her brother. He picked up his shirt, looked at it, and put it back down.

"There's one thing I'm not giving up on," she said. "Not without a fight, and that's your freedom. Are we still on the same page?"

"Like I got a choice," HeartTrouble said. "What you gonna do with them clothes?"

"Get rid of them. And the bag," Ladonis said. "We can't put Tim's bloody bag in Decatur's cabin. My blood might be on it too."

She put clothes on the counter and opened the kitchen-counter drawer. She fished around until she found a bottle of Extra-Strength Tylenol. With a half-filled glass of tap water, she swallowed four pills, then glanced at the clock.

"Jesus H. Christ," she said. "It's almost four o'clock. It'll be daylight soon. We've got to get going."

"You know which room the redneck stayed in on the boat?" HeartTrouble asked.

"I can find out right fast," she said. "I'll pull up the passenger assignments on my computer."

"You right, Donnie," HeartTrouble said. "It'll soon be daybreak. Bodies get found in the daylight. And they leave a trail. We got to cut this one off before it leads to us. How you plan to get rid of the clothes?"

"I thought I'd burn them," Ladonis told him.

"Not around here, I hope," HeartTrouble said. "Start a fire around here and your sididy neighbors will have you locked up."

"I thought I'd take them under the Broad Street Overpass. You know, where those homeless people set fires to keep warm."

"Woman, it's damn near ninety degrees outside," HeartTrouble said. "They don't need no fires to keep them warm."

"Well, don't they set fires to cook? They must set fires in those barrels around there."

Ladonis could feel her body tense up with stress. She couldn't believe that she was standing in her home plotting to cover up a murder. No, not murder. Neither she nor HeartTrouble had set out to kill Decatur.

"You watch too much TV, Donnie," HeartTrouble said. "I've got an idea. Why don't you take them to the Laundromat, Clorox them, then put them in a Goodwill box."

A good idea. Her mother had told her that Clorox could remove motor oil from cement. Too bad she hadn't thought of it.

"I'll wash the bag, too," Ladonis said. "But Bunnie saw me put the bag in my trunk. That deckhand Nate Blenner saw me with it too. And it's all bloody now. I can't risk anyone finding it in a Goodwill box."

"And what about fingerprints?" Ladonis said. "I handled the money and everything else in that bag more than once. Even if there are a hundred prints on an item, with today's technology, the police can retrieve all of them." She looked askance at him. "I read that in a novel."

"Empty it," HeartTrouble said, pointing to the bag. "Dump the bills on the counter. The H too. You got any gloves?"

"In the pantry," Ladonis said.

HeartTrouble put the latex gloves on. He rolled into action, a caricature of a policeman at a crime scene.

"Get me a rag and a couple of Schwegmann bags."

HeartTrouble wiped each wad of money and put the cleaned money inside the Schwegmann grocery bag. He handed Ladonis the empty turquoise bag.

"Wash this too," he said. "But bring it back here, cut it up in as many small pieces as you can. You know that Mackenzie Bakery on the corner down the street?"

Ladonis nodded.

"Well, they keep a big dumpster on the side of the building," he said. "Put some of the pieces there. Then go 'cross the street and dump some pieces in the garbage cans behind that Vietnamese restaurant. And don't forget to wear the gloves."

Ladonis snapped on a pair of gloves and followed her brother's instructions to the letter. She put the bag and the clothes in a garbage bag. HeartTrouble gave her a questioning look.

"Do you have a clothes basket?" he asked.

Ladonis nodded.

"Carry the clothes in the basket," he said. "Look more normal."

"Clean and simple," Ladonis said.

"I'm a simple kind of guy." He eyed his sister. "I leave the hard stuff to the smart people."

Ladonis knew this was her cue to admit that she couldn't be too smart. A smart person would've told Bret where to stick his request. A smart person would've left the turquoise bag where Tim had hid it. She knew she should say those things, but she didn't. She picked up the Schwegmann's bag.

"Now for the hard part," she said.

"No," HeartTrouble said. "The hard part is gonna be learnin' how to sleep at night without seein' that dead redneck."

34

River Rats

Ladonis marched across the Floating Palace's parking lot to the terminal building. HeartTrouble lagged behind her. Despite the early-morning river chill, sweat beads formed on her brow.

"It'll be daylight soon," she said, switching the large Schwegmann's bag from one hand to the other. "We should plant this stuff before the place staffs up. We can listen to the tape later. Tonight even."

"I was thinkin' we ought to listen first," HeartTrouble said, skipping to catch up. "That way we'll know puttin' the money and dope in the redneck's room is where it ought to go."

"There might not be time to do both." Ladonis frowned. "And you should leave before . . ."

"Donnie," HeartTrouble said. "I don't know what you up to, but I want to hear what your friend got to say. I want to know if I'm a have to be lookin' over my shoulder for the rest of my life 'cause of this . . . this . . . white-folk shit." He stopped walking, touched her arm. She faced him. "I wanna know."

"Okay, okay. I get it," she said. "There's a tape machine in the conference room."

⌒

The door was unlocked, and security was nowhere in sight. Ladonis reached for the sign-in sheet, but thought better of it. No one needed to know they were there. Or anything else, for that matter.

"I knew that guard was too young to be reliable," she said. "Keep it quiet and we can sneak upstairs. And, if we're really lucky, without your being seen."

She'd lifted her cut leg and was about to place her foot on the first step when she heard voices coming toward them. She stepped back, took HeartTrouble's hand and pulled him behind the tall receptionist desk at the bottom of the stairwell. The desk wasn't the greatest vantage point from which to spy. However, it was within great earshot range. She could find out who was here and eavesdrop on what they had to say.

"I shouldn't have let my cousin talk me into hiring that loser." The sound of Kasdan's baritone went through Ladonis like a chill.

She leaned forward and caught a glimpse of his tall silhouette. Another man, a head shorter, stood at the top of the stairwell. Not enough light or anything familiar about the second man to know who he was.

"I knew that convict couldn't be trusted." Kasdan spoke again, his tone was more than a little agitated. "Too quick to kill people."

Decatur. He was talking about Decatur. Kasdan and Decatur. Shit.

"The boss owed the dude," the other man said. "Besides he's more worried about you and this trouble you got. He thinks it's more likely you'll be the one to get us jammed up."

"Me?" Kasdan said. "He ought to be worried about the Feds that are out to get him. Their latest probe seems pretty intense."

"Shit, man," the shorter man said. "They've been investigating the boss for years. It's ongoing, and it's always intense."

The boss? Who the hell was the boss? Could Mr. Kasdan be involved with the Mafia? Business, politics and Mafia were known bedfellows in these parts. And that eye-for-an-eye mentality just like the one-deed-deserves-a-turn philosophy was their motto.

"This time," Kasdan said, "it looks like they've got witness testimony that could hold up in court."

Sounded like he wanted this boss guy, whoever he was, to go down.

"Witness?" the other man said. "That hockey honcho from California? We got too much on him. He won't turn Fed ratfink. He loves himself too much."

Hockey honcho? Who was that? Why did she get the feeling she should know who he was talking about?

"I hope you're right." Kasdan's heavy, usually forceful voice, sounded hollow and whiny. "I don't need the media attention. The SEC already has a troublesome presence around here."

"That's why I came," the man said. "The boss wants this cleared up and to keep his name out of it. Hey, you gotta drive me to my car. I parked the limo at the Convention Center and walked here along the wharf. I didn't want some nosy-ass guard to recognize the car and figure out who I drive for."

The man and Kasdan walked down the steps. Ladonis pulled HeartTrouble further under the tall desk, their knees practically in their mouths.

"Who that?" HeartTrouble whispered, tugging at his sister's blouse sleeve.

Ladonis slapped his hand away. Her mind was on a roller coaster. Never in a million years would she have figured Kasdan to be anything but an over-the-hill executive too scared and too bitter to pack it in.

"You hear me, Donnie?" HeartTrouble asked. "Who is that?"

She pretended to zip her lips suggesting that he shut up as she listened to Kasdan and his companion leave the building. She didn't speak or move from behind the desk until she heard the ignition rev in Kasdan's car.

"The tape," she said. "Let's go listen to that tape."

"That's what I told you," HeartTrouble answered.

⁓

Ladonis laid the grocery bag on the conference table, opened the entertainment cabinet and pulled out the sliding shelf where the recorder sat, her lips pressed together. She was unwilling to hear the sound of her voice. Any voice. It wasn't just Kasdan or the tape or the nasty humid air that made her feel like a slimy, algae-covered swamp thing in a B-flick. Decatur did. Decatur was the loser Kasdan and his companion were discussing. And, hearing Kasdan speak of him conjured up his dead body lying under the Woldenberg.

HeartTrouble sat at the table near the bag, his entire body slumped and his eyes so heavy they slanted. He watched her load the tape into the machine, all quiet. It felt strange for them to be in the same room without razzing one another.

The Sony tape player evidently had never been used. Hard plastic still tightly encased the electricity plug. She yanked the packaging off and slammed it onto the floor, glad to have something to throw. If only she could do that to the mess she had. She clicked the recorder to play.

"Bret, man, check out the photo."

Tim's voice. Ladonis fell back into the chair behind her, almost missing the seat. This was going to be hard, knowing she'd never see Tim again. No more lunches. No more swapping books. How had a living, breathing being disintegrated into the Mississippi overnight? Her hand curled into a fist. She'd barely escaped that same fate.

"I took this picture," Tim said, "with one of those tourist throw-aways. Just happened to be eating seafood at Commander's Palace the other night and saw these guys. With everything that's going on with the SEC, I thought what's going on here? So I rushed over to the Walgreen's across the street for the camera thinking you never know when a picture will be worth something. The camera's a piece of shit, I know, but I can see the fellows clear enough, considering I was the one taking the picture. Anyway, do you recognize anyone?"

Ladonis picked up one of the photographs and held it close for inspection. A group of men were standing just inside the double glass doors at Commanders Palace. The ex-governor, and the Mayor's right-hand man Louis Delair. The third man and only a hand on the fourth man.

"See the mayor's right hand man," Tim said. "Louis what's-his-name?"

Ladonis put the photograph down to adjust the tone dial on the audio equipment. HeartTrouble picked it up.

"Next to him," Tim said, "is the ex-governor's son. And beside him is the man himself."

"Hey," HeartTrouble said, shaking the photograph at his sister. "That's the guy who owns a hockey team out in California. Must be the hockey honcho that dude on the steps was talkin' about. I hear him and the ex-governor in hot water with the law about some cheatin' scam or the other."

"For crying out loud." Ladonis snatched the picture from his hands. "What do you know about—"

"Those two on the end, there, I don't . . ." Tim's voice faded in static before getting out more.

"Mafia?" Ladonis whispered, staring at the picture.

"No," HeartTrouble said. "Oil guys from Merdick Oil and Refinery. I saw them on the news the other night. They moved their company headquarters from somewhere in Texas to One Shell Square."

Ladonis put the picture back on the table. She was miffed. HeartTrouble's awareness threatened to undermine the control she wanted to have over the situation. She tuned the tape machine, envisioning HeartTrouble watching news on that antique thirteen-inch black and white Magnavox in the Snugglin' Inn, his home away from home.

"I wonder who that is with his head cut off," HeartTrouble said. "The one standing up. See?"

He brought the picture to her face and pointed. Ladonis pushed the tone lever up and down, her eyes on the picture. The static grew louder.

"The one holding the glass." HeartTrouble pointed to the photo again.

What was he talking about? She leaned in to get a better look.

"Shit," she said, clicking the machine off.

She held up the print. Something about the man seemed familiar. His suit? The shape of his body?

"Somebody's comin'," HeartTrouble said and grabbed the Schwegmann's bag.

"It's probably the guard," she said. "Finally making his rounds. Calm down."

She heard paper crumble, took a quick glance and saw Heart-Trouble push the bag under the chair where he sat.

"You ever have the answer to a question on the tip of your

tongue," she said, "but you just can't get it out?" She noticed something on the picture. "Sweet Jesus! That ring. That's Kasdan."

"Who is Kasdan?" HeartTrouble asked.

"Lamar Kasdan, one of the men on the stairwell. He hired me," Ladonis said. Her voice was all but a whisper. "He said his cousin talked him into hiring Decatur. Didn't you hear him?"

"He didn't call the dude by his name," HeartTrouble said. "He said his cousin talked him into hiring a career criminal."

"So what?" she smirked. "I know who he meant."

"So what," HeartTrouble mimicked.

"I think," she said, "the ex-governor is Mr. Kasdan's cousin. Which would explain why he's moved so far up the corporate ladder without a college degree."

"How you figure?" HeartTrouble said. "That they related, I mean."

"Because," she said. "Looking at this picture, I can see that Kasdan bears a strong resemblance to the former governor."

Wheezing breaths came from the direction of the hallway. Ladonis turned around. Kasdan stood in the doorway. She put her hands on her stomach, which did nothing to stop the fluttering sensation she felt there.

"Decatur said you were too smart for your own good," Kasdan said, entering the conference room.

"Lamar Kasdan?" HeartTrouble said, eyeballing the stately-looking gentleman coming through the door. "Yep, they kin all right."

"Close your mouth, my dear," Kasdan said to Ladonis. "That dumbfounded expression makes you look silly."

"I guarantee the one thing she ain't, is silly," HeartTrouble said, rearing back in his seat and looking up at Kasdan.

"I think I know what you mean," Kasdan replied, walking to the table.

"She a thorn in your side too, huh?" HeartTrouble said.

"Where's Decatur?" he asked, looking around. Kasdan's lips spread into a phony closed-mouth grin. "I was supposed to meet him here. After your rendezvous."

"How should we know where that cracker is?" HeartTrouble shifted his body weight. "What's it to you, anyway?"

"That, my boy," Kasdan said, his temple veins bulging, "is what I'd call a loaded question." He picked up the photo from the table, gave it a quick perusal, then glared at Ladonis. "I see you've uncovered a few things that are none of your business," he said.

Ladonis fired back an indifferent look. Kasdan being here wasn't good. But she wasn't scared yet.

"Don't give me that look. You know what I'm talking about." Kasdan waved the picture at her. "I'm talking about this. And a certain travel bag I know is in your possession."

Her entire body went rigid. Did he expect her to say something? She didn't. She wouldn't. How could she have missed the old man in all of this? Even overhearing him before hadn't made her think he might be behind all this trouble. Or at least involved at that level.

"I knew you were trouble the day I hired you," he said.

"So why did you hire me?" Ladonis said. "Did you maybe need someone to actually do PR work while you ran drugs?"

"You had a look about you," he said. "Poised and eager. And I was right. You took to the job better than anybody I ever worked with."

"Thanks for the compliment," Ladonis said. "I think."

She noticed HeartTrouble sitting stiff and upright in the chair, protecting the bag. Here they were again caught with the bag and needing to keep it out of someone's hands. At least Kasdan had no reason to turn them in to the police.

"As for the drug running," Kasdan said. "Sorry to disappoint you, but the drug thing is Decatur's little sideline."

"Sideline?" HeartTrouble said, leaning forward. The chair moved. Was he going to get up? "Now I see what's going on here." He eased back into the chair. "Why go to Mexico and connive people into slippin' across the Gulf to work for pennies and not haul back a real cash option."

Paddle wheelers and Mississippi river lore symbolized oppression to him. It was his soapbox. Well, maybe his anger could work for them here.

"Sticking your nose where it doesn't belong must run in your family," Kasdan said moving closer to where HeartTrouble sat.

"Kasdan?" a man's voice called out. "That you I hear?"

Ladonis prayed the heavy-booted footsteps she heard closing in on them were the guard's. But Tombigbee appeared, smelly and shabby-looking. His bottom lip poked out from the chewing tobacco under his tongue.

"There you are," Tombigbee said. "You know, Lamar, doing business with you these past days has not been easy." He gave the room the once-over. "I thought you said Decatur was going to be here."

"That man is not exactly trustworthy," Kasdan said. "But we'll have to deal with that later."

Kasdan inched closer to Ladonis, making her move slightly backward. Her foot stopped on something. She glanced down. She'd stepped on the bag. She slid her foot sideways to kick it further under the chair where HeartTrouble sat.

"Hey," Tombigbee said. "You look like the gal I saw driving off from my restaurant the other day." He glanced at HeartTrouble. "You must be the brother." He set his sight on Kasdan. "Where's

Decatur? He was supposed to be here with our money that guy Ganen took."

"We were just getting to that," Kasdan said. "Weren't we?"

"Getting to what?" HeartTrouble said.

"Under the circumstances—" Kasdan said.

"What circumstances?" Ladonis asked. "Anything to do with your cousin?"

Displeasure lines furrowed Kasdan's brow. Just like they did at the mere mention of Bret. She was right. The old guy had cousin issues.

"We go to great lengths to keep my family ties secret," Kasdan said.

"Why?" Ladonis asked. "He was the governor."

Resentment glossed his eyes. No doubt that ticked him off. Knowing Kasdan and his ego, he believed he should've been the head of state instead.

"This is business." Kasdan sighed. "My cousin's business deals are considered shady even to his staunchest supporters."

True. But her mother, a retired state-employed janitor at Louisiana State Medical School and a staunch supporter, had said that the former governor was her favorite politician. Despite his crimes. "He may be a gambler, a whore and a thief," Mrs. Washington would say. "But, when he was governor, he shared the spoils." Of course she was referring to the cost of living salary increases they received during the ex-governor's glory years. And judging from the op-ed articles printed daily in the *Times Picayune*, many citizens shared that perspective. Shady, corrupt, what the hell? It all went down as doing what you had to. Still, Ladonis had a hard time rallying behind the man.

"Enough," Kasdan answered.

He seemed to be filling with anger or resentment. Then, as if he had reached the full mark, Kasdan rushed her and took hold of her by the wrist. He turned and nodded at Tombigbee. The big man dashed over and pulled HeartTrouble by the collar from his seat. HeartTrouble staggered forward. He pushed his body onto Tombigbee's, pushing him back, away from the chair. Kasdan gave Ladonis' wrist a hard yank.

"Ouch," she cried.

HeartTrouble made a side step, getting further away from the chair. Then Tombigbee pulled out a gun, cocked it and aimed at HeartTrouble's head. HeartTrouble threw up his hands.

"Cool it, man," he said. "You could hurt a brotha with that thing." He turned to Kasdan. "Look, man, let us go. Your secret is safe with us."

Kasdan laughed. Ladonis had never heard him laugh before. Never heard that snorty sound that didn't go with his lordly mannerisms. This was a whole new Kasdan. Or she was seeing him for the first time in full light.

"You amuse me, young man," Kasdan said.

"I don't see nothing funny about any of this, Lamar," Tombigbee said. He wiped at the sweat beading up on his forehead. "I came here for my dough and Decatur's head on a platter. I don't see either one."

"I knew that dude was a loose end," HeartTrouble whispered too loudly.

"Who you callin' names?" Tombigbee asked.

"Not you," HeartTrouble said. "I'm talkin' about What's-His-Face." HeartTrouble snapped his finger. "You know, Decatur."

"A loose end?" Kasdan said. "Yes, I believe you're right. Decatur . . . was a loose end."

Deliberateness filled Kasdan's voice when he said "was." Decatur, lying dead in the water, flashed before Ladonis, a vision so real, she had to close her eyes. Did Kasdan know or had he figured it out because she and HeartTrouble were still alive?

"You see," Kasdan said to HeartTrouble. "Great minds do think alike. But enough of that too." He turned to Ladonis. "You were seen coming out of Tim's cabin with a bag. I want it. Now. Or I'll have my trigger-happy friend blast your brother's brains to the river rats."

Ladonis' heart pounded in her chest. Kasdan tightened his grip, practically separating her wrist from her hand. She looked away at HeartTrouble, Tombigbee's gun barrel at his forehead.

"What makes you think I know what you're talking about?" she groaned.

"When the Boy Wonder insisted you handle the press, I told Decatur to watch you. He said you had it. Was certain."

"Okay. Okay," Ladonis said. She needed more time. They needed to work their plan and put the contraband in Decatur's space. "But we gave it to Decatur."

"Don't toy with me," Kasdan said. "Decatur's no rocket scientist, but he's no idiot either. If he had it, you wouldn't be here and he would."

"How somebody like you," HeartTrouble asked, "end up partners with that dude?"

How had that come about? Even in a corporate setting, Decatur looked out of place and acted like a mobster. And, in death, he was still scarier than any Magnolia Project thug she'd ever encountered.

"It was a favor to my cousin," Kasdan said. "Though I probably shouldn't have given that outlaw a position of integrity. The man has—or, dare I say?—had none."

Had Kasdan just winked at HeartTrouble? The old guy was enjoying himself. At their expense.

"You mean," HeartTrouble said, "a governor of the state of Louisi—ana heads the green card scam?"

"Of course not," Kasdan said. "It takes real brains to run such an operation."

"A brain, huh?" HeartTrouble said. "And that would be you, right?"

Ladonis glanced at her brother. What must a small-time con artist think of a professional con playing the game for such high stakes? His fierce gaze surprised her.

"Aren't you the smart one," Kasdan told him.

"Too damn smart if you ask me," Tombigbee offered, re-aiming his pistol at HeartTrouble's head.

"Enough of this," Kasdan said. He shoved Ladonis toward the door. "I want that bag you confiscated from Tim's room."

Ladonis landed on her knees. Tombigbee pushed HeartTrouble. He stumbled to where his sister was and offered her a hand. Kasdan pushed him away.

"You went to a lot of trouble to keep your sister alive, didn't you?" Kasdan said to HeartTrouble. "Let's see if she'll return the favor."

"What are you talking about?" Ladonis asked.

"Here's the deal," Kasdan said. "Tombigbee here is going to take your brother onboard his tug, and you're going to take me to that bag." Kasdan pulled her to her feet. "If I don't have the bag in my possession within thirty minutes, Tombigbee is going to do to your brother what somebody did to Ganen."

"Let's go, Brother Dear," Tombigbee said, mimicking Kasdan's tone.

He guided HeartTrouble to the door at gunpoint. HeartTrouble looked at her. His stare blended scorn, impatience and, believe it or not, affection. And, for the first time since she used to walk him home from kindergarten, she felt like his big sister. She had to take care of him.

"Wait." Ladonis rushed over to the chair where she'd kicked the Schwegmann's bag. "Here." She held out the bag. "Now, let him go."

Tombigbee grabbed the bag. His grubby hands took hold as if he'd just been handed a life line. He looked inside.

"This is it," he said. "What now? What'll we do with these two?"

"I didn't hear the foghorn," Kasdan said. "Is the tug here or at the Robin Street wharf next door?"

"Here," Tombigbee said. "I've got a . . . a catch on board and didn't want it too far away."

"Shit," Kasdan said. "I told Decatur not to . . . How many?"

"Three young ones," Tombigbee said.

Ladonis watched HeartTrouble's slumped shoulders lift. Tombigbee was referring to smuggled Mexicans, and he knew it.

"Fish?" HeartTrouble said. "That's what you call slaves nowadays?"

There was no fear in his voice, only anger. Not good. Kasdan had the bag. She wanted them to make their getaway. But that wouldn't happen if HeartTrouble's anger took root. How many times had he told her that he was relegated to street con artistry because of the lingering prejudices of slavery? How many times had he shown deep anger when talking about slavery anywhere in the world, especially close to home? HeartTrouble took a half step toward Tombigbee. She touched his arm and he eased back.

"Shut up." Tombigbee waved the gun at him. "Smart ass."

"HeartTrouble, please," she whispered.

She knew the demon HeartTrouble was fighting. He'd always said to her and anybody who would listen that it was easier for white people to keep him down and out of sight rather than forgive themselves for being the descendants of chattel slave owners, the worst kind of oppressors known to mankind. And she'd answer him—if he believed that, why did he let them get away with it?

"Come on. Take the bag and get out of here," Kasdan said. "Somebody might start to wonder why your tug is docked here at this hour during lay-up."

"What about them?" Tombigbee nodded toward Ladonis and HeartTrouble.

"I'll take care of them." Kasdan held his hand out for Tombigbee's gun. "Get going. I don't want to arouse suspicion."

"Where are you taking us?" Ladonis asked.

"To the boat," Kasdan said. Kasdan dragged Ladonis to the stairwell by the wrist. He pressed Tombigbee's gun into HeartTrouble's back, forcing him to walk ahead. "I think it's only fitting that you have the same demise as Tim."

Ladonis tripped on the bottom step near the building's exit, but Kasdan yanked her up. She winced from the pain in her leg. Kasdan pushed first her through the door to the outside, then HeartTrouble. She struggled to balance her body on one leg, took a couple of limping steps, and her feet slid on the slick pavement. Kasdan responded by gripping her wrist again, then pushing her body toward the paddle boat's gangplank.

Tim was dead. Decatur was dead. Kasdan was a crook. Bret was . . . And she and HeartTrouble were once again staring at death. But she still didn't have the answer to the question she had started out to find. Why had Tim died?

⌒

Ladonis and HeartTrouble crossed to the other side of the vessel, walking side by side through the wider observatory. Kasdan strode behind them, gun in hand and aimed at them. Ladonis glanced at HeartTrouble, hoping to catch his eye. But HeartTrouble gazed ahead, his eyes glassy and mad, like that day when Vincent Deedo, the neighborhood bully, and his friends had chased her through the project threatening to cover her with caterpillars. Caterpillars gave her the creeps. Like Decatur and Tombigbee and especially Kasdan.

Once again she was outside, HeartTrouble still silent and Kasdan still in command of the situation with that gun in his hand. Her eyes darted around the wharf. Why weren't there any people around? Where was everyone? Where was Bret? Especially Bret. She'd called to tell him she'd located the bag, and he'd said he'd meet her.

"Looking for someone?" Kasdan asked. "I sent the guard home. Now move it." He shoved her again, toward the narrow stairwell. "Hold on to your sister's shirttail," he ordered HeartTrouble. "If you let go, I'll shoot her in the back."

"So what's the going rate for fish?" HeartTrouble asked, his voice almost raspy with rage.

Why couldn't HeartTrouble keep quiet? They couldn't run anywhere. There was no one around. Him on a rant wasn't going to make any of this easier. But of course. They could swing into an argument. Either with each other or get Kasdan mad enough to lose some concentration.

"Why?" Kasdan said. "You want to get into the business? Sorry, we got all the people and connections we need."

"Their employers," Ladonis began, "are too greedy to pay fair wages to their help." Trina had talked about how little money even legal Mexican workers made. "But the smugglers make a lot of money, don't they?"

"You can get what?" HeartTrouble said. "Eight grand an immigrant?"

"No, not so much," Kasdan said in a quietly proud voice. Like maybe what he was doing wasn't a crime. "I get a commission, sure. But these are people willing to work."

"Oh, I get it," HeartTrouble said. "They willing to do the work for a illegal green card that we black folks won't do for nothin' anymore, right?"

"They are willing to work, period," Kasdan said. "And their employers are—"

They were at the stairs now. She glanced at her brother. Heart-Trouble's glazed eyes showed his aggravation. The more stairs she climbed, the more anxious she got about what was going to happen. And the stairs to the next level up were just ahead. Not much time to do something. One more wrap around on this level, and they'd be at the stairwell headed for the top deck and a long fall into that paddle wheel.

"We fly over the Gulf on pontoon planes," Kasdan said, "partly because they can get below the radar, partly because they can land in the swamps where shrimp boats pick up our passengers." Pride filled his voice. "The trick is to carry a few, three, maybe four passengers at a time, not a truckload." A reference to how Mexicans were smuggled into Texas and California and other border towns, no doubt. "You know our port in Morgan City," he said. "I call it the entering center."

"Entering center?" HeartTrouble asked. "Like the trading block in *Roots*?"

"That's where they get green cards and are transported to oil fields, shipyards," Kasdan said, as if HeartTrouble had said nothing.

"Some work in the cane fields. The women get to work as nannies and housekeepers."

Who would've thought that she'd be even remotely involved in transporting indentured slaves into the free world in the new millennium?

"That's some cold-blooded, low-down shit, Man," HeartTrouble said, clenching his fist, advertising his contempt. "But think about it, Dude. Your boy, What's-His-Name, Tim, found you out, didn't he? So did my sister. Believe you me, the cops gonna be next."

The expression from Kasdan's frown was downright scary. A frightening look Ladonis had never seen before. HeartTrouble had struck a nerve. Maybe she had a chance to discover something she wanted to know.

"When did Tim find out about all of this?" Ladonis asked.

"Tim found out about Decatur and the drugs," Kasdan said. "I tried to assure him that I'd take care of it, but he wasn't having it." Kasdan licked his thin lips, his eyes wandered a bit. "He and Bret were up to their eyeballs preparing financials and other disclosure documents for the SEC and worried that, if word of drug trading on board got out, the boats would be dry-docked."

She slowed her pace. The stairwell to the next deck up loomed ahead, inching death at them like that passing paddle wheeler had pushed water at them under the Woldenberg. Should they make a run for it now? No. She had to know more.

"What all did Tim know?" she asked. "Did he know about you?"

"Tim said he had to get the proof to oust Decatur," Kasdan went on. "He said he had to use proof rather than accusation to get that louse out quickly and quietly to protect the company."

"Tim was right," Ladonis said.

"Of course he was right," Kasdan told her. "And I told Decatur to stop picking up passengers until after the SEC had cleared the boats for a gambling license."

Ladonis stared at HeartTrouble. Her brother's face looked blank, not angry. She knew that the wheels were turning. That he was trying to figure out how to get free.

Kasdan stopped at the foot of the stairwell. This was the last leg of their journey to the top. Was it the end of Kasdan's story as well? It couldn't be.

"Tim called me the day before he died," Kasdan said. "He told me he was taking an overnight trip on board to get the evidence he'd needed to fire Decatur. Said he was going to hand it over to Bret and Velcroy the next day." Kasdan looked tired, his face droopy. "But when he asked me why I never told anyone that the ex-governor was my cousin, I knew."

"Knew what?" Ladonis asked. She heard an air of bitterness in his voice. Noticed the way he dropped his hand holding the gun.

"That he'd found out more," Kasdan said.

"More?" Ladonis asked. "Like what?"

"He knew that my mother had been seduced and impregnated by the son of an important river man, who died in a barroom brawl before he got around to marrying her." He lowered his voice. "Not that he would've married her. He was promised to some heiress. Pretty much a married man before he actually was."

Wow. Kasdan, the old man, was an outside child. A real outside child. Grandma Lucille was an outside child and her mama had had one hell of a time getting her inheritance because of it. Her relatives believed that since Grandma Lucille was born outside of marriage to a man that was already married, whether she had his DNA, his name or not, she was not entitled to any part of his estate. A conservative tradition that ticked Ladonis' mama off because she said slave owners' children were treated that way. And Kasdan, a white man, was in the same situation.

"I'm sorry," Ladonis said and she meant it.

"And," Kasdan said, "I'm sure Tim found out that my grandfather, a previous owner of this vessel, refused to own me. I was his outside child. His child, but not."

Grandma Lucille often talked about how her father would pass her on the road when he was with his wife and other daughter without so much as a nod. She said it hurt because everybody in town knew she was his, including his wife. She said she always felt better, though, when he'd sneak her a nickel when she passed the fire station where he worked as a volunteer fireman.

"A nickel?" Ladonis had asked. "What could you buy with a nickel?"

"A lot," she'd whisper. Her Grandma Lucille, usually fiery and full of pride, would lower her head. "A lot."

Kasdan looked down at the floor now. He was also without his trademark pride and anger. His moment of sadness was quickly replaced with anger. The old Kasdan was back.

"And Tim probably found out that I own two pontoon planes and have clearance to fly them in the no-fly zone over the Gulf."

"Thanks to your cousin, no doubt?" Ladonis said. Was that the "nickel" that his family had given him?

"That's the least he could do," Kasdan said. "For his father's sister's bastard son."

Kasdan was all rage. He was back to his sneering self. Angry with everyone and particularly his place in the world. Jesus. It was just like Grandma Lucille said—if you don't like yourself, you spend your life making sure that no one else does.

The sound of water splashing up against the still boat seemed louder. Soon they'd be on the top level overlooking the paddle wheel. Even though the blades weren't moving, they were sharp. She gazed out into the still waters shimmering under the cascading moon. She looked at HeartTrouble, pleading—willing—him to think of something, hoping that she would if he didn't.

"I knew that I was going to be investigated next," Kasdan said. His eyes were scanning the stairs and deck around them. "That I'd lose my job and my boats."

"Your boats?" HeartTrouble said. "How they get to be yours?"

Kasdan's face transformed—beet-red cheeks, bulging eyes, thumping temples. In that moment, he lost all semblance of the calculating Kasdan she'd grown to loathe. He looked as if he'd flipped over to the other side of sanity.

"These boats belong to me," Kasdan said, pounding his chest with the hand that held the gun. Then he turned the gun to her. "Get moving," Kasdan said, shoving her yet again.

She froze, turned and stared the old man down. It was now or never.

"No," she yelled. "I'm what's standing in your way. Forget the paddle wheel. Shoot me. Do it here and now. Do what you have to do to get what's yours."

"What's wrong with you, Donnie?" HeartTrouble said.

Kasdan cocked the gun, the sound like a fire starter, lighting her up, fueling her into action. She lifted her bad leg and kicked him. She went for the groin but hit his shin. Pain shivered through her, but she kept her balance. She turned to her brother.

"Get out of here. Run, HeartTrouble. Run."

Kasdan leaned down a bit, trying to steady his hand to fire the gun. Ladonis got her strength together and pushed his arm. The gun fell. Kasdan backhanded her hard across the face. She went down, holding onto the railing. HeartTrouble swung his leg like a golf club at the gun. The gun slid past her into the Mississippi. HeartTrouble stepped up on a ledge near the railing, maybe reaching for her. She wasn't sure. But, before HeartTrouble could do anything, Kasdan rushed him, and he fell backward into the water.

"HeartTrouble?" Ladonis cried. "Oh, my God. He can't swim."

"Good," Kasdan said, bent over holding his stomach, backing away from her and the railing. Like she had the strength to push him over that railing. But she didn't care about him, she wanted HeartTrouble. She stumbled along the deck, searching the water for some sign of her brother.

Feet on the deck. Was someone coming? She followed the sound and saw Kasdan struggling to get away, his body still bent over. He pivoted and faced her, his face contorted with pain or anger or both.

"I told Decatur to kill you," he said, winded. "I wish he had. But I should have known that rodent couldn't follow orders. If he had, he wouldn't have killed Ganen."

Ladonis felt a sharp pain in her stomach. She opened her mouth, but words wouldn't come out. Decatur had killed Tim. And Tim was dead because he had discovered Kasdan's secret. And Decatur was . . . Oh, God. She'd solved the mystery and gotten rid of Tim's killer. Before she even knew it. But had she killed her brother too?

35

Perjured

Detective Travers drove up in front of the Floating Palace's passenger terminal. Never mind the "No Parking" sign. He was NOPD. City laws excluded NOPD. Everybody knew that except his partner who he spotted knocking on the building's sash door.

He hopped out of the car and slammed the door. Why was Wellsburg here? Had his partner read the forensic report? He would've called if he had. Wouldn't he? Wellsburg looked at Travers, waved and walked to the dockside of the building. Travers had seen that off-the-rack three-piece suit his partner wore in a Lord and Taylor newspaper ad. Looked just as good on the model.

"I spoke to that preacher," Wellsburg said.

"Preacher?" Travers said, struggling to keep up. He crossed from the dimly lit parking area to the dark and cold spot between the office building and the boat.

"Remember the call last night?" Wellsburg said. "The preacher with the tip?"

"Oh, yeah," Travers said. "What's his angle?"

"Don't know yet," Wellsburg said. "That's why I'm here."

Travers looked out at the water and saw nothing but darkness. Why hadn't he worn a jacket? It was always cold on the docks before sunrise.

"He must've said something to get you here at this hour," Travers said.

The scent of Dial soap on Wellsburg's skin was strong. Travers couldn't use Dial. Made him break out in a rash.

"What's with the third degree?" Wellsburg said. "The man told me he had information that'll solve this murder. Asked me to meet him here at 7 A.M." He looked at his watch. "I'm early."

Wellsburg may have been agitated, but Travers was mad as hell. And, if Wellsburg's flat tone hid how perturbed he was, Travers made sure his tone imitated calm disregard. He wanted to follow up on his gut feeling and connect the CEO to Honey Man. And he wanted to do it his way, without this guy breathing down his neck. That fair and impartial bull was for judges, not cops.

"The question is why are you here so early?" Wellsburg said. "It wouldn't have anything to do with your fixation on a certain CEO, would it?"

"We're partners, remember?" Travers said, mockingly. "I got word that you were here."

"Any law says I have to believe you?" Wellsburg said.

Any law says he shouldn't have a crack at that CEO without his partner chastising him with ethics? Travers swallowed this retort, his day already off to a bad start. He'd planned to lean on that CEO and zero in on the heroin ring he suspected operated from one or both of the riverboats. Now he had to spend valuable time convincing his partner there was a drug connection.

⌒

Travers followed his partner onto the *Magnolia Belle's* gangplank. He heard footsteps, looked over his shoulder and waited for a figure to appear. Bret Collins rushed through the dark spot up to them, panting as if he'd finally reached the end of a jog.

"Didn't have time to get it together, huh?" Detective Travers asked the corporate leader, dressed even more casually than he was. Aside from the faded jeans and wrinkled pullover shirt, the damned CEO looked as if he hadn't slept or shaved in days.

"You people work the strangest hours," Collins said to Detective Wellsburg, catching his breath. "Do you ever sleep?" When Wellsburg didn't respond, he looked at Travers. "What about you?"

"Forget the small talk," Travers grumbled, moving closer to the area lit from lights coming from the boat's main deck.

"Okay," Collins said, tucking in his shirttail, skipping to catch up. "What brings you guys here before sunrise? Do you have a suspect?"

"Maybe," Travers said, watching Collins' eyes. His favorite instructor at the police academy believed that eyes were like truth serums. The man spent a great deal of time teaching him how to read them. Collins' eyelids lowered into their sockets, convincing Travers that the young CEO was hiding something.

"Meaning what, Detective?" Collins asked.

"We found a zipper hook," Wellsburg said, pulling a plastic bag from inside the pocket of his suit jacket. "On the Dixie Deck near where your Mr. Ganen went overboard. According to forensics, that hook is off a pair of coveralls like the ones your deckhands wear."

Travers had a hard time pretending not be surprised. Even he wouldn't have kept his partner in the dark about a forensic report.

"Really now, detectives," Collins said. "I'm sure there are any number of our deckhands and other workers onboard with torn zippers."

"I'm sure you're right," Wellsburg said. "But we still have to check it out."

Always the diplomat. How could Travers trust a guy like that? He glanced away. Was that a shadow he saw moving on the upper deck of the boat?

"I didn't see your security guy," Travers asked. "Any idea where he is?"

"Shift change," Collins said. "I'm sure someone will emerge soon."

Collins' body swayed from one side to the other. Travers witnessed the motion. The CEO was nervous.

"Do any of your deckhands chew tobacco?" Travers asked. He passed his partner a subtle, yet glowering look. He was determined to uncover the connection he was looking for.

"Certainly," Collins said. "A lot of the rural, country boy types come to work on board with that habit."

"Tell me something," Wellsburg said. "Ganen was holding a stiff piece of black fabric in his hand. Probably off a baseball cap. Any ideas about that?"

"Most of our deckhands wear baseball caps," Collins said. "If you're here to accuse someone, I hope you have more to go on."

Travers couldn't ignore the I'm-in-charge look his partner gave him. What was his problem? Was he trying to make him look like a fool in front of this guy?

"I bet you do," Travers said.

He could no longer hold in his contempt. But for whom? The CEO or his partner?

"I say that, Detective," Collins said, "because the caps became an unofficial part of the deckhands' uniforms when we made a deal with the Saints football team."

Travers turned so that he had a full view of Collins' taut face, his tightly drawn muscles.

"The caps were gifts," Collins said, "from the team's owner, one of our most satisfied customers. Publicity, you know."

Travers squirmed, letting out a soft groan. The CEO was nervous about something. Travers was sure of it. But the guy didn't sound like it.

"The Floating Palace sells Saints caps in its gift shops," Collins went on to say, "and the Saints use The Floating Palace's souvenir calendars that feature pictures of the boats, as giveaways, a token for us doing business with them. A little win/win arrangement that gets sweeter every time a Saints fan books a cruise. And when a steam boater adds a Saints game to his or her New Orleans itinerary."

Travers watched Collins' expression and shoulders drop despite the intrinsic luster in his voice. Like a candle burning low. What was he hiding?

"For that I bet you got season tickets," Travers said, hoping to get a rise out of Collins. "I know how you guys operate."

"Yes, we did get a couple of season passes," Collins said. "And raffled them off and gave the money to Toys for Tots."

The CEO's tone, laced with scorn as well as desperation, blew over Travers like a fierce wind. Travers was rattled, but only unleashed a frown and fiery eyes in response. If he'd been partnered with anyone other than Mr. By-the-Book, he'd give that smart mouth CEO a gut punch.

"We know Ganen struggled with somebody," Wellsburg said. "And I believe it was a deckhand who saw him last. A Nate Blenner, I recall."

Blenner? Travers had suspected that Blenner guy knew more than he'd let on. Did he have a stroke of conscience and called his pastor? Did that forensic report point to the deckhand?

"Don't try to deny it," Travers said, blowing his own wind of arrogance. "Because like my partner said, we know that happened." He was desperate to lean on this guy.

"Why would I deny it?" Collins said. "I have no idea what happened to Tim."

Travers gritted his teeth. So far, he hadn't intimidated the CEO, and he didn't like that one bit. Footsteps moved toward them.

"You security?" Wellsburg asked the tall, robust, black man who came into view.

The man, who sported a straggly mustache and gray whiskers, nodded his head, "yes," and put a toothpick in his mouth between rotten-brown teeth.

"Where have you been?" Travers asked.

"Got here just before you," the man said, gnawing on the toothpick. "But I had to take a crap."

Water splashed. Travers' body twitched. His eyebrows lifted.

"Something's moving out there," Wellsburg said.

"Probably fish. Gaspergou," Collins said.

"No. Mo' like catfish," the security guard said, conjuring up a big, tawny smile. "Tryin' to figure out what all the commotion about."

Who cared what fish was out there? Travers pivoted, slapped his leg. He had to get on that boat.

"I want to inspect Ganen's room again," Travers said. "See if we missed something. Then I want to speak with all the deckhands on board." He gave Wellsburg a sly look. "Nate Blenner in particular." He couldn't allow the so-called "good cop" to be the one to get the drop on the killer.

"Anything in particular you're looking for, Detective?" Collins asked, looking at Travers.

"Only a corporate asshole would ask that," Travers said. "Is there something in particular I ought to be looking for?"

"Only a dumb cop would ask that," Collins said, again matching Travers' animosity.

"Let's go," Travers said to the guard. He looked at Wellsburg. "Care to join us?"

Wellsburg's professionalism might have chained him to the appearance of police camaraderie, but the glare of distrust showed through his eyes. Travers answered his partner's silent contempt with a sardonic grin. He'd deal with the consequences of the bad blood between them after he had that CEO locked up.

"Wait up," the security guard said. "There's a Reverend Sweeney in the terminal. Said he was supposed to meet a detective here?"

"Shit," Travers mumbled. By the time he got the goods on the CEO, this would be a cold case.

"Come with me," Wellsburg said to his pouting partner. "You too, Mr. Collins." He looked at the guard. "Get the keys to Mr. Ganen's room and find that deckhand, Nate Blenner, and meet us at the cabin."

Travers didn't like the authority he heard in Wellsburg's voice. Particularly when he addressed him. Most of all, he didn't like not knowing what Wellsburg knew and he didn't.

"That the Reverend?" Travers asked, pointing to a large white man. Another man stood beside the Reverend, twirling the rim of his cap between his fingers. Blenner. Mr. Religious. "Is that that deckhand, Blenner?"

"Looks like him," Wellsburg said.

Reverend Sweeney with his broad shoulders and thick thighs looked like a football player toting a Bible. He wore a large silver cross around his invisible neck. Looked like a giant statue standing beside the deckhand. The Reverend moved toward the policemen, his hand outstretched.

"I'm Reverend Sweeney," he said. "Detective Wellsburg?"

"You said you could solve this murder." Wellsburg took the man's offered hand, but looked squarely into Nate Blenner's eyes. "This got anything to do with what really happened?"

What was going on? Was his partner following a hunch or did he have the goods on this guy?

"Tell him, Nate." Reverend Sweeney turned to Nate Blenner, resting against a table below a huge painting of the *Bayou Queen*. "Tell the detective what you told me."

"You witnessed Ganen's death, didn't you?" Wellsburg side-stepped in front of the Reverend to face Nate Blenner.

"Yes sir," Nate Blenner nodded. "I did."

"That's not what you said when we questioned you," Travers said, placing himself so close to Nate they could've kissed. "You're telling us now that you perjured yourself?"

"What's that, Reverend?" Nate asked, fear flashing through his eyes. "What he mean?"

"He's asking if you lied before, Nate," Reverend Sweeney explained. "That's all. Just tell him the truth."

"Well, did you?" Wellsburg asked. "Did you lie before?"

"Well, sir," Nate said. "If by not tellin' you everythin' I knowed is lyin', then, yes sir, I believe I did, sir. I lied."

"Before you say anything further . . ." Wellsburg shot a glance back at his partner. "I want this done right. By the book." He faced Nate Blenner. "You have the right to remain silent," he said. "Anything you say can and will be used against you in a court of law. Understand?"

Nate Blenner nodded. Travers glanced over at Collins, whose eyes glared keen and expectant, like a wolf about to pounce. The detective noticed something else too. The CEO's baby blues were also sad, like his mother's had been when she sat by his dying father's bedside.

A door flung open. The sound of large feet thumped and slid across the floor. Travers turned. A small crowd of riverboat workers in various shades of orange made their way into the terminal.

"Shut up Preach," a deckhand called out. "You ain't gotta say nothin'. You didn't do nothin' none of us wouldna done."

"What the hell . . ." Travers said.

36

Dirty Secrets

Ladonis hobbled along the edge of the boat leaning over the rail, calling for HeartTrouble. The sun rose, but it was a cloudy morning, and nothing but a powdery blankness came into view. What she imagined, however, was a horrible vision of HeartTrouble lying somewhere along the river, being eaten by rats. What was she going to tell Mama? She heard voices coming from the wharf. Maybe someone who could help her find HeartTrouble.

The guard, Big Blake was coming toward her waving. Big Blake was another Magnolia Project alumni whom she'd helped find a job. HeartTrouble took issue with what he called her Uncle Tom Employment Agency, supplying "The Man," as he put it, with hard-luck brothers to oppress. She'd take any and all of her brother's razzing now if he were okay.

"Hey, Donnie," Big Blake said, chomping down on a toothpick. "Was that a shot I heard? What's goin' on like that, Sistah?"

"HeartTrouble," she cried, pointing to the water. "He can't swim."

"Yes, he can," Big Blake said.

"What are you talking about?"

"We learned at Shakespeare Park," Big Blake said. "When we was kids."

"He can swim?" She grabbed him by the shirt.

"Yeah," Big Blake said. "He can swim, and he gone home." He took her hands into his. "I lent him my ride."

Her knees went limp. Big Blake held her up. HeartTrouble wasn't dead. She hadn't killed her brother. But she needed to see him, needed to talk to HeartTrouble. Especially now that Kasdan had said that Decatur had killed Tim.

"You better have a good reason for being up here," Big Blake said. "Because the cops, the young boss, they all on the way to Mr. Tim's cabin."

"I do," she said, reeling from relief. "Bret—I mean, the young boss—is expecting me. But I'd rather he didn't find me on the boat."

She wasn't worried about Bret. But the police were a different matter. They might want to know what she was doing on board at that hour of the morning. She looked around for Kasdan. Did he know that the cops were here? Would he tell them about Decatur?

"Listen," she said. "I don't know what my brother told you, but—"

"HeartTrouble just said he needed to get off the dock without being seen," Big Blake said. "And that I should come get you. What about that shot I heard?"

What shot? That gun had just gone into the river. No shot. Maybe the sound Big Blake'd heard was the explosion of her fear when HeartTrouble had gone into the water.

"There wasn't any shot. Honest," she said. "There was a gun. But it's in the river now. Nothing you need to worry about."

"You good peoples," Big Blake said. "You and your bad-ass brother. Long as nobody shot or dead, I'm cool."

Ladonis grabbed Big Blake in a thank-you embrace. Depending on what Kasdan was up to, she might still get out of this with her life intact. Whatever that meant. Considering what Kasdan had to lose, she had to assume that he wouldn't mention the bag, her or HeartTrouble. If he did, what would she say about Decatur? No, she wouldn't think about that. Kasdan wouldn't give her away if she didn't give him away.

"Listen," Big Blake said. "I can get you to the parking lot without anybody seeing you and you can come in through the front door. That way nobody will know you been here all this time."

Her leg started throbbing again. She leaned down to check her leg. A red spot showed on the bandage, but not too red. Despite her kung fu moves, the cut hadn't bled badly. But the pain was acute.

"Did the cops see HeartTrouble?" she asked, hopping along on her good leg.

"No," Big Blake said. "They came up afterwards."

"But they didn't they see him?" She felt a thumping heartbeat of panic.

"They didn't see nothin'," Big Blake said. "Not even me. By the time I showed up in their faces, HeartTrouble was in my car on his way home."

Big Blake led her to the water-side of the neighboring Robin Street Wharf about a half a block away. He stopped at a small, tin, prefab shed, the city's Mardi Gras storage place. Ladonis leaned over to check the bandage on her leg.

"What's the matter with your leg?" Big Blake said. He lifted a piece of torn tin in the back of shed and ushered her in.

"I hit it earlier, and it's just now starting to hurt," she said.

She stooped and pulled herself through the hole. Big Blake followed. Once inside, Big Blake moved one of the many crates of Mardi Gras beads and opened the door. She exited the shed into the Robin Street Wharf. Like the parking lot next door, it was a large, open, dark space filled with massive Carnival float decorations.

She followed Big Blake outside and into a mist of rising daylight through the darkness to Tchopitulas Street, the front side of the dock. Familiar now with her surroundings, she headed toward Pelican Street Wharf and the Floating Palace's parking lot. She may have been on familiar grounds, but she was in an unfamiliar predicament. Was she headed for safety or the beginning of the end of life as she knew it?

"You go in," Big Blake said at the entrance. "I have to go back on the boat to Mr. Tim's cabin. That detective told me to meet them there."

Ladonis hugged him again. She would go to her car that she'd cleverly sandwiched between two company mini-vans at the far end of the lot, and fix herself up. She didn't want those detectives to become any more suspicious than they probably were. Especially that Detective Travers. He had a way about him that made her feel as though he knew she was hiding something.

⌒

Ladonis walked up to the terminal door, grateful that HeartTrouble was safe. She had to keep it that way. So now what? And where was Kasdan? She stepped inside and froze. Of all the men in the lobby she expected to see—the two detectives and Bret—she gasped when she saw Preacher Man and that television minister, Reverend Sweeney. But no Kasdan. He was the only other person who could tip the cops off about her involvement. The rat had to be more concerned about his own hide than Decatur's. Otherwise she was screwed.

"Ladonis Washington, right?" Detective Travers made his way to where she'd planted herself at the door. "What are you doing here?"

She couldn't speak, seeing Preacher Man talking to the police. What if he said something about her, her and Tim's bag? She'd have to tell them she heard him say he hated—what had he called him?—a she-man. Suppose the police didn't know Tim was gay. Would she be the one to out him? After all she'd done to protect Tim? Then Bret rushed over to her. Thank God.

"I told her to meet me here," Bret said, his tone sharp. "She's PR. Whenever there's a crisis of any kind, we have to stay on top of it. To make sure that the information that reaches the public is accurate and serves the best interest of the company."

Ladonis' eyes jumped. Did Bret just snap at a New Orleans policeman? Was he nuts?

"Big job," Travers said to her.

"I can handle it," she said, making sure she didn't sound intimidated. But then Kasdan walked up, and all that self control went to that cut in her leg. A sharp pain hit so hard, her eyes watered.

"And I guess," Travers said to Kasdan, "you're here to make sure she gets her job done right."

"Indeed," Kasdan said. "I was in my office watching the fish jump in and out the water, waiting for her to arrive."

Ladonis' body stiffened. Bastard. She stared at Kasdan with all the disdain her soul could muster up. How could such a contemptuous man have control over her future?

"Now that we're all here," Detective Wellsburg said, looking at Preacher Man.

The nervous deckhand squeezed his eyes shut, hunched his shoulders, and took a loud, deep breath.

"It's okay, my son," Reverend Sweeney said. He laid his hand on Preacher Man's back. "God will be with you. Summon up your strength from Him."

"I know, Reverend," Preacher Man said. "I done prayed and prayed on it. Praise the Lord." He lifted his head, cleared his throat and looked straight at Detective Travers. "Detective, sir . . ."

Ladonis moved closer to a pillar and leaned against it taking the pressure off her leg. Grief and apprehension were heavy on her heart. What was he going to say? Would he implicate her?

"You have the right to have an attorney present so that you don't incriminate yourself," Detective Wellsburg said. "Do you understand? Do you want an attorney?"

"No, sir," Preacher Man said.

"Why?" Ladonis whispered.

She didn't think anyone had heard her. But Preacher Man looked at her, his eyes blazing. He was going to accuse her. She wanted to run away, but her body wouldn't move.

"Tim was a homo," Preacher Man blurted out. "And he made a pass at me."

Oh, shit. Ladonis glanced at Bret. Had his worst nightmare come true? Would everyone assume Bret and Tim were lovers, the way she had? What else would Preacher Man reveal?

"Thou shalt not," Preacher Man said, "lie with mankind as with womankind. It's in the Bible. Gospel according to Leviticus. Praise the Lord." He twisted the rim of his Saints cap. "He deserved to die. I shoulda killed him. But I didn't."

An English transfer student in an Ancient History class Ladonis had taken at LSU had argued once that the Bible could be translated to justify an evil deed just as well as a good one. And that she had too much respect for Jesus to be a Christian because of that. "Christian interpretations of biblical history," she'd stated, "are all over the place. And, more often than not, contradict what Jesus stood for." Preacher Man gave that argument credibility.

"What does that mean?" Detective Wellsburg said. "You should have, but you didn't?"

Ladonis clenched her fist, gritted her teeth. It meant he was a zealot. A crazy who couldn't tell the difference between God's law and his own self-righteousness. What about "Thou shalt not kill?" That was in the Bible too.

"Shut up, Nate," a deckhand called out. "You ain't gotta say nothin'."

"You shut up," Travers told the deckhand.

"Look, Mr. Blenner," Detective Wellsburg said. "Your friend is right. You don't have to say anything without your lawyer."

"Yes, sir," Preacher Man said. "I know that's my right, but Jesus is my lawyer and He is here with me. I feel Him. Praise the Lord."

Preacher Man glanced over at Reverend Sweeney who indicated with a swift nod that he should go ahead and speak. But Preacher Man wasn't in any kind of a hurry. Ladonis fought the urge to walk up and shake the words out of him. The lines on Bret's face painted a picture of wonderment, disbelief. To think she'd thought Bret had killed Tim. Thank God, he hadn't.

"I knowed somethin' was wrong the minute I laid eyes on Mr. Tim," Preacher Man said. "I thought maybe somebody died. I recollected the time his Ma passed. He came on board then, and moped around for days. He looked like that. Like he did the day his mama passed. Praise the Lord."

Travers moved in. Kasdan's body shuddered. Was Preacher Man going to mention Decatur? Kasdan seemed as concerned as she was. Shit. He should be.

"It had been rainin'," Preacher Man said. "And the riverbank was nothin' but mud. Mr. Tim moved through that mess like that plank walk we laid down wasn't even there. Praise the Lord. I said,

'What's wrong, Mr. Tim? Another bumpy flight?' He was always gripin' about them old-timey propeller planes they use on short trips out of New Orleans."

"Preach," the deckhand called again. "You ain't got to help them nail your coffin. The son-of-a-bitch got what he deserved."

"One more word from you," Detective Travers said, pointing his finger. "And you're going to get what you deserve." He looked at Preacher Man. "Go on."

"My shift was over," Preacher Man said. "I was headed outside for a smoke and some fresh air. Praise the Lord." He spoke to the floor, sliding that cap of his around in his hands. "I heard some-body laughin' real loud in the Prop, you know, the bar," he said. "Sounded like a party, so I looked in through the glass. It was Mr. Tim, sittin' at the bar by hisself, drinkin'. He drank straight out the bottle and he started laughin' again. Next thing I knowed, he'd picked up that bottle and came out the bar on the deck. He stood over the paddle wheel lookin' down at it like he was tryin' to figure it out or somethin'. Praise the Lord."

Ladonis locked eyes with Preacher Man and held his gaze. She remembered the way his hands had shook when he had read about Tim in the newspaper. The dread she'd seen on his face. The clues had been all there.

"Where were you?" Detective Wellsburg asked.

"When he came out," Preacher Man said. "I moved to the side out the light so he couldn't see me. I didn't want to embarrass him. He was leanin' over that rail and laughin' up a storm. But he didn't sound like he was happy, you know. Sounded almost like he was cryin'." He cleared his throat, then hacked loud and long. "He was stinkin' drunk. But he took another swig of liquor, then tossed the bottle in the water. He almost went over too, so I stepped out to lend him a hand. Praise the Lord. Next thing I knowed, he was all over me. He said, 'I'm a dead man. How about you and me, huh, Nate? One last fling?'"

Preacher Man looked down. He didn't look at anyone, not even his Reverend Sweeney. Just he twisted his cap's brim.

"We tussled." He spoke to the floor, his voice loud with passion. "But I got the better of Mr. Tim. Held him back over the railin' by the neck. Praise the Lord. I was so disgusted, just the feel of his skin on my hands made me sick." His voice grew softer. "All I had to do was let loose, push his legs up and over, and the world would be rid of his sin and evil."

Had she thought about getting rid of Decatur when he had held her at gunpoint under the Woldenberg? She couldn't remember. What if she had? Decatur was evil. Tim was just gay.

"I took one hand away," Preacher Man said. "But that she-man, he just looked at me. I thought he woulda begged or somethin', but he didn't say a word. Just stared up at me. Made me so mad. Praise the Lord." Preacher Man clenched his fists and looked up into Detective Travers' eyes. "I was gonna grab him tight again. But then I heard somebody comin'. So I turned to look. Mr. Tim leaned up enough to get from under my grip."

Who had been coming? The captain? Another deckhand? No, if what Kasdan had said was true, it had been Decatur. Ladonis looked at Kasdan who stared at Preacher Man, a smug expression on his face.

"Instead of hittin' me," Preacher Man said, "or somethin' like a real man would do, Mr. Tim smiled at me. I wanted to pick him up and throw him in the water, but somebody was steady comin' our way. So, I walked off." Preacher Man had another coughing fit, though not as intense as before. "But you know what that creature did?"

"What did Mr. Ganen do?" Detective Wellsburg said.

Mr. Ganen? Was the detective making a point to the holy roller or someone else? Ladonis followed Detective Wellsburg's gaze to Detective Travers, who rocked back and forth, glowering at Bret.

"The she-man started laughin'," Preacher Man said. "I took a couple a steps at him, but Mr. Decatur was there."

Decatur. Confirmation. Decatur had killed Tim. Kasdan knew it. And she knew what had happened to Decatur. Her moment of truth.

"Are you saying," Detective Travers said, "that Decatur was with Mr. Ganen after you almost threw him in the river?"

"Yes, sir," Preacher Man said.

"Mr. Blenner," Detective Wellsburg said. The look Detective Wellsburg gave his partner could've started World War III. "Did you see what happened between Mr. Ganen and Mr. Decatur?"

"Well," Preacher Man said. "Mr. Decatur went right up to Mr. Tim and pushed him in the chest. 'Freak,' Mr. Decatur said, 'you're a dead man.'"

"What did Mr. Ganen do?" Detective Wellsburg said.

"Mr. Tim," Preacher Man said, "he told Mr. Decatur he was a criminal of the worst kind. That his days of runnin' the company into the sewer were over. He said, 'Screw you, Decatur.' Then Mr. Decatur said, 'Punk, I ought to kill you right now.' They kept on arguin', saying more and more of the same, so I decided to leave and go to my cabin."

"Are you saying," Detective Wellsburg said, "that you didn't see Mr. Ganen fall overboard?"

"No, sir," Preacher Man said. "I didn't see him, sir. No, sir. But, when the boat stopped, and the captain said somebody went over, I knew it was Mr. Tim."

"How?" Detective Wellsburg said. "How did you know?"

"I believe," Preacher Man said. He spoke to the floor again. "I believe I heard him hit the blades. And when I heard the noise, the boat slowed."

"Did you go back to see what caused the noise?" Detective Travers asked.

"No," Preacher Man said. "I didn't. I shoulda. But I didn't."

He should have, but he didn't? What kind of explanation was that? And what about her? She should've left that bag where Tim had hidden it, but she hadn't.

"Why?" Detective Travers said. "Why didn't you tell us this when we first questioned you?"

"Because," Preacher Man said.

"Because what?" Detective Travers said, in that pissed-off, intimidating tone of his.

Preacher Man responded like a bewildered child. No words, just wide-eyed panic. He looked over at the Reverend who offered up another swift head nod. Preacher Man took a deep breath.

"Because," Preacher Man said, "I didn't want nobody to know." He looked at one detective, then the other.

"To know what?" Detective Travers said, placing himself real close to Preacher Man. "You have no idea how much trouble you're in if you don't tell us the truth."

"I didn't want nobody to know he was, you know, like that," Preacher Man said. "I didn't want nobody to think that I . . . Praise the Lord. We used to hang out like, you know. Down on the gang-plank. In the mess hall. We was always talkin' and laughin' bout stuff. I didn't want nobody to think I was like that too. Praise the Lord."

For crying out loud, Preacher Man thought homosexuality was contagious. So what? She'd thought homosexuality was a mental illness. And HeartTrouble believed that men being with other men was another affront to the black man's manhood. Tim was none of that.

"Then why are you telling us now?" Detective Wellsburg said. "What people think doesn't matter to you any more?"

"No," Preacher Man said. "I mean, yeah." He looked at his Reverend Sweeney again. "When I read in the paper that the police said Mr. Tim was pushed, I figured Mr. Decatur musta done it. Praise the Lord. So I called my pastor, told him what happened and he said I had to get in touch with you."

"That's right, Detectives," Reverend Sweeney said. "I advised Nate to tell you everything he knew, for his own salvation."

Ladonis watched Preacher Man's eyes water. His hands kneaded that damn hat. How could this be? Tim gone. Decatur dead.

"At the time," Preacher Man said. "I really wanted Mr. Tim to die. That's my sin. Pastor said I had to face my sin and repent. Otherwise, meet my Maker with another man's blood on my hands. But I didn't kill him." He met Detective Travers' gaze. "I swear before God, Mr. Decatur was the last person to see Mr. Tim before he went over."

He crossed his heart. Ladonis frowned. Preacher Man turned his head and stared into Ladonis' glare.

"I didn't want to kill him," Preacher Man said. "I just wanted to get him off me." He cleared his throat. "And I'm really sorry I didn't say nothin' about it before."

Detective Wellsburg walked up to his partner and got in his face. His eyes glaring, jaws clenched. What in the world was going on between those two?

"Have Decatur picked up," Detective Wellsburg said. "Now."

Jesus. Pick up Decatur? Decatur was dead under the Woldenberg.

And she was responsible. But he'd killed Tim. Had justice been served?

"Yeah, yeah," Detective Travers said. "Let me have it. If I hadn't released the guy, he'd still be in custody, right?"

Ladonis couldn't help but notice the anger brewing in Bret's misty eyes. Nor the tension that eased from Kasdan's shoulders. Nor the smirk that crossed the old guy's lips when he looked at her. Was that look to remind her that she'd better not talk about the drugs and Mexicans he'd smuggled into the country via a national historic treasure? That he would make sure she'd have to explain her part in Decatur's disappearance if she did? How could she protect HeartTrouble if she ratted him out? She had to keep his dirty secret so that he would keep hers.

"Nate Blenner." Detective Wellsburg walked up to Preacher Man. The deckhand didn't take his eyes off the floor. "You have to come with us to police headquarters to make an official statement."

Preacher Man nodded, gave the Reverend a pleading look, and trotted off alongside Detective Wellsburg. Reverend Sweeney followed right behind. Detective Travers walked up to Bret standing beside Kasdan, his eyes shooting darts at Bret. Was the detective disappointed? Had he suspected that Bret could have been the killer? She had.

"Well," Travers said to Bret. "You were right. Looks like Decatur is the killer."

Bret just stood there. Ladonis glared at Kasdan, the thought of the Mexicans tugging at her conscience. Indentured slaves. The Floating Palace's outside children. Never to be acknowledged. Lord, help her, she prayed the same for Decatur's body, that it would never be found.

"Yes," Kasdan said to Detective Travers. "Now, can we go home?"

He gave her a quick, sly glance. Kasdan thought he was safe now, and he probably was, if she and HeartTrouble were to be safe as well. She sighed. No one's success or well-being should ride on the back of another human being's dignity, alive or dead. No wonder HeartTrouble was always so pissed.

37

The Whole Truth and Nothing But

The sun shining through the kitchen window pointed out a sticky spill on what Ladonis had thought was a clean counter top. Ladonis sprayed Windex and wiped down the dark granite as hard as she could. Her neighbor's cat sat perched on the fence outside her window, watching as if to mock her. She really wasn't into housekeeping, and that cat seemed to know it.

"You promised to be done by the time my guest arrived." She turned her anger on HeartTrouble, who was measuring a shelf.

"It's a shame, you know that?" HeartTrouble said, straining to be heard over the music blasting from her stereo close by him.

"What are you griping about now?" Ladonis said, retying the head scarf around her uncombed hair.

"It took damn near a year," HeartTrouble said, "and somebody white comin' over before you fixed this place up. But don't worry, your bookshelves gonna be built before she get here. And I'm gonna help you unpack the books from them boxes too."

Ladonis' glare said he'd better and a lot more. Not all of it bad or critical. She sipped Chardonnay straight from the bottle, not wanting to dirty glasses she'd just put away from the dishwasher. Every time she laid eyes on her brother these days, she thanked God.

"You drink too much," HeartTrouble said. He stopped to gulp down the last of a Miller beer.

"Look who's talking," she said.

She took another swallow. Eight months had passed and she still hadn't found a place for her memory of Decatur—somewhere besides her conscience—for him to rest. The wine did blur her visions of him.

"That just prove I know what I'm talkin' about," HeartTrouble said.

"When I want your advice," she said, "I'll ask for it."

Some things wouldn't change between them. HeartTrouble couldn't show concern, and she'd better not acknowledge appreciation. They still had to argue about everything.

"I'm a man," HeartTrouble sang, turning up the stereo volume. "I'm a hootchie-coochie man."

"When do you think you'll be done?" Ladonis asked, putting her hands over her ears. John Lee Hooker didn't need a chorus to make him sound bad.

"What's the matter?" HeartTrouble said. "You need a hootchie-coochie man?"

"Don't go there," Ladonis said, pointing her finger at him.

"Get off your high horse, girl," HeartTrouble said. "Me and John Lee will be out of here in no time."

"Good."

Ladonis picked up a hammer and picture hook lying on the coffee table. She walked to the wall without bookshelves, to the spot where she'd made a mark to nail the hook.

"Who would've thought that your worst enemy would be your first guest," HeartTrouble said. "And that you two would be workin' together."

"Yeah," Ladonis said. "Who'd a thought."

HeartTrouble was talking about her and Bunnie Sinclair. Her Grandma Lucille had warned her that grudges wasted a lot of time and energy. And Tim had said that grudges were stumbling blocks. That if you carried one too long, you ran the risk of falling and never catching up with yourself. So she had decided to make peace with Bunnie. Her timing had been right too. Bunnie had felt plenty bad about the trouble she'd caused Ladonis. She was ready to change her attitude toward her coworker too.

"Hey," HeartTrouble said. "I read about you and your boss in the *Picayune* yesterday. The piece said y'all gotta a big gospel show comin' up on the historic *Bayou Queen*."

Ladonis was still amazed at how intently he kept up with current events. If he'd developed his mind, instead of his street hustle, who knew what he could have become. Maybe even a politician who could have changed some things.

"What did it say about me?" Ladonis said.

"It said that you was the contact person," HeartTrouble told her. "They went on and on about that white dude though."

She expected the media to give Bret more play. But she'd thought up and fought to produce the slave-music centennial cruises. And the $15.5 million in new revenue the Floating Palace earned from their production. But the less fuss made over her accomplishments, the less she reproached herself. Besides, she wasn't eager to fill in details of back-story on how she manipulated her big break.

"That old guy screwed up," HeartTrouble added. "You proved there was good money in doing it right."

He was poking fun at her, Ladonis was sure. But she liked it. Kasdan had walked away, all the way to Europe, last she'd heard. But HeartTrouble didn't believe that he had escaped punishment.

"He might've escaped jail," HeartTrouble had said, "for sellin' them people. But, believe you me, there ain't no way in hell he got off scot-free. Too many of the city's big wheels had to be in on a scam like that. They the kind of people who have their own ways of dealing with screw-ups."

HeartTrouble was right. Kasdan couldn't get away from his benefactors in crime any more than she could recapture the natural goodness she'd given up. And that she'd keep giving up, as long as she hoped that an evil-doer like Kasdan didn't get caught. A whole truth and nothing but that she never wanted to surface.

"You need to get some plywood," HeartTrouble said.

"For what?" She hung a lithograph of Mardi Gras Indians— blacks dressed in homemade full Indian festive dress—on the wall.

"Hurricanes and storms, that's what for," HeartTrouble said. "And they headed this way. With all these glass doors and windows, you might have to board them up."

"Storms, huh?" Ladonis said.

"Um, um," HeartTrouble grunted.

He lifted a handful of books from a box and placed them on a shelf. Ladonis threw herself on her precious new gold and rust-colored loveseat and stretched out. She watched her brother empty another box of books and add them where he'd put the others. It didn't matter that she and HeartTrouble were on different life planes. It didn't matter how much they argued. She knew that whatever challenges she faced, even a hurricane, HeartTrouble had her back.